AF253198

Hues of Summer

The First Inspector Lamoureux Mystery

James S. Holmes

ISBN **978-0-473-44579-9**

GB
Great Bear Books

Hues of Summer

London, Summer 1924

They got into the apartment soon after one o'clock in the morning. The first two waited in the darkness while the last of them stepped inside and locked the door. Moonlight shone in through a glass panel in the ceiling, illuminating a thin corridor between the sofa and the grand piano. They waited a few moments, letting their eyes adjust to the light, then moved off quietly towards the bedroom.

The young woman inside had not been asleep long, having lain awake for some time, still feeling uncomfortable with the novelty of the surroundings. If Stephen had been there, she had thought, or anyone else for that matter, sleep would surely have come much sooner. But at last, she had dropped off, only to be woken up less than an hour later by the sound of a familiar voice and a knock at the bedroom door.

She sat up and pulled the covers closer to her, unsure at first whether she had dreamt it. Looking down by the side of the bed, she noticed that there was no light coming in through the quarter-inch gap beneath the door. When no further sounds came, she decided that it must have all been in her head. She laid her head back down on the pillow and closed her eyes.

A second knock came, much louder this time, rattling the door and sending reverberations around the room. She pulled once again at the mess of the thin cotton sheets and sat back up.

'Hello?' she said, her voice lilting upwards as she reached for the bedside lamp. She clicked the switch and shaded her eyes from the sudden light.

'Catherine?' came the voice again from beyond the door.

She sighed in irritation as she angled her feet into her slippers, tightened her dressing gown and got up to open the door.

The room outside was dark; the blackness broken only where the moonlight cut in onto the top of the grand piano.

She combed the wall with her fingers, stretching to locate the brass toggle, and then leant out a little further.

There was a swish of fabric from somewhere behind her. Her head shot forward, resonating from the assault to the back of it. She raised her hands to cover herself. Then another black leather fist swung up from in front and landed solidly beneath her ribcage. She crumpled and hit the floor.

A set of fingers clenched tightly around her wrist, dragging her forward across the narrow hallway. Then another hand grabbed at her face, crushing both nostrils and causing blood to start drifting into her sinuses. She clawed at the first set of hands as they slid down her torso, managing to get a finger inside one of the gloves, but the advantage was short-lived. The grip tightened, pinning her legs together and throwing her over onto her back.

As she was dragged further across the room she could feel the leather fingers dig painfully deeper into the soft hollow of her left cheek. An arm moved up to her stomach, lifting her higher before throwing her back down again onto the edge of the Egyptian rug.

Moonlight flashed above her but was quickly drowned out by the soft yellow light fanning out across the ceiling, coming in from the outside landing. She kicked out a leg and struck a side table and heard the dull thump of mahogany and the crack of crystal.

A knee jammed heavily into her sternum, reminding her of her other concerns, as the landing light slunk away again. She looked up and saw a metallic glint turn swiftly then swoop down into a sharp, cold pressure that spread out across her throat. As the air rushed into her lungs it brought with it a deep, primordial sense of relief. The grip on her arms and face loosened.

Again, there was movement above her. Her airways were now awash with blood. She tried to sit up but choked and fell flat again. The main light came on.

Blood was now flowing out beneath her, soaking into the thick pile of the rug and pooling at the ridges of the parquet floor. Above her, a crimson reflection on the lens of a closely held box camera obscured the face of a black cloaked figure. Somewhere behind it, the pale green opaline lightshade affixed to the ceiling now shone with a ruddy luminescence.

A few more clicks and the darkness returned. A few careful footsteps and again the light from the landing crept in and slipped away. She coughed and spat. A key could be heard turning outside the door. Then nothing more.

Her pulse fluttered and faltered as it quickened in the darkness, each wave weaker than the last.

One

Justin had barely slept, as was so often the case these days. He had left home early, taken the omnibus south from Bayswater Road then changed buses, and headed back north across the river. It was a sunny morning; the kind he remembered longing for back in the frozen mid-winter trenches of Picardy. He sat calmly now, watching the white sunlight speckle sharply on the surface of the Thames.

The bell rang from below. Justin looked at his watch and saw that he was running late for the third time this week. But he was not at all worried. It's just a game, he thought, as he sat on the upper deck, watching the Houses of Parliament draw near.

The bus jolted to a stop. That was it, his time was up. Reluctantly, he stubbed out his cigarette in the ashtray and went downstairs.

Something about being out in the street seemed to heighten his ever-present sense of living in two different worlds. In his line of work, they were both constantly visible, but only one of these worlds seemed to be endowed with the famous optimism that had reputedly spread since the signing of the armistice. Motorcars were now commonplace; chrome and black and the distinct smell and sound of the engines. But other than that, the country seemed to have very little to show for nearly a decade of fighting and peace.

Justin stood by the side of the road and looked up at the Palace of Westminster. It was here that it had all begun – and where it had so cynically been kept going, if some were to be believed. But all that was a world away now – pale faces of downy prickles, blanched and petrified as their sentences were read out – only the guilt of it remained, resurfacing painfully whenever he found he had slipped and briefly allowed himself the luxury of forgetting.

He reached into his pocket, pulled out another cigarette and crossed over to Victoria Embankment. Standing on the curb at the other side, he inhaled deeply and did his best to shake off the images. A cheek here, an eyebrow there, it was never quite the full picture. Yet somehow, it was always those faces. Despite the copious images of horror his mind had the luxury of choosing from, it seemed to care little for change.

But this was no time for reflection.

He stubbed out what remained of his cigarette, dropped it into the gutter and headed towards New Scotland Yard.

Justin passed under a row of trees lining the embankment and felt a nudge at his shoulder. A man dressed in overalls had appeared, swinging his leg over the seat of his bicycle as he dismounted. He looked angrily back at Justin, seemingly intent on provoking an altercation. Then, as he made the connection between Justin's smart suit and the imposing buildings that lay ahead of him, the look in his eyes dulled. Nudging his battered old bicycle back onto the road, he raised his cap apologetically, and quickly moved away.

'Everywhere cunning,' thought Justin with a wry smile, 'everywhere small feuds and hatreds…feebleness of purpose.' The words of H.G. Wells had stuck with him ever since he had read them, itching in a dugout near St. Martin-Cojeul. Just like those other memories, they seemed independent of him, creeping up on him at inopportune times.

He passed through the wrought iron gates and on towards the imposing redbrick turrets, then went up the steps and pushed through the double doors.

The desk sergeant raised his head and they nodded to each other in passing. The night shift was just clocking off. Justin stopped one of the sergeants as he was ascending the stairs.

'Anything I want to know about?' he said.

'I shouldn't think so, sir. Bit of a quiet one. The new Crossleys are in the basement though – came in this morning. You should sneak a gander, sir, while they're still all shiny and new.' Justin checked his watch.

'Andrews in?'

'Yes, sir, but he's not been out of the lair since about eight o'clock.' Justin considered his options.

'No, it's too late, I'd better not.' Nodding farewell to the sergeant, he continued up the stairs.

Justin dropped his hat into the paper tray on his desk and lit himself a cigarette. DI Richards, sitting at the desk opposite his, glanced down at his watch and frowned.

'Has he been out yet?' said Justin, nodding towards Detective Chief Inspector Andrews' door.

'Not since I've been here,' said Richards. The broad silhouette of the chief inspector was just visible through the mottled glass. Justin sat down.

Richards appeared at Justin's shoulder with half a Woodbine hanging from the side of his mouth. He dropped a folded newspaper onto the desk, having ringed the one he wanted.

'*Phaedra Star*, three-thirty. I've marked it here.'

'I see. And what makes it a *star* exactly?'

'I don't know about a star, but it's a dead-cert from what I've been told.' Justin eyed it suspiciously.

'All right then.'

'Your man'll take that, won't he?' He passed Justin a folded note.

'He'll take whatever you give him. I, however, am going to have to start charging at this rate,' he replied. Richards walked back over to his desk.

Justin pushed the newspaper to one side and picked up his post, opening the first of the two envelopes and pulling out a set of accounts. *H.S. Sibley and Sons* read the heading on the facing letter. With a laboured sigh, he slipped the papers under the folded newspaper on his desk.

'I should get a sergeant onto this,' he said, shaking his head. Richards looked up.

'That the case you brought with you?' he said.

'I'm sick to death of it. He wants me to see it out,' said Justin, nodding towards the chief's office.

He thought about getting a cup of coffee but decided to deal with the post first. Picking up the other envelope – intrigued at it having been postmarked at Windsor – he tore it open, begging it to contain something more urgent than the bloody Sibley case.

He spread out the three grainy images it contained and began to study them, a little confused. Though the pictures were not very clear, there was a familiarity about them; something seemed to draw his attention to them, something he was not quite able to place. Then, as he picked up the clearest of the three images and looked a little closer, his breathing ceased.

In one of the photographs he could clearly make out the image of his own face in profile, then the blurred décor of the Turkish baths, and finally, the nude male figure facing him, half hidden in shadow.

He put the images face-down on his desk, trapping them under his forearm while he checked the envelope for a note. As he tore at the thin brown paper, Richards looked up from his desk.

'Everything all right?' he said. For a moment Justin looked blankly at him, unable to answer. Having found nothing more in the envelope, he quickly searched his pockets for his keys, found the right one and locked the articles away in his desk draw. He turned to face Richards.

'Fine. Just trying to find something, that's all.' Richards went back to his work.

Justin could think of nothing but his own stupidity. Picking up the newspaper on his desk, just to give himself something to hold onto, he got up and left the room.

In the toilets, he splashed his face from the cold tap and looked at himself in the mirror. Rubbing water into his eyes, over his nose and mouth again and again, he attempted to slow his breathing. As his heart continued to pound with ever greater speed, he found himself struggling for air. The door swung open.

'Sir,' DS Kettering nodded to him as he entered, and continued absent-mindedly over to the urinals.

Justin straightened himself up and pretended to dry his hands calmly on the soggy hand towel. It was as though Kettering's presence had been enough to save him, leaving him no option but to regain some control. He wiped his face with his sleeve, adjusted his waistcoat and tried to clear his throat. He knew he would be all right now. Stuffing the newspaper under his arm, he went back outside.

He got back to find DI Woodbridge leaning over his desk.

'How are things, Justin?' he said. It was a perfunctory gesture; the fact of which Justin was glad. Woodbridge did not wait for an answer. 'I need those Sibley files. All right?' he said.

'Take them. Take the lot!' said Justin, sweeping them towards him across the desk.

Woodbridge had almost twenty years' experience over Justin and it showed, both in the looks he gave him and in his tone.

'You look a bit flushed, young man,' he said. 'Are you feeling all right?'

'Yes, fine,' he said, giving the files another push. Woodbridge turned and left.

'I've just remembered,' said Justin to Richards, 'I needed to pick something up.' He put on his Homburg. 'If Andrews asks, I'll be back within the hour.'

'Remember that wager,' Richards called after him, though not so loud that Andrews might hear.

'How could I forget?' said Justin, patting his pocket and letting the door swing shut behind him.

Sitting in the back of the taxi cab on the short ride over to Bloomsbury, Justin tried to work out how in hell it could possibly have happened. It was the price of his stupidity in a moment of weakness, he said to himself, but that offered no explanation. The curtains of the cubicle had been closed to ensure their privacy – he was sure of that – even though the evidence clearly suggested otherwise. It was not like him to forget these things; some habits are simply too ingrained to be compromised. And that was one of them.

He got out and paid the driver, then ran up the marble steps and knocked on the door. He stared straight ahead at the brass lion-head knocker, trying to ignore the sense of exposure he felt out on the street.

Taking a step back, he checked to make sure that the bulbs in the hallway were on; a sure sign there was someone at home. The window-bars of the fan-light sat across them with the colour and sheen of a spider's web. He waited a moment longer, then gave another impatient knock on the big red door. Finally, it opened.

A servant, whom he did not recognise, led him into the drawing room and politely asked him to wait.

Through the door at the back of the room, Justin could hear the brusque voice of Lord Henry conversing with another guest. Henry's was a voice that had never once sounded out of place on the parade ground at Sandhurst, and one which for many years had been renowned for striking fear into the new recruits.

'I'm all for making them pay-up,' Justin heard him say, 'but they can't pay anything if they haven't got the means.'

'Of course not,' came the reply. 'Horrendous really, for the people. It's little more than enslavement.'

'Well, this is it. It was probably the plan in the first place, I'm afraid to say. They can't do much without resources and infrastructure.'

Justin went over to the drinks cabinet and quickly swallowed a large measure of whisky. It went down easily.

Becoming impatient, he removed his hand from the chair that he had been nervously tapping it against and looked for something – anything – in the room to divert his attention.

The house had been kept in a style consistent with its late-Georgian exterior, and he always found the sense of nostalgia it provoked in him to be a welcome escape. It always seemed to Justin that there was something reassuring about the past, no matter how bad it had actually been.

For the most part, the three windowless walls were covered with paintings – all of them originals – leaving, in several places, little more than an inch of Regency stripe between them. A gigantic gilt mirror hung above the fireplace, having the effect of doubling the room's size.

At the window, Justin pulled down the hanging cord of the nets, peered outside and saw that the sun was now well over the rooftops. He would have to get back to The Yard soon, he thought.

'It's coal to Newcastle…' said a voice in the next room.

'…or unemployment to Manchester,' came the reply.

'Quite.' There was the sound of laughter.

Justin checked his watch. 'Come on!' he said under his breath.

He lit a cigarette and flicked through the collection of records perched next to the gramophone in one of the alcoves. A recording of English medieval pieces sat next to a selection of Bach. Justin knew that with his love of the Catholic Elgar, Henry was already flying close to the wind with some of his acquaintances. But having a German on display? In the current climate, that took more than a healthy dose of courage.

Justin picked up one of the sleeves and gently slid the disk out. '*The Original Dixieland Jazz Band,*' read the label in proud gold type. At any other time, this might have amused him. Sliding the disk back into the sleeve, he carefully replaced it at the back of the pile.

'Well, I'm awfully sorry, Colonel, but I must prepare for the afternoon session,' came Henry's voice, growing in volume as he reached the door.

'Oh, of course. I mustn't keep you. It's been good to catch up,' came the reply.

'And who's in here?' The door opened.

'Inspector Lamoureaux, M'Lord,' came the servant's reply from out in the hallway. Justin's hand moved involuntarily to straighten his tie. Even after all these years, he still felt a reflexive need to make himself look more respectable in the presence of Lord Henry Cunningham.

'Oh, good.' Henry's face appeared at the door. 'Any news on those pieces?' he said, catching Justin with his familiar marble-eyed stare. But before Justin could answer, he had already turned back to the colonel in the hallway and said, 'Some little bastards got into the manor house and stole my Constable! I think they chose it on purpose just to be impudent!'

'Good God, how awful!' the colonel said, leaning into the room and revealing the pipped shoulders of his military tunic. 'I hope you're making a concerted effort to catch them!' he said and leaned back out again. 'They can be terribly lax in these matters,' Justin heard him say from beyond the door, 'even when it's a genuine treasure. As soon as you get hold of them you ought to give them the birch!' Justin could not be entirely sure as to which 'them' the Colonel was referring.

'We have some very important information,' said Justin.

'Thank goodness for that,' said Henry.

'Anyway, I must be off,' said the colonel, moving along the hallway.

Justin finally heard the front door go, after a few more seemingly interminable pleasantries. Lord Henry appeared, putting his finger to his lips as he strode over towards the window. The net curtains flickered as he watched the colonel trot down the steps and off along the pavement.

'Good Lord!' he said a moment later, his voice suddenly much gentler and smoother as he turned to face Justin. 'Do you know, I thought the old girl would never leave!'

The change in his demeanour was instantaneous. Everything about him, even his gait as he crossed the room towards Justin, seemed like an expression of relief. The ferocious army officer had taken on a good-natured gaiety;

not feminine, but somehow more graceful, like a prisoner
released. Somehow Justin always found himself feeling sorry
for him.

'Too early for a wee dram?' purred Henry, reaching for the
decanter.

'Never,' said Justin.

'Good man. Actually, no…' said Henry, drawing back his
hand and addressing the servant, 'bring in the good stuff will
you.' The servant, staring across at him wide-eyed, did not
dare move. 'Oh, don't worry about him,' said Henry,
pointing to his guest, 'the inspector here is a *very* good friend
of mine.' The young man's shoulders dropped noticeably as
he smiled and left the room.

'Another new one?' said Justin. Henry raised a single
eyebrow in reply.

'Light me a cigarette would you, darling?' said Henry,
pointing to the silver box on the mantelpiece. 'I've been told
not to by my doctor, but what does he know about it?' He
sat himself down. 'Very little I should expect,' he added,
perhaps somewhat hopefully.

'I've got a bit of a problem,' said Justin, passing him the lit
cigarette.

'Well, we all know that, dear,' smirked Henry. 'Do take a
seat.'

'I mean it. This is serious.' Justin sat down. Henry leaned
back on the sofa and took a long drag on the cigarette.

'I should have known you'd want something from me,' said
Henry, 'turning up at this time of day.'

The servant returned, placing a silver tray, a cut crystal
decanter and two glasses on the table then went and stood in
the corner. Lord Henry sat looking expectantly at Justin.

'Well, what is it?' he said. Justin looked across at the
servant, and back at Henry. Though enjoying his friend's
discomfort immensely, Henry eventually gave in and
dismissed the young man.

'You needn't worry about the likes of *her*,' said Lord Henry
turning back to face Justin again after watching the servant

leave the room, 'she's fully confirmed. Now what's got you into such a state? Business or pleasure?'

'Someone sent me some pictures today in the post. Personal ones. The type you don't want. They landed right on my desk.'

'Oh, I see,' purred Lord Henry. 'How dreadfully naughty!' He poured two large measures into the glasses and passed one of them to Justin.

'They were sent straight to Scotland Yard, Henry! You understand what that means. No note or anything, just the photographs.' He swallowed half the glass.

'And how incriminating are they, exactly?'

'Unmistakeable, once you realise what they are.'

'Oh dear, dear, dear,' tutted Henry.

'They were taken at the baths on Harrow Road,' said Justin, pre-empting Henry's next question. Henry's eyes widened.

'You decadent little bitch!' he said. 'That's a little risky, isn't it?'

'I know, I've been bloody stupid!' said Justin, rising to his feet and gulping down the rest of his drink. 'You don't seem to be taking this very seriously.' Henry drew back a little.

'I think you'll find I'm taking this incredibly seriously!' he said. 'It's not every day someone so dashing offers me some exotic images of themselves *in-flagrante*. I demand that you stop teasing me so mercilessly this minute, name your price and be done with it.'

Justin stared down at him. The silence was long enough for the sound of a passing motorcar to come into the room and shrink away again.

'Oh, come on, Justin,' said Henry. 'Sit yourself down, you're not the first person to get caught sniffing the daffodils. We've all been there at one time or another.'

'And you've forgotten that I'm a detective inspector?' he replied.

'No, not at all. Have you forgotten that I was a major general? Egad, Justin, this is the nineteen-twenties!' he said with a wave of his hand. 'This kind of thing isn't what it once was – you know it's practically compulsory in Berlin! I must admit though, the traditional method, other than getting caught in the act, of course, was the incriminating letter, which one could always claim to be a forgery or a symptom of madness. I can see how a set of photographs could be a bit more problematic.'

'Yes, just a bit. And a lot more shocking for whoever's hands they happen to fall into, I should think. Anyway, this isn't Berlin. My department is supposed to be working alongside the vice squad, who are hoping to bring in another lot of "Piccadilly Pansies," as they so enjoy calling them, any day soon.'

'Well, aren't we all, dear?' smiled Henry.

Seeing how anxious Justin was becoming, he tried to affect a look of concern. Nevertheless, he could not resist having just a little more fun.

'And is that what you think you are then, officer?' he whispered, leaning forward, 'a *pansy*?'

'Please Henry, I really don't have time for this,' said Justin. He reached over and poured himself another whisky. 'Do you have any idea what would happen to a disgraced officer inside?'

'One can only dream,' replied Henry, but he could see that Justin's anger was now rising to a dangerous level. 'All right, I apologise,' he said, draining his glass. 'You will not be disgraced or ruined or any such thing, Justin. It would simply not be allowed. You're a decorated officer or have you forgotten? The public sees you as some kind of war hero, or some such nonsense. No-one with the MC ever gets more than a wrap on the knuckles for something like this; the establishment simply couldn't afford the embarrassment.'

'And what if my colleagues found out? My career would be finished.'

'Oh dear God, how awful,' replied Henry. 'How utterly terrible! But seriously, would you miss it? I could match a policeman's pay twice over. In fact, you could be my next manservant. I should have you measured up for a new waistcoat while you're here.'

The room went silent again and Henry finally relented.

'Look, you've come to the right place,' he said. 'I know exactly how troubling this kind of thing can be. You're not the first person to come to me in this predicament. In certain circles, I'm what you might call, "The Fixer."' He got to his feet and lit another cigarette at the fireplace. 'I had exactly the same problem once,' he continued, then broke off. 'Are you here on business or pleasure?' he said suspiciously.

'This is certainly not pleasure, Henry.'

'I shall ignore that little remark!' He continued, 'In any case, let's just say that I once had a *friend* who had exactly the same problem. Now, this friend of mine was himself a pillar of society – a Lord, Knight, Duchess or something – and was *extremely* well connected.' A hint of the old military man returned as the story went on. 'Anyway, unbeknownst to the little bastards who were trying to hold him to ransom, his tentacles reached a lot further than they ever imagined, and, as was the case, there was very little chance of this information reaching any receptive ears. Now, this friend of mine not only blocked all avenues of publication, but also rather quickly managed to dish out his own variety of justice. Do you catch my drift?'

'It must stay within the law, Henry.'

'Oh, must it really? Well then, that makes it easy. Why don't you take your little photographs along to your superiors and ask them to sort it out for you?' Justin sank back into his chair. 'Look,' continued Henry, 'I know it's a shock when it happens the first time, but pretty soon you'll have to learn to fight your corner just like the rest of us. Leave it to me for now, Sergeant, and I shall see that you have no more trouble.'

'I'm an inspector these days,' said Justin, as he drained what was left in his glass. Henry returned to the couch.

'You know, you do make life very difficult for yourself, Iustus. Where did you school again, was it Oxford or Cambridge?'

'Neither.'

'Good Lord,' said Henry in mock outrage. 'You mean to say that I've opened my door to a member of the great unwashed? I must admit, I myself was sent down in disgrace…but then so was Shelley,' he said with some pride. 'Anyway, you are decorated by your King nonetheless, and yet you spend your days messing about with the lowest possible of castes. God knows why you do it! Underpaid, under-privileged…and I dare say under-sexed! How depressing.'

'Perhaps it's good for the soul,' replied Justin.

'Well, don't expect Jesus to get you out of this one.' Henry sat back and sighed. 'And don't give me that old rubbish again. I know exactly what you're thinking, and you need to get over it. It was the army, Justin, and we were at war! The next time some little upstart decided to take a nap while on duty, it may very well have been your last. It was your duty to report them, and let's face it, it wasn't you who pulled the trigger, anyhow. As for the others, cowardice costs lives. Anyway, you had other men to think about…not usually a problem for you, I might add,' he said, raising an eyebrow. 'Good God, back in my day they would have got the bayonet there and then.'

'Perhaps that would have been better.'

'It's time to let it go, Justin. You have medals for your gallantry, and they are well deserved! Now for the love of God, be a man!'

It was an argument Henry was used to winning and it felt odd to Justin, hearing the words he had so often said to himself, coming from the lips of someone he trusted.

'I should be leaving,' he said getting up. 'Thanks for your time and assistance.'

'Anytime Justin,' said Henry with genuine affection. 'I shall see to it that this little problem of yours goes no further.

And…in return, I dare say a few of my acquaintances would appreciate some more information concerning these up-coming raids.'

'I'll let you know the places to stay clear of, Henry,' said Justin, making for the door.

'Very good. It's always good to have a man on the inside,' he replied with a smirk and a final twitch of the eyebrow.

Two

The air in the office was already heavily stained with tobacco smoke. Justin wafted it away as he sat down at his desk, opened a nearby window and lit a cigarette. Richards came into the room.

'He's looking for you,' he said.

'Andrews?' said Justin. Richards nodded.

'Fuck.' He muttered the word under his breath as he checked his watch. It was twenty to eleven. The door of the chief inspector's office swung open.

'Cambridge!' came the voice of the Ulsterman. 'In here!'

Andrews' sturdy frame was a mixture of muscle, and muscle that had long ago turned to fat. He had a solid look about him, deep chested and bullish, and wherever he went it always seemed as though his feet were somehow rooted to the ground. Justin went in and closed the door.

'Sit down,' said Andrews.

Justin pulled up a chair as Andrews tossed a manila envelope across the mess of paper on his desk. The paper had been torn open. Justin looked up at Andrews and then back down at the envelope as he slowly pulled out its contents.

'You feeling all right?' said Andrews. A moment or two passed.

'Yes, sir,' said Justin, as relief spread through him. He took a deep breath and scanned the single sheet of typed, headed paper in his hand.

'Where've you been, anyway?' said Andrews.

'I had to pick something up, sir. I told Richards–'

'What, for Sibley? Aye, well you can drop that for now; there's more important things. This is gonna have to be quick – I'm far too fucking busy.' He pointed at the sheet of paper. 'That there's come over from Vine Street. A young woman, in some flat overlooking Green Park. I want you to head straight over there. I'd be out there myself, but he's got me heading up all sorts; you know how it's been. Anyway, Lisson's in court today and besides, they're a bunch of toffs round that way anyway, so you'll do quite nicely. You've got the address,' he said, again pointing to the sheet. Andrews got up and moved towards the door. 'There's rumours I'm getting called back over to Ireland. I'm none too happy about it, but anyway, duty's duty. So, I might not be here to see this through, which is why I want you to take charge of it proper. Get Richards if you need him or get Lisson when he's back, but you know how short we are…take Bennet if you have to.' He opened the door, looked out and saw DC Cameron passing by. 'There's officers at the scene, but you can take Cameron with you for now – it'll do him good.'

'Yes, sir.'

Justin stepped out of the office as the door closed behind him.

Detective Constable Cameron sat waiting for Justin in the car downstairs. His hooded eyes, as always, added a laconic expression to his pleasant, rounded features, as he sat watching two mechanics working under the bonnet of the vehicle opposite.

He reached down and rubbed a grey scuff mark off the top of one of his shoes and was reminded of the fact that his daughter desperately needed a new pair. Maggie had been on at him again. Yet another growth spurt, he could so clearly picture her saying. She was right though; you can't have your little girl running around with no shoes on. Still, everything's a cost these days, he thought. He scratched an itch buried somewhere beneath his neatly trimmed auburn beard.

Cameron had promised his wife that he would pick up a tin of corned beef from the shop on the corner on his way home. Bully beef – just like he was back in the army. It was at times like this he was struck by the stark monotony of what his life had become.

Justin climbed into the passenger seat beside him.

'All right, I've got the address here; it's round the other side of Green Park,' he said as he shut the door. Cameron started the engine and pulled out towards the ramp, stopping behind an old Crossley Tender that was blocking the exit.

'What are they doing?' said Justin.

'I think somebody's been a little bit stupid,' Cameron replied.

From where they were sitting, it looked as though someone had tried to drive the thing out before the radio frame had been fully collapsed. The timber had split, and the wire had crumpled against the underside of the doorway.

'Idiots!' said Cameron, his voice sounding resigned rather than angry, softened somewhat by the gentle undulations of his Aberdeenshire accent. He tooted the horn. A mechanic turned and waved him away then swung back angrily to face the uniformed officer in the van. Cameron tooted again. The driver of the Tender slammed the door and reversed back down the ramp, as the two of them continued to argue.

The brightness of the morning struck them as soon as they got outside. They drove up through Westminster under a clear blue sky and then on to Green Park. The engine was loud enough to drown out any attempt either of them might have made at starting-up a conversation. It suited them both fine. Justin spoke only momentarily to give directions.

They parked-up and took the lift to the top of a new apartment block, where a uniformed officer let them into the flat. The mechanised ratcheting of a camera could be heard from along the hallway as they made their way into the apartment.

The body of a young woman was lying on its back in the centre of the room, the bottom half of the torso resting on a thick rectangular rug. Blood had spilled out onto the parquetry, staining the floor with a dry brown crust. A doctor was standing over it, as was the newly appointed police pathologist who was busy taking pictures. Justin showed them his identity card.

'The cleaner found her,' said the doctor without further introduction. 'Quite a struggle seems to have taken place, by the look of it.'

'So I can see,' said Justin, kneeling down by the side of the corpse. The body lay so still that he half expected it to move at any moment. 'How long has she been dead?' he said, standing up again. The doctor finished packing his things away in his bag as though he had not heard him.

'Difficult to say,' the doctor replied, eventually looking up. 'That's a question for the pathologist here.' He nodded towards the other man, who had now moved over to the upended table to photograph a broken whisky decanter. 'I'm only here to make it official.' He put on his hat and handed Justin his card. 'I shall be at my office until five o'clock this evening. Call me on the telephone if you need me.'

The pathologist came back over as the doctor turned and left.

'Doesn't seem right when it's a woman, does it?' he said.

'When is it ever right?' replied Justin.

'Pretty too,' said the pathologist.

The girl's eyes were still open, staring up through the skylight above.

'Hasn't anybody thought to cover her face with something?' said Justin, kneeling again next to the corpse.

'Not until she's been photographed,' he replied. 'New procedure. I'll do it soon.'

'Well, can we at least close her eyes?' said Justin, as he attempted to gently stroke down the lids with the palm of his hand.

'They won't close now, I'm afraid,' said the pathologist. 'The coroner will have to see to that.' Justin rose to his feet.

'I'll go and speak to the other officer, sir,' said Cameron, heading off into the hallway.

'There must have been more than one attacker,' continued the pathologist. 'Luckily it doesn't look as though she was interfered with.'

'Yes, how very lucky,' said Justin. 'And by looks of it, she bled out?'

'Yes, and I'm afraid she probably knew about it too. There are signs of pressure around here,' said the pathologist, pointing his pencil towards her throat. 'That's from the obvious trauma. And around the wrists; scratches mostly, the left one's broken, as is a section of the skin. It looks as though she was pinned down rather than bound. There's the very beginning of some bruising to the face and torso mostly. The nose is fractured. And then there's the obvious throat wound.'

Justin got up and went over to the window of the apartment and looked out at the sun-lit tree-tops of Green Park. To the left of him, next to an empire sofa, was a small circular side-table, on top of which sat a small elephant's foot which had been hollowed out, lined expensively with silver, and further decorated with some recently extinguished cigarette butts.

'Is there any sign of the murder weapon?' said Justin.

'Not that I can see,' said the pathologist. 'It wasn't the glass,' he said pointing to the broken decanter. 'It's a nice clean wound.' Justin came back over to the body.

'Oh, and there's a firm bulge in the abdomen,' continued the pathologist. 'It could be from internal bleeding or from something else, but it's most likely she was pregnant. We won't know until after the examination proper.'

'Lovely,' said Justin, nodding his head. Cameron returned to the room.

'I've got the officer's notes, sir. It doesn't look as though anything's been taken, though the owner hasn't been informed yet,' he said.

Justin looked up at the wall and the plush lion skin that was stretched out across it. Below it, on top of a rosewood plinth on the mantelpiece, sat a twin set of carved ivory tusks depicting a hunting scene. If it had been a robbery, they would have been the first to go, he thought. As it was, even the expensive wireless and gramophone had remained untouched.

'And who might the owner be?'

'We don't know yet, sir,' said Cameron. 'The apartment changed hands fairly recently. Uniform are following it up.'

'Isn't there a porter in a place like this?'

'Three, sir, day and night. Two young ones and an old one.' Cameron looked down at the notes the uniformed officer had given him. 'The one that took over this morning says that his colleague wasn't here for the handover.'

'Is he usually?'

'Yes, sir. It was the older one's shift last night and he's always here.' Justin took another look around the room.

'Do the porters have keys to the apartments?' he said.

'No, only to the main building and the communal areas.'

'We'll need to track down the porter from last night.'

'His name's Paolo Scutari,' said Cameron. 'He lives nearby, on his own apparently. He was supposed to be retiring at the end of September. He's been called on, but there's no answer as yet.'

'Do you know if there was a replacement set up for when Mr Scutari retired – someone who may already have access to the building?'

'Not according to the bloke downstairs, sir.'

'Well, there's no sign of a break-in, so she could have let them in herself. Either that or the door was forced when she opened it. We need to speak to that porter. Tell the constable to keep at it.' He looked down again at the corpse. 'In the meantime, we need to find out who she is.'

'Her suitcase is still next to the bed, sir.'

'Good, let's take a look at it.'

But for the disturbed bedsheets, and the glass of water on the bedside table, the bedroom seemed otherwise unlived in. Justin lifted the suitcase onto the bed and unstrapped the lid.

'A change of clothes…sensible underwear…a Bible…that's the lot,' said Cameron, narrating the search. 'Nothing to say who she was.'

Justin checked the drawers and the wardrobe next to the window, but they were empty.

'That's all right, we'll take this with us,' he said, picking up the suitcase. 'We're going to need statements from all of the neighbours – try and cause them a bit of trouble and hopefully they might be able to tell us something. I'll contact the landlord from the station as soon as uniform gets back to us. He can fill us in on who she was and what the *hell* she was doing here.'

Justin stood at his desk back at the office, holding the telephone, waiting for the operator to put him through. His call was answered after only a couple of rings.

'Good afternoon. My name is Detective Inspector Justin Lamoureaux of Scotland Yard. May I please speak with Lord Jeffrey Keating?'

'I'm afraid he's out at the moment, sir,' said the voice at the other end of the line. 'May I ask what it concerns?'

'I'm afraid I can't say at the present time. Is there anyone else I could speak to? It is rather urgent.'

'I'm afraid not, sir. Lord Keating is otherwise engaged, and the Lady has gone to London. I'm afraid they will both be unobtainable until later in the day.'

'Well, could you get the message to one of them as soon as possible please? Either of them will do; she may be able to get in contact with her husband.'

'Certainly, sir. I'll see what I can do,' he replied. Justin hung up the phone.

He lifted the girl's suitcase up onto his desk and opened it again. It was a part of the job he had never gotten used to. The act of looking through innocent people's things always seemed so unjustly invasive. And there was also something particularly pathetic about the sight of a murdered girl's few meagre belongings. Strangely relieved to have found nothing of any note, he refastened the buckles and slid the case back under his desk.

The Keatings' servant had clearly been as good as his word, as Lady Keating arrived unexpectedly at Scotland Yard within the hour. DC Cameron showed her into one of the interview rooms and then alerted Justin.

'M'Ladyship's here, sir,' he said with a strangely mischievous grin.

'She's here? God, that was quick,' said Justin. He checked his watch. 'I wanted her husband really, but I suppose she'll have to do.'

'A servant got a call to her at some boutique or other, so she came straight in, sir.'

'Fine. Is she able to contact her husband?'

'I haven't asked her yet. I thought you might like to, sir,' he said with a wry smile. Justin looked at him, slightly perplexed, as he put his papers away in the desk.

Down in the interview room, he found Lady Keating sitting in one of the wooden chairs, depositing the ashes from her cigarette into the little ashtray on the table. He looked in at her through the wired glass.

'*That's* Lady Keating?' he said, turning to Cameron, who was leaning with his back against the wall.

'Aye,' he smiled.

'She's not old enough to smoke, is she?'

'I don't know, but she's quite a beauty, wouldn't you say?' said Cameron. He turned and sneaked another look at her through the window. Justin nudged him away.

'You found that porter yet?' said Justin.

'Still no luck, sir,' said Cameron, moving back to the wall.

'And uniform have broken in?'

'Aye. He's not there.'

'All right. We can deal with that afterwards.' Justin went into the room.

'Lady Keating?' he said cautiously.

'Yes,' she replied. Justin pushed the door closed behind him.

Lady Keating pulled at the fingers of her satin glove, removed it and then shook Justin's hand.

'Detective Inspector Lamoureaux,' he said, pulling up a chair opposite. He lit a cigarette, leaving the open pack on top of the desk. 'Are you able to contact your husband at all? I need to speak to him rather urgently.'

'Not until later this afternoon, I'm afraid. He has business on the estate.'

In her light summer dress, and with her neat blonde bob poking out from under the brim of her hat, Justin thought he had never seen anyone look so out of place as she did under the harsh light of the single hanging bulb.

'Is it anything I could help you with?' she asked. Her voice had a maturity to it that made her seem wiser than her years. Wearier perhaps.

'Well...' he began.

Lady Keating sobbed quietly, trying to take in what Justin had just told her, but her attempt to maintain her poise only heightened the impression of her vulnerability. As she sank back further into her chair, Justin poured a cup of water from the jug and slid it across the table towards her. Then, not knowing what else to do for her, he sat back and waited, and lit another cigarette.

'If you could get some word to your husband as soon as possible, it would be a great help,' he said to a face hidden behind a blue handkerchief. She nodded in reply. 'We need to know who the girl was and what she was doing there, Lady Keating.'

Lady Keating withdrew the handkerchief from her eyes.

'I can help you with that,' she said. 'That would have been Catherine, our housemaid. She went to stay there yesterday.' Her voice faltered.

'What was she doing there?' he said and waited while she took a sip of water.

'The servants are allowed the use of the flat on their days off – as long as we don't need it ourselves, that is. It gives them a break from the estate.'

'I see. And when was she due back?'

'Tomorrow afternoon.' She folded the handkerchief and placed it in her lap.

'Is there really no way of contacting your husband, Lady Keating? We need someone to have a look around the apartment; that way we can tell for certain whether or not it was a robbery. Would you mind doing so, if he can't be contacted?'

She looked up at him unhappily.

'God, I don't think I could. What about the body?'

'Oh, no, the body will have been removed to the morgue by now. I wouldn't expect you to help with the identification.'

She shook her head as if the thought alone appalled her.

'My husband should be back at home shortly, I can call him there. But in the meantime, I can come with you to the apartment if that will help.'

'Yes, it would. Thank you, Lady Keating.'

At the apartment, they found that the body had been removed, just as he had promised. Nothing else had been touched. The solid crust that had formed over the surface of the Egyptian rug was now beginning to crack, greying slightly at the edges where the sunlight had baked it in. Lady Keating entered the room, looked down and immediately turned away from it.

'Cover that up, will you,' said Justin to Cameron, placing himself between her and the rug. Then he turned to Lady Keating. 'I'd like you to have a good look around the apartment please. We haven't found any sign of damage or forced entry, nor of anything having been taken, but only you and your husband can tell us that for certain. Was there anything of value here they might have been looking for?'

Lady Keating was now holding her handkerchief up to her mouth as if there was something contagious in the air.

'Nothing I can think of,' she said. 'Nothing of mine anyway. We only bought this place for convenience; for when Jeffrey had business at The House or if we needed to stay in town over-night.'

'How often would that be?'

'Oh, we stayed here once, just after we bought it. Jeffrey, maybe only a couple of times after that.'

'Maybe?' said Justin. Lady Keating looked at him, hesitating before she answered.

'I think twice. Possibly more. He comes up to London a lot,' she said moving over to the window. 'I must get some air.' She leaned in close to the open casement, took a few deep breaths and then reached into her handbag for her cigarettes.

'So you don't use the place much?' said Justin, moving up next to her.

'No. Though we should have. I've always loved Green Park.' She lit a cigarette. 'I've always dreamt of living somewhere overlooking it.' She turned and looked mournfully about the room. 'We shall have to sell the place now, after this. I certainly couldn't stay here. We'll just have to get rid of it.' She sighed and turned back to the window. 'I'd prefer not to stay here much longer, if you don't mind.'

'No, of course. I understand,' he said.

Justin escorted her through the flat and was not surprised that she was unable to tell him if anything was missing. In the bedroom, she ran her fingers over the still crumpled sheets on Catherine's bed, and began to cry. They came out of the room in silence just as the telephone across the room started ringing. Cameron answered it.

'I don't know why anyone would want to hurt her,' said Lady Keating, turning to Justin as they went back across to the open window.

'Lord Keating's at Vine Street, sir,' said Cameron, calling out across the apartment.

'Get someone to bring him over right away,' replied Justin.

Lord Jeffrey Keating arrived ten minutes later. A man in his mid-sixties, Justin thought that he had the unmistakeable air of the upper-class ex-military about him. Khartoum at a guess, he thought…or perhaps Ladysmith. Either way, his demeanour suggested that he had never really left it.

He emerged from the hallway, stopped to look down at the mess on the floor and then signalled to Justin to follow him.

'They told me at the station to come and see if anything's missing,' he said, going into the bedroom and tossing back the sheets on Catherine's bed, before moving on to the wardrobe. 'How the bloody hell I should know is beyond me,' he muttered to himself. 'Was there anything here? It looks pretty empty.'

'There are a lot of expensive items in the flat, sir,' said Justin. 'I understand they are all yours?'

'Of course they're mine. Everything in the flat's mine,' he replied.

'Are you aware of anything missing?'

'No, I can't see anything in particular,' he said, squinting at Justin suspiciously. 'You sound a bit too well educated to be a policeman.' Justin ignored the comment.

'So, there's nothing missing, sir?'

'I don't know – I don't think so,' he said with little concern.

They came out of the second bedroom. Lord Keating went over to where the corpse had been, knelt down and lifted the sheet from on top of the rug.

'Don't touch that please, sir,' said Cameron. Lord Keating's nostrils flared as he looked up at him.

'It's my bloody rug!' he said replacing the sheet.

'It's a crime scene now, sir,' replied Cameron.

'What a bloody mess,' sighed Lord Keating, looking about the room. 'I suppose you want me to identify the corpse?'

'If you wouldn't mind, sir,' said Justin.

'All right then. See to it that my wife gets back home safely, will you?'

Lady Keating was standing by the window, looking out across the park, most of which now lay in shadow.

'Are you all right, Joanna?' He put his arm around her.

'Yes Jeffrey,' she said, continuing to smoke what must have been at least her fifth cigarette.

'Dreadful business this, for a woman,' said Lord Keating, turning to Justin. 'You should have waited for me to arrive!'

He turned back to his wife. 'I'll see to it that they get you home.'

'Yes, we can take you back,' said Justin.

'I'll wait for you, Jeffrey,' she said flatly, still staring out at the view as though trying to commit it to memory.

'We'd better get going then,' said Lord Jeffrey, turning and leading Justin out of the apartment.

At the morgue, Justin chose to forego the usual delicacies and instead took Lord Keating straight in to see the body. The attendant pulled back the sheet, exposing the battered face and shoulders.

'Blimey,' said Jeffrey, leaning in a little closer. 'Yes, that's her,' he added without a hint of concern. 'What are all the marks on her skin from?' He pointed to her torso and lower arms.

'She lost too much blood for any bruising to fully form,' said Justin.

'Yes of course.' Lord Jeffrey shook his head, tutting. 'Terrible shame. Never a pretty sight, is it? I suppose you missed out on the war, didn't you, being in your line of work?'

'I was at the Somme,' Justin replied flatly.

'Ah, well,' said Jeffrey seeming a little taken aback, 'you'll be used to all this by now then.'

'Not really.' Justin nodded to the attendant and escorted Lord Keating out.

'How well did you know her, sir?' said Justin, as they walked back out towards the car park.

'She was just one of the staff,' replied Jeffrey, searching his pocket for his car keys. Lady Keating was waiting patiently in the passenger seat of the motorcar, looking out at them.

'Can you think of anyone who would have wanted to harm her in any way?' said Justin.

'Good Lord, no. She was a quiet little thing, never said much really. She was the one I would wheel out if we had respectable company at dinner. But then how would I know

her private business? We weren't tennis partners you know.'
Lord Keating got into his car and half-closed the door.
'You'll want to talk to Stephen,' he added. 'He knew her
best. Or at least one would hope so – they were getting
married.' He shut the door.

Justin wrapped his knuckles against the window. Jeffrey
lowered it.

'And he is?' said Justin.

'My servant at the house, of course. Good fellow. Oh, and
come to think of it, I would very much appreciate it if you
could break the news to him – particularly after what you've
put my wife through this afternoon.' He started the engine.

'I'll get someone on to it.' Justin started to move away,
unable to cover his irritation any longer. Then he turned
back to face Lord Keating. 'We'll need to interview each of
your staff members, anyway,' he added, hoping to make clear
the inconvenience of it all.

'Very well,' said Lord Keating. The engine chugged as he
shifted gears.

'And we'll need statements from both you and your wife.'

'Very well,' he said, stressing the words this time. Justin felt
a little better. He waved as the car jolted backwards and then
pulled out onto the road.

Cameron pulled up a chair at Justin's desk and slapped his
notepad down in front of him.

'I've spoken to the officers at the scene, sir, and they've
come back with pretty much nothing.'

'Nothing at all?' said Justin. Cameron shook his head.

'One old lady said that there were workmen in and out of
the building all day long, but she couldn't give us a
description. No-one else seemed to notice them. She said
they were in blue overalls or maybe white, she can't be
certain.'

'Excellent, I'll inform the press. Was there much work to
be done on the building?'

'The porter reckons they're in quite often; a couple of carpenters. Trouble with the doors throughout the building, he says.'

'So, they have keys to all the doors?'

'No, just the communal ones – stairways and the like.'

'We'll need to follow up on that, anyway. With builders' tools you could probably gain access to the apartments quite easily. Have there been any reports of anyone else seen in or near the building, particularly yesterday evening?'

'Nah. None, sir.'

'All right then, we'll make a list of all the neighbours' names – check that they can prove their whereabouts for yesterday evening. It's getting late now; we can sort this out tomorrow morning. Maybe a little hassling will help jog some of their memories. You and I can drive over to the manor house and get straight on with interviewing Lord Jeffrey's staff.'

'Anything to see M'Lady again, sir.'

'Yes, something like that.' He feigned a smile. 'I'd rather see her than her husband.'

'Aye. It makes you mad doesn't it – a beautiful young woman like her and an old codger like him.'

'Does it?'

'It does me. Still, I suppose she must see something in him.'

Justin was back at his Bayswater flat inside the hour. As he put the key in the door, he looked back suspiciously along the empty street. Once inside, he dropped his keys onto the cabinet and reached into the back of it for a new bottle.

In the living room, he placed the half-filled tumbler down next to the gramophone and then fingered through his collection of records. He justified the fact of having come across several of them by nefarious means by telling himself that even the best of men must have at least some vices. After some deliberation, he finally settled on Sibelius, wound the handle on the gramophone and gently lowered the needle.

He finished the glass in two goes, gave himself another decent slug of whisky and looked down at the manila envelope in his hand. A couple more sips and he found himself reaching into his jacket pocket and pulling out a small glass bottle of barbiturates.

Twice before he had built up a tolerance for the drug, and both times he had found it easy enough to wean himself off it. Sleep was the real problem. For weeks on end he would be unable to drop off, until he went back to the bottle.

A smaller dose would do the trick for now; maybe just one tablet or a double drop. His liver would welcome it home with gusto, and tomorrow morning he would have trouble waking up.

Too much alcohol and he would have black-outs. Too little, and his mind would never stop turning. He looked again at the envelope and the grey sheen of the images, just visible through the tear in the paper. Taking two tablets out of the bottle, he placed them on his tongue and washed them back with a large gulp of whisky.

Minutes passed as he sat there, surrounded by the music. Everything around him seemed to be softening. Looking at his watch, he decided that it was probably still just the effect of the whisky. He got up and lit a cigarette then slid the photographs out of the torn envelope and sunk back into the comfort of his chair.

Looking at them now, they seemed less clear. Anonymous even…perhaps…little more than a set of colourless abstract impressions. He began to wonder if he could get away with denying that it was even him. But what if there were others?

The whisky bottle toppled over at his feet, rousing him ever so slightly as it landed on its flat, square edge on the rug. He reached down and picked it up. It was all right – the lid was on – nothing was lost or broken. The record still span. He looked up at the curtains – their faded green marked by years of tobacco smoke and a lack of attention – swaying ever so slightly with the movement of the air in the room. They fell still again.

It was safe, this existence. Or at least it had been for a while. He propped himself up in the chair and lit another cigarette.

His actions in France had earned him medals, due to his ability to blind himself to danger. He smiled at the thought. Tossing the photographs onto the coffee table, he put another pill on his tongue and washed it down with a swig straight from the bottle.

Three

As his hand brushed his head, his eyes opened, and he found himself facing the wallpaper. The dream he had been having was still with him, playing like a film as he turned and looked around the room. The alarm rattled away on the bedside table.

He had been pushing hard on the timber, trying to dig it down deeper into the ground, but the water had kept on coming; trickling, rolling over the stones as it followed the curve of them, smooth and glassy in the sun. The sound of birds, pecking at something nearby, had been getting closer, unnerving him. Or perhaps it had been gunfire at a distance? He was unsure now. Either way, with only an air rifle lying empty across his lap, there was little he could do about it.

He looked down at his pillow and the sheets, still very much under the spell of the Luminal, and wondered how he had managed to get there from the living room. He had been sitting in his chair, and then what? The alarm was still ringing, he realised. He reached out and turned it off.

The morning sunlight was creeping in through the curtains and crossing the adjacent wall. He sat up on the bed and cast his mind back to whatever it was he was supposed to be doing.

In the bathroom, he splashed his face with cold water and stared into two very bloodshot eyes. Everything belonged to another world. He showered and shaved quickly, not wanting to look too long at his own reflection. Then he got dressed, parted his hair at the usual side and lit the first cigarette of the day. As the modest intoxication swayed him gently, he finally felt able to leave the flat.

He stopped at a café in Westminster and swallowed two cups of coffee in quick succession. The bright sunlight dazzled him as he stepped back out into the street, and he stood for a moment feeling its warmth on his skin.

A van rattled past as he crossed Parliament Square. He followed the road up past the gothic clock tower, and then on towards the Embankment and Scotland Yard.

Justin sat down at his desk and was greeted by a note from the pathologist, confirming that the girl had indeed been pregnant at the time of the killing.

'Good morning, sir,' said Cameron, appearing at his desk.

'Yes, good morning,' he replied flatly. The telephone rang.

'Should I get that, sir?'

'Please.'

Justin rubbed his eyes as he sat down in his chair, almost certain now that he had forgotten something important. Richards looked over from his desk.

'Did you place the bets?' he said, his voice only just audible over the hum of the office.

'All bets are off,' Justin replied.

'Why's that?'

'They just are,' said Justin, shaking his head. Richards went back to his work.

'I think you'd better take this, sir,' said Cameron, coming over and passing him the receiver.

'Inspector Lamoureaux,' he said into the mouthpiece, taking a few moments to rest his back against the chair. 'We're on our way.'

The brambles had been cut back to expose the area where the body had been found. The place had been chosen well, hidden from view at the back of the apartment block by the thick foliage of the deciduous trees.

'The dogs found him, sir,' said the uniformed officer, hunched under the branches. Justin uncovered the face of the corpse then quickly replaced the sheet, shielding his nostrils from the smell of the nascent decomposition.

'Same night, was it?' said Justin, addressing the doctor several feet away.

'I should think so, wouldn't you?' he replied.

A dark, pitted wound on the porter's left temple made it clear exactly how he had been despatched.

'Well, that's my job done,' said the doctor. 'The pathologists will be here soon, I expect. I don't know why they bother calling me in.'

A thought came to Justin, and he decided to walk him back to the house.

'Doctor, as you're here, I was wondering if you could help me with something. I need a prescription and I was wondering if you could–'

'I keep office hours,' said the doctor, 'I could probably fit you in later on if you come down to the surgery.'

'I don't really have time for that, I'm afraid,' said Justin, 'not with the investigation.'

The doctor gave him a quizzical look.

'I remember you. Weren't you involved in the Thompson case?' he said.

Justin nodded vaguely, not wanting to commit himself without knowing how it might affect his request.

'There are some questions I want answered about that,' said the doctor. His tone had changed to one he might use when addressing a respected colleague.

'I'll see if I can tell you, if you help me out,' replied Justin.

'Like that, is it?' he said with a sigh. 'Very well then. That whole case was a bloody mess if you ask me – no wonder your lot are so tight-lipped about it,' he said, and they went inside to discuss it.

Ten minutes later Justin was back outside, striding briskly across the lawn.

'The property manager has just been out and identified the porter's body, sir,' said Cameron, looking up.

'Good. I don't think we were in any doubt about that anyway, were we? We can take Mr Scutari off the list now, I think,' he said flippantly. 'Where's the property manager now?'

'He vomited on the lawn just behind you, sir. Then he went back inside.'

'Hopefully I can catch him before he leaves,' said Justin, feeling well enough now to smile as he lit a cigarette. 'Let's get in there, shall we?'

They made their way back round the side of the building, towards the big oak doors of the main entrance.

'Let's just wait here for a moment,' said Justin, breathing in the fresh air and his own tobacco smoke. He could feel his heart racing.

'Looks like the coffee's finally kicked-in, sir,' said Cameron. 'You were looking a bit peaky this morning, if you don't mind me saying.'

'Yes, our friendly doctor's sorted me out – given me something a little stronger.'

'Aye, I thought as much, sir.'

Justin saw a car pull up in the drive as he looked over Cameron's shoulder.

'I don't believe it,' he said, as Detective Inspector Lisson climbed out.

'Lamoureaux!' shouted Lisson as he approached them. 'Good to see you,' he said, lighting a cigarette. 'Chief wants us together on this one.'

'The court case has finished then, has it?' said Justin.

'Yeah, yeah,' smiled Lisson, 'he'll swing.' He turned and surveyed the surroundings; the street, the car park, and finally the building. 'What are we up to here then?'

'It's just got a bit more complicated,' said Justin. 'The Detective Constable here will fill you in,' he said turning to Cameron. 'I have to make a quick phone call.'

Justin stood in the foyer, prodding the air with his finger as he spoke into the telephone receiver.

'You said I could have Richards instead, sir,' said Justin, to the sound of Detective Chief Inspector Andrews' impatient sighs at the other end of the line.

'I said you could have one of them, but that was yesterday. Lisson's far more experienced and I need Richards on another job. Anyway, *I'll* be the one deciding who does what. You've not had your stripes long, son, and working with someone like Lisson might do you good.'

'Well, I'll need to keep the constable with me, sir.'

'Aye, you can do that. It's a double murder now. Lisson can take care of one side and you two work the other. Look, I know what Lisson's like, and I know you can't stand him any more than the rest of us, but he's a good copper. I won't give him seniority – although I should do – but I need you two to co-operate with each other. He can take the porter, and you, the girl – he doesn't have the social graces for much else.'

'All right, sir,' said Justin.

'Of course it's all right. You'll both do what I bloody well tell you.' Andrews put down the phone.

The front door of the building opened. Cameron and Lisson appeared in the hallway.

'Everything all right?' said Lisson.

'Of course it is,' replied Justin.

They took the lift up to the top floor and he showed Lisson around the apartment.

'There are no witnesses, sir,' said Cameron to Lisson, as the latter stepped over the remnants of the broken decanter and brushed his hand over the tiger skin on the wall.

'No, well these are just city boltholes for most of this lot,' replied Lisson. 'This place is probably empty most of the time.'

'There should be a law against it,' said Cameron. Lisson nodded.

'There's no chance of that,' said Justin, the image of Lord Henry creeping into his mind.

'That's probably what yours is, isn't it, Lamoureaux?' said Lisson, giving Cameron a sly nudge. 'A city escape. Gives you a break from the stress of all that fox-hunting and pheasant shooting, doesn't it?'

'We need to get over to Horsham,' said Justin, turning to Cameron and ignoring the remark.

'Aye, sir,' replied Cameron, hiding a smile.

'Yeah, you two get off,' said Lisson, 'I'm going out the back to have a look at this dead wop.'

Heat radiated off the engine and warmed the car quickly as they headed out of London. Justin felt a sense of relief as they left the city. He opened the passenger window to give vent to the gathering tobacco smoke.

Gradually the buildings thinned out, giving way to hedge-rows, parched grey bark and green pasture. The sky spread out in the absence of brick and concrete, and the sun shone down unhindered, adding a two-toned shimmer to the trees' leaves. London was not designed for the summer, Justin had often thought; its grey angularity somehow better suited to the flatness of winter. Out here, everything fitted – everything other than the small-mindedness and games they had just left behind.

'He doesn't seem too bad, sir,' said Cameron raising his voice over the rising and lolling growl of the engine. Justin shifted his attention back inside the car.

'Lisson?' he said, having to think to catch up. 'No, he *seems* all right.'

'You two've had run-ins before then, sir?'

'Once or twice. You'd be hard-pressed to find someone who hasn't with Lisson. Still, it's all in the past now.'

'I thought he'd be worse – from what I've heard of him.'

'Oh, he's just warming up. Don't believe any of that man-of-the-people nonsense.' He took a last drag on his cigarette and dropped the butt out into the wind. 'You'll see.'

They passed a village green with a small local pub nested on the edge of it and carried on along the country lane. Then, finally reaching the property, they turned off and passed under the boughs of two huge oak trees whose upper branches met in the middle, forming a natural arch.

The Tudor manor house – still visible somewhere beneath a series of whimsical upgrades – was set back from the road, reigning over a vast circle of lawn and a loose gravel driveway. They parked-up just short of the portico, where a male servant was already standing in the open doorway.

'Good morning,' said Justin, introducing himself and Cameron as they approached.

The servant nodded his greeting.

'Please, come in,' he replied. 'Lord Keating is expecting you.'

His demeanour seemed inappropriate, thought Justin; far too affable, considering.

'May I ask your name, sir?' said Justin.

'Yes of course, I apologise. My name is Stephen Hollis. I'm the head servant here. I heard there has been some kind of trouble at the Green Park property. Nothing important, I hope?'

Only now did Justin remember that he was supposed to have sent out an officer to inform him. He took off his hat and looked out across the lawn.

'I would like to speak to you for a moment, Mr Hollis, if you don't mind,' he said, fidgeting with the rim of his Homburg. 'Is there somewhere we could go to talk?'

They sat down in the panelled room and Lady Keating appeared in the doorway. Justin motioned to her to join them and she pushed the door gently shut behind her.

There was silence in the room after Justin had finished speaking. He had seen the expression before; half seeing, half dreaming, a whole personality trying to bore down into itself for protection.

Lady Keating moved over to the drinks cabinet and poured Stephen a brandy. Justin followed her over.

'I think it might be best to get a doctor in to see him,' said Justin. He did not want to make the same mistake he had made all those years before. She looked across at Stephen, who was sitting forward, his face masked by his hands.

'I will do,' she replied. 'Perhaps he could do with something a little stronger.' She looked down at the glass in her hand and took it to him.

Stephen raised his head and swallowed the drink silently, then covered his face again. Lady Keating placed a reserved but comforting hand on his shoulder then followed Justin and Cameron out of the room.

'I need to speak to your staff all together,' he said as he pulled the door to, 'but I'd make sure someone stays with Mr Hollis, if I were you.'

'Yes, of course. I'll stay,' she replied. 'Some of the staff will be free within the hour. I don't know if they will be able to tell you much, I'm afraid – Catherine was one for keeping her business to herself.'

'That's all right. I need to know as much as possible about the arrangements at the flat, especially now it's a double murder.'

'What?' she said sharply. 'There was a second murder?'

'Yes, I'm afraid so. One of the porters, Lady Keating. His body was found early this morning, hidden in bushes at the back of the property.'

'But, when did this happen?' she said.

'The same night, most probably. Did you know him at all?'

'No.' She shook her head. 'God, no, I didn't even think of the porter. I've only ever seen an old gentleman there, a very pleasant man, foreign – French or Italian, I think.'

'Yes, that would be him,' said Justin.

Lady Keating looked fearful, almost as though she were looking straight through him. A groan came from within the room.

'I can call the doctor for you, if you would like?' said Justin. She broke out of her trance.

'No, it's all right, I'll do it. I have something I can give to him in the meantime,' she said, producing her own small bottle of sedatives from her cardigan pocket.

'Very well,' nodded Justin, surprised to see them in the possession of someone so young. 'Be careful with those.'

'I always am.'

Justin and Cameron went off along the hall just as a young, pale-looking maid was coming down the staircase. Lady

Keating asked her to gather everyone in the kitchen, and then went back into the room. Justin and Cameron followed the girl.

'I can't believe he wasn't told about it,' whispered Justin, hearing the drawing-room door close behind them.

'It's bloody disgusting,' said Cameron.

'I forgot to get someone onto it – it's my own bloody fault. Still, it's done now. But I can't believe they still had the poor bloke working.'

The cook and the pale young maid had already seated themselves on two stools at an old pine table in the centre of the kitchen. The electric light from a single shaded bulb shone down from above, casting a pale-yellow tint onto the lower quarters of the whitewashed walls. It was still too early for the sun to creep in, but the vibrant green of the lawn seemed to lend its energy from beyond the window. The wooden worktops were crowded with plates and cooking implements in preparation for lunch, half obscuring the view of the glimmering pond and the summer house at the back of the garden.

Justin stood up, introducing himself and Cameron. Just then, a door at the back of the room opened and a second male servant appeared. Justin looked at him for a moment as he tried to place him, before realising where he had seen him before. Smiling discreetly, the servant pulled a chair up to the edge of the table.

'Is that everyone?' said Justin.

'It is,' said the cook. Justin cleared his throat and told the staff what had happened.

There was a gasp, some nascent sobs, a head down with mouth covered, a hand to a cheek. Watching each of them intently, Justin saw nothing in their reactions that seemed at all out of the ordinary.

'For your own safety I'd like you all to remain here at the house, at least for the next few days,' he said. His attention was drawn to the cook, who seemed to be muttering something under her breath. Then the pale girl covered her

mouth with her hand, rose quickly from her chair and ran
out of the room. The male servant seemed the least affected
by the news, so Justin turned his attention to him first.

They sat down at the long dining table in the next room,
the officers taking one side, the servant the other. At the end
of the room was a set of French doors, illuminating the burr
of the polished oak table between them. Justin lit a cigarette.

'I believe we've met before,' he said. The servant looked
back at him, surprised at his openness.

'Yes, that's correct,' he replied. 'My name is Samuel
Wallace. I was employed at Lord Cunningham's house in
Bloomsbury until quite recently.'

'That's right,' said Justin, offering Samuel his cigarette
packet. Samuel took one, lit it and blew the smoke up into
the air.

'Why did you leave his service?' said Justin.

'Oh, I just felt that spending some time outside of the city
would make a nice change. It was Lord Cunningham who
advised me about the vacancy here, actually. I had no
particular reason for leaving, he's a very good person to
work for…but you know how it is.'

The bemused frown on Cameron's face might have
demanded further explanation if Justin had had the courage
to look at him. Luckily, he did not.

'All right,' said Justin, 'can you tell us exactly where you
were on Wednesday evening?'

'Yes, of course,' said Samuel, still smirking at Justin's
discomfort. 'I was here all evening, as was Sandra; that's the
other girl – and I imagine you've already met Stephen. Betty
was also here, in the kitchen.'

'Just your own whereabouts will be fine for now, thank
you,' said Justin.

'Well, Lord Jeffrey, you see, had a small gathering and we
were all needed. All except Catherine, of course. Everyone
was here apart from that poor girl,' he said with a grimace.

'And why was she not needed here?' said Justin.

'I wouldn't know about that,' he replied.

'Who were the guests that evening?'

'Sir James Dempsey and his wife were here, also Anthony Cotton, the art curator, and a few others.'

'And they had dinner with Lord and Lady Keating?'

'Yes, that's correct.'

The room fell quiet as Justin finished scribbling something down in his notepad.

'What time did they leave?' he said.

'Around half-past ten, I believe.'

'What happened then?'

'Lord and Lady retired to bed. The rest of us cleared up and then also went up to bed. Nothing out of the ordinary.'

'And have you noticed anything unusual since you've been here?' said Justin. 'Anything at all that may have hinted at some kind of friction in the house; disagreements between the staff or between anyone else?'

'I can't say that I have, although I've only been here a short time. There was certainly nothing that evening; in fact, I can barely remember much about it, it seemed so ordinary.'

'Did you know the deceased at all?' said Cameron who was sitting back in his chair now, arms crossed in front of him.

'No, not really. She seemed rather a quiet, shy type of girl. I haven't really had much of a chance to get to know anyone just yet.'

'And have you been to the flat in Green Park?' said Justin.

'No, and I can't say I'd want to now, either. I only came over from the house at Bloomsbury a fortnight ago and, you see, I have other arrangements for my days off.'

Cameron turned his eyes to his notepad.

'Do you like working here?' said Justin abruptly, his tone having something of a threat about it. Samuel looked across at the door before answering.

'Well, I would have to say yes, wouldn't I?' he said. Justin understood.

'Well, thank you, Mr Wallace,' he said. 'We may need to speak to you again at some point.'

'Anytime officer,' he replied and left the room.

'Looks like you've got an admirer there, sir,' said Cameron.

'Never you mind about that,' replied Justin. 'Lord Keating told me he would use Catherine especially when he had respectable guests round, so why wasn't she here?' Cameron shrugged.

There was a knock at the door and the young maid walked in. She had a nervous look about her as she sat down, still fondling a soggy handkerchief.

'And your name is?' asked Justin.

'Sandra MacGuire,' she replied. She looked thin and frail, undernourished even, with an unhealthy shade of grey beneath her eyes.

'You sound like a Londoner,' he said.

'Yes, Bermondsey,' she replied.

'And how long have you been working here?'

'About a year and a half. No…closer to two years now.'

'Did you know Catherine well?'

'Well enough, I suppose,' she said with a shrug.

'How well is that?' said Cameron.

'We worked together, but that's all. She kept herself to herself and I minded my own business.'

'What about Stephen?' said Justin, noticing her eyes widen at the mention of his name.

'We ain't really friends or nothing, but I know him better than I knew her.'

'How old are you?' said Justin.

'Nineteen,' she said. She looked tense now, sitting as far back as the chair would allow.

'Smoke?' he said offering her the packet. She shook her head as though disgusted by it. He lit one for himself.

'Do you know why Catherine was away from the house on Wednesday?' he said.

'It was her day off.'

'It's just that Lord Keating told me that Catherine usually serves when there are important guests at the house.'

'He asked me to serve on Wednesday,' she said. 'It was supposed to be my night off instead of Catherine, but we swapped shifts.'

'When did he ask you?'

'Last weekend. I arranged it with Catherine so that I would go when she got back at the end of the week.'

'Have there been many guests over this week?'

'Only Wednesday night.'

'Have they been here before?'

'Not that I know of,' she replied.

'Do you spend much time outside work with the other staff members?'

'Not really. I suppose no-one really feels like it much after being here all week.'

'No, I know what you mean,' said Justin, tipping the ash from his cigarette into the ashtray. 'Do you also stay over at the apartment on your nights off?'

'I did, yes, most days I'm off, since they've had it. I'm not going back there now though.'

'No, I don't think you'll have to,' said Justin. 'And they trust the staff to look after the apartment properly in their absence?'

'Yeah, why not? We look after this place well enough.'

'Yes, of course you do.'

'It's a nice escape from this place. Or at least it was.'

'Did you ever stay there when Catherine was there?'

'A couple of times. She was usually working if I wasn't.'

'Naturally. But do you know why Lord Keating asked you to work that Wednesday night instead of Catherine if that was supposed to be your night off?' Suddenly she started to look agitated.

'He just did,' she replied. 'It's up to him who works and who doesn't.'

'And how do you like working here?' said Justin.

'Same as anywhere else,' she said.

'Nothing special then?' he added. Her eyes shot across to the door, as she again indicated the negative. Justin sat forward, so he could speak more quietly.

'What did you mean when you said that the apartment was an escape from here?' he said.

'It's just a bit of privacy. It's just good to get away sometimes,' she said, refusing to meet his gaze.

'Tell me, Miss MacGuire, do you ever have visitors to the flat when you're there?'

'What do you mean?'

'Friends, family…anyone else?'

'No, of course I don't. It's not allowed.'

'Of course not,' said Justin. 'We're just trying to assess who might have known how to gain access to the property, Miss MacGuire. It might give us a clue as to who might have done this to poor Catherine.' She looked back at him blankly.

'No-one I know,' she said.

'No, I'm sure it wasn't. Do you know if Catherine ever had visitors?'

'I doubt it. She was just a quiet girl. A nice girl.'

'How about Stephen? Were they often there at the same time?'

'They weren't allowed to be there together,' she said.

'Why ever not? They were engaged to be married, weren't they?'

'Lord Keating doesn't like it.'

'I see,' said Justin. 'You know, you were lucky it wasn't you at the apartment that night.'

'I know,' she said quietly, looking down at the handkerchief in her hand.

'Is there anyone you can think of who might have wanted to get at you instead? That's not something we're overlooking, Miss MacGuire,' said Justin. 'If there's anyone you can think of who may have wanted to harm you, it's vital that you let us know.' She thought for a moment.

'No, I shouldn't think so,' she said quietly.

'Very well,' said Justin. 'We may need to speak to you again.'

Justin waited until she had left the room before speaking. She pulled the door to behind her. Cameron got up and shut it.

'There's something wrong here,' said Justin. 'It's obvious. I want to know why Jeffrey switched their shifts that evening.'

There was a knock at the door.

'Come in,' said Justin. The cook came in and sat down, gathering her apron neatly around her. 'And your name is?'

'Betty,' she said quietly, with a strong Yorkshire accent.

'Surname?' said Justin, looking up from his notebook.

'Marsden,' she replied. Justin could not help but notice the weary look she had about her.

'Do you also use the apartment on your days off, Mrs Marsden?' he said.

'No, it's not for me' she replied calmly. 'I've got my room here out back, that's enough for me. What do I need London for?'

'That's a good question,' he said. 'How well did you know Catherine?'

'Not very. But she was a nice enough girl, kept herself to herself,' she said, shaking her head. 'The Lord seems to take them young these days.'

'Yes, He does,' he said. Something about the way she said it seemed to suggest that the tragedy was not wholly unexpected. 'Forgive me if this sounds like a bit of an odd question,' he said, 'but, how did you feel when you heard the news of her death?'

'What on earth do you mean? It's a tragedy, of course,' she said, before adding, 'but these things do happen, don't they.'

'Do they?' he replied.

'Listen, officer,' she began, 'I had two little-uns once – a boy and a girl. Both of them have passed on,' she said.

'I'm sorry to hear that,' he said.

'Nothing for you to be sorry about, lad. But that's not all. I had an older lad too, went off to France, along with his dad.

Only the old man made it back – until he caught the Spanish Flu. So, it's just me now, and I expect I'll be meeting-up with them all soon enough. There's no point crying about it now,' she added. 'It'll be your time as well before long, no doubt.'

'Yes,' said Justin. 'There's no escaping it in the end.' He felt humbled by her answer. He put the lid back on his pen and closed his notebook. 'I'm not sure how much you can help us, Mrs Marsden, but we need to get hold of whoever did this to young Catherine. Is there anything you can think of that could possibly help us in our enquiries?' She looked out across the room.

'There are always rumours flying about with these young girls, officer. Who's to say what's true and what isn't?'

'What kind of rumours?'

'It's not my place to say. And anyway, they might as well play the game while they still can in this lifetime. I say good luck to them – it's only God who's fit to judge.' She ran her fingers momentarily over the crucifix at her neck. 'Some people have misery thrust upon them in this world, while others end up creating their own problems – that's the only trouble,' she said.

'How do you mean?' said Justin. She leaned-in a little closer.

'If you ask me, judging by all this marriage business all of a sudden, I'd say she'd got herself into mischief. Not that that's got anything to do with all this other business, you understand, but I wouldn't be surprised if it were the case.'

'Actually, as it turns out, she was pregnant,' he replied.

'Yes, well it doesn't take a detective to predict that. It does happen. And she was a good enough girl, really.' She leaned closer still. 'Not like that other one; she's an unsavoury character, if you ask me.'

'Is that right? She seemed quite timid to me.'

'Well, you know what the young girls are like these days. Still, I'm not judging.'

'What about Stephen, Mrs Marsden?' he said.

'He's a good enough lad, though he drinks a bit too much sometimes – comes back from the village every now and then worse for wear. Lord Keating wanted rid of him for it at one point.'

'Have a lot of staff been and gone while you've been here?' said Justin.

'The young girls do. Some of them aren't up to much. And there was another lad here a while ago, but he went; Lord Keating wasn't happy with him. You'd have to ask him why. Only Stephen's been here for any decent amount of time.'

'What did you mean about Sandra being an unsavoury character?' he said, pretending to consult his notes.

'Why don't you stick to one line of questioning? It's confusing,' she said.

'I think the answer's in the question,' he replied. She gave him a suspicious look but then smiled.

'Well, you'll have to ask her about that,' she said, gathering her apron round her. 'If you don't mind, officer, I do have a few things to prepare before lunch.'

'Of course,' said Justin. 'We'll call you back if we need to speak to you again.'

She got up and left, pulling the door to behind her. Justin got up and closed it.

'Why do none of them shut the bloody doors behind them?' he said, sitting back down at the table. Cameron shrugged.

'What now, sir?'

'We might need to speak to Sandra again, but–'
The door fell open slightly.

'Come in,' he said in a loud voice, but no-one answered. Justin got up and looked out into the hallway, but there was no-body there. Then he gave the door a firm shove.

The muffled chimes of the grandfather clock rang out in the hallway as the clock struck two. It was Lady Keating's turn to be interviewed. She walked over to the table and pulled out a chair, nervously smoothing her grey tweed skirt as she sat down.

'I'll get someone to clear that for you,' she said, looking down at the half-filled ashtray.

'It's no bother,' said Justin, moving it across the table, out of their line of sight. 'I understand you had some guests over on Wednesday night?' he said.

'Yes, just some old friends of ours,' she said.

'And what time were they here till?'

'I think until some time after ten,' she said, looking out through the French doors towards the summer house, 'but I can't be too sure.'

'How long have you known these old friends?'

'Since we were married,' she said. 'Over four years now. But they've been friends of Jeffrey's since long before that.'

'How did you and your husband meet?' he said. She looked at him, a little surprised at his line of questioning.

'I fail to see its relevance,' she said.

'It probably isn't all that relevant, but we need to piece together as much information as we possibly can. It seems highly likely that the attack on Catherine was premeditated. Most intruders wouldn't feel the need to go as far as they did with her. Our job is to find out why they did.'

'Yes, of course,' she said. 'Jeffrey and I met when I was working at The Ritz hotel. He often used to stay there when he had late sessions at The House of Lords, and I suppose I must have caught his attention. We would bump into each other sometimes.'

'Indeed,' he said. 'And what was your position there?'

'I was a maid,' she said. Then, noticing the expression on his face, she quickly added, 'It was nothing like *that*, you understand.'

'No, of course not,' he said shaking his head, 'it's just that I never saw you as a maid. You're not really the type. You were privately educated, surely?'

'No, not at all,' she said, relaxing enough now to almost force a smile. 'Jeffrey and I are from very different backgrounds.'

'It doesn't sound that way,' said Cameron, 'if you don't mind me saying.'

'The elocution lessons weren't wasted then,' she said, turning to him. 'They were a present from Jeffrey.'

'That's very generous of him,' replied Cameron. Justin gave him a scornful look.

'So, you were working at The Ritz,' continued Justin, 'and so, does that explain your love of Green Park?'

'Yes, it does,' she replied. 'You see my parents both passed away when I was quite young; my mother when I was twelve and my father a year later. I was alone here, you see. We were immigrants from Poland. Once they had gone, and I found myself working at The Ritz, Jeffrey became a kind of benefactor, I suppose – when I had no-one else.

'So, you were married quite young?' said Justin.

'Yes. We got married in Scotland, actually,' she said turning to Cameron. 'It's different up there.'

'I understand that Stephen and Catherine had planned to get married,' said Justin, 'it was announced fairly recently, is that correct?'

'Yes, in the last couple of weeks,' she replied.

'And they both seemed happy about this?'

'Of course,' she shrugged, 'why wouldn't they be?'

'Well, you see, Catherine was expecting a child, so there's more than one reason why they may have decided to get married.'

Lady Keating looked down at her hands, and her eyes started to well-up.

'I'm sorry if I upset you, Lady Keating,' he said.

'No, I'm sorry,' she said producing a handkerchief from her pocket. 'I had no idea, that's all. It just gets worse, doesn't it?'

'Let's talk about Wednesday night for a moment. Everyone was here at the house, apart from Catherine. Why was she not here?'

'You'd have to ask Jeffrey about that; I don't deal with that side of things.'

'Yes, I have a number of things I'd like to ask your husband, actually, Lady Keating. Can you tell us anything about Sandra? Does she go down to London very often, to visit family, for example?'

'I don't think she has any family,' replied Lady Keating, 'at least she's never mentioned them.'

'Her as well?' he said.

'What do you mean?'

'Oh, it just seems a little coincidental that's all, as far as the family backgrounds go – Mrs Marsden, Miss MacGuire, yourself – no-one seems to have any. Does Stephen have a family?'

'I'm really not certain,' she replied, 'We keep a respectful distance from all our staff.'

'Of course,' said Justin. 'So, your husband hires all of the staff here?'

'That's correct.'

'There was another male servant who used to work here, wasn't there? Your husband got rid of him.'

'Yes, why do you ask?'

'Are you expecting your husband to return home at any point today?'

'I really don't know. He has business at Parliament, so I shouldn't expect he'll be back before seven or eight. Were you intending to speak to Stephen while you're here?'

'That depends on what kind of state he's in.'

'I could go and check for you,' she said. She got up and left the room.

'What do you think, sir?' said Cameron, getting up to make sure that the door was closed behind her.

'I think that either Lord Keating likes to surround himself, for some reason, with tragic cases, or that he has a heart of gold,' he replied. 'There's something not right about this whole set-up. Does Jeffrey strike you as being the altruistic benefactor type?'

'I wouldn't have thought so, sir.'

There was a knock at the door. It opened, and Lady Keating reappeared.

'You can speak to Stephen now, if you wish,' she said.

Stephen, it seemed, was yet to move from the couch. A fresh snifter of cognac, seemingly untouched, sat on the coffee table in front of him where he still sat, cradling his head in both hands. The curtains had been pulled shut, adding to the sense of morbidity in the room. To alleviate the boredom of watching over him, Sandra had begun to lightly dust the bookshelves in the half-light.

'My condolences once again, Mr Hollis,' said Justin, coming into the room and taking a seat opposite him. 'I'm sorry to bother you at this time. We could come back later, if you'd prefer?'

'Now's as good as ever,' said Stephen, in a slow, defeated tone. His pupils were dilated, the blue of his irises barely visible under his drooping eyelids.

'When did you last see Catherine, Mr Hollis?' Justin began.

'Wednesday morning,' he said eventually. 'I put her in a cab for the station at around noon.'

'And you were expecting her back this afternoon?'

'Yes, of course. You already know this, don't you? She would have been on her way back now.'

Stephen drained an inch of the cognac that was sitting in front of him and then lowered his head into the palms of his hands. Justin slid the glass a little further away from him.

'I'm sorry I have to ask these questions, but can you tell me how long you two had been personally involved with one another?' said Justin. Stephen raised his head, his eyelids drooping ever lower.

'About a year,' he said, inhaling deeply then reaching across and draining the rest of the glass. 'We were getting married. I hadn't spoken to her yet, but I had made plans for us go to

America and make a new start. It would have been better for the child.'

'Yes. I'm sorry,' said Justin, 'but I do have one last question. Do you know of anyone who might have wanted to harm Catherine in any way?'

Silence fell into the room.

'No,' he said eventually. 'And I don't think I can answer any more of your questions.' His elbow slipped from his knee and he jolted forward, catching himself just in time. Justin put a hand out to steady him.

'I understand. Thank you, Mr Hollis,' said Justin. Cameron followed him out to the car.

Back at the office, the skeleton night crew was just beginning its shift. Justin made some telephone calls and arranged for a public appeal to be put out in time to catch the next morning's papers, while Cameron chased up the officers at the apartment in Green Park. The door opened and Inspector Lisson walked in.

'You should be out of here by now,' he said, coming over to Justin's desk.

'So should you,' replied Justin. 'Anyway, what have you got then?' he added. Lisson pulled up a chair.

'Not a lot yet,' he replied. 'No-one saw anything, no-one suspects anyone. Looks like an inside job. How about you?'

'Not much to go on really, but I've got my suspicions.'

'Of who?' said Lisson.

'I don't know yet. There are some things I still need to check out.'

'Well, don't piss about for too long. If you're going out there tomorrow, maybe I'll come with you. You look like you could use a more experienced head.'

'No,' said Justin, addressing Lisson, 'I don't want you there.'

'Well, that's not very nice is it, Inspector?' he replied in his most patronising tone. 'I should think you'd be grateful for the help. Anyway, Andrews wants us both on it.'

'I think you'll find he's happy for us to work apart for the time being…and so am I,' said Justin.

'Why the aggravation?' Lisson put his hands up in a gesture of innocence.

'You know exactly why. Let's not pretend, shall we?' Cameron came in and pulled up a chair at the desk.

'Yes, Constable?' said Justin. Cameron cleared his throat.

'There were a couple of cars spotted around Hyde Park Corner way, late on Wednesday night,' he began. 'They seemed to be travelling together. It's unusual at that time of night and it was an especially quiet night as well. We're probably clutching at straws, but we've not really got much else to go on, sir.'

'Who spotted them?' said Lisson.

'Just some passer-by; he came over to the apartment block about an hour ago and spoke to one of the officers. He can't say what type of cars they were, and he's given no description of the drivers, but he wanted to mention it anyway.'

'It sounds like nothing,' said Lisson.

'Well you can chase that up tomorrow anyway,' said Justin. Lisson turned to him.

'Two cars, no description, and they've probably got nothing to do with it? That should take me all of five minutes,' he said.

'It looks to me like you've got your work cut out,' said Justin. Cameron passed Lisson a sheet of notepaper with the contact details of the witness written on it.

'I'll see what Andrews thinks,' said Lisson, screwing up the paper and stuffing it into his pocket. He pulled the door shut behind him as he left.

'You really don't like him, sir,' said Cameron.

'Nope.' Justin reached into his desk drawer and pulled out a bottle of whisky. He spread his notes out on the desk and poured them both a drink. Cameron read through the notes.

'Lord Henry Cunningham, sir?' he said with a smile.

'What?' said Justin, looking down at the sheet of paper upon which he had scribbled the name.

'I thought the lads were just joking,' Cameron muttered to himself.

'What do you mean by that?'

'Well, I knew you were posh, sir, but not *that* posh.'

'Oh, I see. He's a good friend of mine – from the army,' he said dismissively. 'How's the whisky?'

Cameron nodded his appreciation and they both read through the notes together.

'What are you thinking so far, sir,' said Cameron, taking a large gulp of the cloudy, faintly coffeeish liquid in his mug.

'I get the impression that it's not a very happy household in Horsham. There's something I find slightly disturbing about it.' Justin took a large swig from his own mug, peered into it quizzically and put it back down. 'These things don't happen by accident. Whoever they were, they must have known she would be there if she was the intended target. By all accounts she seems to have kept herself to herself; no family, according to the Keatings. Maybe Mr Hollis can tell us a little more about her friends, if she had any. We'll need to interview Mr Hollis again anyway when he's in a better state of mind, and probably the other girl too, what's-her-name – Miss MacGuire. I'll speak to Henry, Lord Cunningham I mean, about the new male servant, but I don't think he'll be much of a lead. And I'll get some background information from him on Lord Keating. I don't particularly like the man and I wouldn't be surprised if he knew more than he's letting on,' he sighed. 'People in his position are used to getting away with things.'

'Aye, I'm none too keen on him either, sir. It's always possible that Catherine wasn't the intended target though. Maybe it was meant as an attack against the Keatings, rather than against the girl.'

'Yes, there is always that. I think we're going to have to get to know them a bit better, unfortunately,' said Justin. He looked down at his watch. 'I expect you should be getting back to the wife and kids,' he said, offering-up the whisky bottle.

'I suppose I should be, sir…but I won't say no,' said Cameron, holding up his mug. 'Christ, that last one reminded me of the army.'

'Petrol tea?' smiled Justin. 'Yes, I remember it well.'

'Aye, it got into bloody everything,' replied Cameron. He took a large swig.

'Who were you with?' said Justin.

'Second Highlanders, from 'fifteen onwards,' he replied.

'*Cock O' The North* and all that?'

'Aye, that's it,' smiled Cameron.

'You would have been up at Mametz then. I was commissioned into the Welch, Third. You were probably whistling distance from where we were.'

'Aye, we would've been, sir.' He took another gulp. 'I heard you got the MC.'

'Yes, I did. It's a bit of a long story,' he said, looking down and swilling round the contents of his mug.

'Aren't they all,' replied Cameron. 'I caught one up at the wood.' He undid the button of his shirt sleeve and rolled it up to show Justin a pink twisted channel on the lower half of his left bicep. 'Straight in out the back,' he said almost proudly. 'Missed the bone completely. I was quite pleased with that; got a short rest out of it.'

'That was a stroke of luck. You seem to have survived fairly intact, other than that.'

'Aye, better than some.' Cameron put down his mug then got up, unhooked his jacket from the hanger and came back carrying a large book.

'Don't want to forget this,' he said, sitting back down.

'What's that you're reading, the code of conduct?' said Justin.

'Nah. Fiction's for the wife, sir,' he replied. 'Dr Gross. German, believe it or not. Something to read on the way to-and-from.' Justin eyed the book warily. 'Apparently a good investigator needs to possess "the vigour of youth, energy ever on the alert, robust health…liveliness and vigilance" sir.'

'Oh, good. We'll be all right then.'

'Aye.'

'What about good old-fashioned gut instinct?'

'Well, nothing beats that, sir. Still, I'm sure the rest of it can't do any harm.'

'I'm not so sure about that,' he said. 'Did you ever want to go on to study? It seems you were cut out for it.'

'I did, and I was going to,' said Cameron proudly. 'I even won myself a scholarship, no less.'

'So, what happened?'

'The usual story. The first child came along, then the war…' He shook his head, 'it's too late for all that now.'

'Oh, I don't know.'

'I do. You can't do much with a family in tow.'

'Did you plan to have a child?'

'We planned the second and third ones, if that's what you mean,' he said, taking a sip from his mug. 'You're not married are you, sir?'

'No, I seem to have avoided it so far.'

'What about your pals? Are they all married?'

'Some of them are.'

'You're best off out of it, sir, especially with the surplus since we got back, eh?' he said with a wink. Justin quickly finished what was left in his mug and picked up the bottle.

'I shouldn't,' said Cameron unconvincingly, as Justin held it over his mug.

'Come on,' said Justin, 'you're a long time dead.'

He poured two large ones and held up the half-empty bottle.

'It brings out the truth, does whisky,' he said and clinked his mug against Cameron's. 'Never trust a man who can't handle his drink.'

'Aye. And never trust an Englishman who thinks he knows about whisky,' said Cameron. Justin laughed.

'Touché,' he replied. Cameron put down his mug.

'Aren't you a bit too well-bred for a policeman's job, sir?'

'Well, I had a fairly comfortable upbringing, I suppose,' he shrugged.

'You suppose, sir? I think you'd know if you hadn't. May I ask what happened?'

'A similar thing that happened to both of us,' he said. 'Or maybe not quite.' He thought for a moment. 'I have my reasons. It's all just a game in the end.'

'How do you mean, sir?'

'Oh, I don't know. Everything. Sometimes it all just seems like some big joke.'

Cameron swilled the liquid round in his mug.

'I don't quite get what you mean, sir.'

'I mean, you might as well do something with your life that means something; or at least attempt it.'

'And that's why you're doing *this*?' said Cameron, with a look of bemusement.

'I suppose so. It makes a difference – it's easy to forget that sometimes. And I suppose I enjoy it, as long as I make sure I don't take it home.'

'Well, that's fair enough,' said Cameron, 'but there's no escaping much these days.'

'No, there isn't.' Justin took another sip and placed the mug down on his desk. 'Don't laugh if I tell you this, but my only real escape is to get out into the country. The city will suffocate you, if you let it.'

'And you find that it helps?'

'Absolutely. You get far too wrapped up in all the details otherwise – you can see it all the time. Everyone gets too caught-up these days.'

'But do you not get bored, sir? If there's one thing I miss, it's being out with my pals.'

'To be honest,' he sighed, 'I look at people and I just see them holding each other back. You can see them constantly reining each other in. It's the same with the blokes here. This bloody job's enough for me to deal with. I'd rather just be left alone.'

'Aye, well don't get married then, sir.'

'I assure you, I'll try not to. But it'll catch up with me one day, no doubt.'

They sat in silence for a moment.

'Anyway,' said Justin, 'how did we get onto this?'

'I don't know, sir.' Cameron looked at his watch. 'I'd better head off now or I'll be in trouble. Thanks for the drink.'

'No problem. We'll get back out to Horsham tomorrow – try to find out what that old bastard knows.'

Cameron took the tram north from Westminster then caught the omnibus to Holloway Road. He sat down next to the window and found himself struggling to keep his eyes fixed on his book, as he rocked back and forth. It was not for lack of focus; each time his eyes involuntarily left the page, he re-read the line just as soon as he became aware of it. But somehow, despite his efforts, the sentences seemed to have lost all meaning and the voice in his head trailed off of its own accord. He gave up and closed the book.

Turning his attention to the view through the window, watching pub after pub go by, he fought the urge for another drink. Then, having won the battle, he alighted at his stop and drew in some long, deep breaths of the diesel-heavy air, before making his way along the pavement towards his flat above the newsagents.

After struggling with the key in the lock, he realised that the light in the hall was already off, which meant that everyone was already asleep. He swore under his breath, grieving for the nightcap he had passed up. But it was too late now. Knowing this, the feeling of sobriety returned to him, almost instantaneously.

In the kitchen, at the top of the bowed and worn stairs, he found his dinner sitting on the table, cold and uncovered. He pulled up a chair and ate the powdery potatoes and peas that had been smothered in the thinnest of gravies and looked ahead at the wall with its cracked paintwork and chipped beige tiles.

How many families must this place have seen? he thought, as he put the plate in the sink and went into the bedroom where his wife was already asleep.

Maggie stirred as he gently pushed the door shut behind him, then turned away from him and closed her eyes. He undressed quietly by the light at the side of the bed, his eyes drawn to the open end of his pillowcase that was facing towards her. It was as if the open sleeve was somehow inviting her closer towards him, and, as he looked down at it, he wondered why it rankled with him so. Unable to resist the urge any longer, he picked up the pillow and turned it round to face the other way, and immediately felt better.

He could still taste the whisky as he lay in the dark picturing the clear golden liquid, turned murky in the unwashed mugs. It was something of a novelty these days, he thought; long gone were his days of drinking. Not on a policeman's pay.

He remembered something Justin had said, something about other people holding you back.

A bus went past, sending a draft into the room and disrupting the shade of the curtains.

It's all one big joke, the inspector had said – or something to that effect. I suppose that's what the job does to you. And then that old bastard Keating with his elocution lessons. What a bastard. And what a beauty.

His eyes were closing now. He was starting to feel a bit sick. He rolled onto his side and fell asleep.

Four

'That dashboard's vibrating,' said Cameron, as they waited for the traffic to resume movement.

'The mechanic's probably been tinkering with it,' replied Justin. Another dose of the doctor's prescription had now kicked-in and his heart was beginning to pound. He pressed both palms down on top of the shuddering panel to stop it from moving. 'It is what it is,' he said with a shrug.

Cameron shifted gears and moved out to overtake the other vehicles.

'Ah, my head!' he said, rubbing his temples as they stopped in traffic once again.

'I didn't think we got through that much,' said Justin. 'I thought you said you were Scottish.'

'Aye…aye. I used to be. I don't have much time for the drink these days, sir.'

'So I see.'

'These late nights, they're going to get me into trouble.'

'That's part of the job, I'm afraid,' said Justin, 'I hope you told her that.'

'That's what I said, but you know what they're like.'

'She probably thinks you're leading a double life.'

'Aye, if only!'

A heavy grey mass had gradually swept in overhead, continuing to darken the sky as they got closer to the house in Horsham. They turned off of the main road and onto a country lane, and the view opened-up across the fields.

The sky began to empty, thudding down onto the roof of the car in a barrage of heavy droplets. As they drove on, the yellowish lights of the manor house came into view, shining dully, as they passed in and out of sight above the undulating hedgerows.

The public appeal had attracted a small group of reporters, which had arrived early and huddled together beneath the oak archway. As the car slowed to turn onto the property, a couple of them emerged from their makeshift shelters, and a camera swung out across the windscreen.

'Speed up,' said Justin. Cameron pressed down on the accelerator and the car slued up the gravel drive.

The front door of the house seemed to open by itself as they made their way towards it.

'Good morning,' said Sandra, hiding herself behind the door, away from the cameras.

They stepped inside, and Lord Keating appeared in the hallway. Staring silently at them, he turned and motioned for them to follow him into the drawing room.

'Have a seat; make yourselves at home, why don't you,' he said bitterly. He waved his finger at the maid and she left the room, pulling the door shut behind her.

'I would offer you refreshments,' he continued, 'but I'm afraid we're a little under-staffed.' He checked his watch and went over to the drinks cabinet to pour himself a sherry.

'Is Mr Hollis here, sir?' said Justin, taking a seat on the sofa.

'No, he is not,' said Jeffrey with his back still turned to him. 'He was in no fit state to do his job properly, so I told him to take a few days off. That other little pansy has driven him off somewhere, probably hoping to have his way with him in a moment of weakness, no doubt. Only the girl's here, I'm afraid.'

'That's all right,' said Justin, 'it was you we were after.'

'Yes, and you're not the only ones.'

Jeffrey moved over to the window and looked out towards the congregation beneath the trees. The rain had stopped, and there was even a break in the clouds through which the sunlight shone down, illuminating Jeffrey as he stood behind the curtains.

'This is your doing, I suppose?' he said, pointing at Justin. 'I fail to see why you needed to involve the press.'

'We needed to put out an appeal for information, sir,' he replied. 'I'm afraid the inconvenience, to yourself and to us, is of little importance. While the assailants are still at large they may kill again.'

'And they won't be the only ones – this is a bloody nuisance!' he said, peeping out again towards the archway. 'They were up at the front door this morning like Jehovah's bloody Witnesses; pointing their cameras about and loitering around the Bugatti. That's the last thing I need.'

'I should imagine it is, sir,' said Justin.

'I set the dogs loose out back and told the lot of them to bugger off! It was quite amusing actually. They'll be getting a blast of the old Lee-Enfield if they come up my driveway again!'

'Please don't do that, sir,' said Cameron in his usual laconic way.

'What do you want anyway?' said Jeffrey, sitting down on the sofa opposite them and lighting a cigarette.

'A number of things actually, sir,' said Justin. 'There are a few things troubling us which we'd like to clear up.'

'Go on,' said Jeffrey.

'I'm sure I don't need to skirt around the details with you, sir. It's partly to do with the nature of the attack. We've discounted burglary as the motive and, given the efficiency with which the assailants moved into the apartment and back out again, it seems quite unlikely that it was committed purely on the off-chance.'

'What exactly do you mean?'

'Well, sir, the attack was unnecessarily vicious, and it has all the hallmarks of being planned well in advance. Do you mind?' said Justin, lighting a cigarette. Lord Keating leaned forward and prodded the ashtray towards the middle of the table between them. Justin continued: 'Now, as far as I understand, Catherine had no family of her own, and neither did she seem to have many friends outside of this house. So, for the attack to have been planned out, the assailants would have had to have known when she would be at the property on her own.'

'You mean to say you believe someone in this house was involved?' said Jeffrey.

'Not in the actual attack, as it seems that everyone's whereabouts is accounted for. But whoever did this, if she was indeed the target, would have had to have known her days off from work.'

'*If* she was the target,' said Jeffrey.

'Yes, well, the fact that there was no break-in at the property suggests that either she let the assailants in or that they let themselves into the apartment. Do you see where we're heading, sir?'

'Have you considered the possibility that maybe one of the porters could have been involved?'

'That is a possibility, sir, yes. But they don't have the keys to the apartments.'

'Not officially,' he said dismissively.

'Unless you know otherwise?'

'No. It's just a possibility, that's all.' Jeffrey was sitting forward now, his attitude becoming increasingly defensive.

'Yes, we'll keep that in mind, sir. Your maid here, Miss MacGuire, told us that the house staff don't take the same days off each week; is that correct?'

'Yes, it is. Their days off are rotated.'

'But Catherine was supposed to work that evening, wasn't she? That is, until you asked her to swap shifts with Miss MacGuire.'

Jeffrey sat for a moment, looking agitated and rubbing his eyes.

'You told me yourself, sir, that Catherine was the girl you would have on when you had important guests round for dinner,' continued Justin.

'Yes, well you see our guests that evening are old friends of mine,' said Jeffrey, his tone picking up as if he was relieved to have stumbled across the right answer. 'I don't mind who serves when the guests are close friends.'

'So, why did you ask the girls to swap shifts that evening?'
'I didn't ask them to, they asked me,' he replied.
'Who did?'
'Both of them.'
'Not according to Miss MacGuire,' said Cameron.
'No, wait a minute,' said Jeffrey, 'it was Catherine who asked. She approached me that afternoon.'
'Right,' said Justin, pausing for a moment. 'See, Miss MacGuire seems to think that it was at the weekend and that they were both asked by you.'
'Oh yes, that's right,' replied Jeffrey, desperately trying not to look as though he were backpedalling.
'So, which is it, sir?' said Justin.
'Oh, I think I remember now, it was indeed at the weekend. Yes, that's correct.'
'Are you certain of that?'
'Is it that difficult to remember, sir?' added Cameron.
'No, it was Catherine who asked me at the weekend,' he replied. 'It was only mentioned in passing. It wasn't important at the time,' he shrugged. 'I then told Sandra to swap with her.'
'It's a shame we can't check with Catherine,' said Justin, turning to Cameron.
'Isn't it,' he replied.
'The problem we have, sir, is this,' Justin continued, 'it seems that if she was the intended target then somebody must have known she was going to be at the property, and, at the moment, all we have is the fact that you asked the two girls to swap shifts.'
'I just told you, it was Catherine who asked me. Sandra must be getting things muddled up, poor girl – she's really not the brightest.'
'Yes, that may very well be true. But the fact remains that it seems as though someone was intentionally targeted. Whether that was Catherine or Sandra, we don't know, but nevertheless, someone must have allowed the assailants access to the apartment.'

'Though she may very well have let them in herself,' Jeffrey reminded them.

'That is a possibility,' replied Justin.

'It's more than a possibility, officer, so I suggest you re-evaluate your tone with me,' said Jeffrey. He was up on his feet now next to the chimney-breast, lighting another cigarette. 'If you must know, I was perfectly happy for the girls to swap shifts when Catherine asked me because…let's just say that one of my guests that evening had taken somewhat of a shine to young Sandra. Having her serve him that evening was, oh…I don't know, sort of a private joke.'

'Is Miss MacGuire in on the joke, sir?' said Cameron.

'That is irrelevant,' he replied.

'Which friend was it?' said Justin.

'Also irrelevant,' said Jeffrey. He stood up and ran his hand down the front of his cardigan to flatten-out the creases. 'Now, if you don't mind officers, I do have some important business—'

'Please excuse us, sir, we didn't mean to cause offence,' said Justin in as innocent a tone as he thought necessary to placate him. 'We just have a few more questions to ask, if you don't mind.'

'Well, get a move on,' said Jeffrey, sitting back down on the couch.

'One thing that did attract my attention, sir, was the fact that when we arrived here yesterday morning, Mr Hollis was still unaware that his fiancé had been murdered. Now, I do apologise for the fact that I was unable to get someone out here to inform him, but at the same time, it does seem a little odd that no-one else had told him. Cruel even, wouldn't you say, given the fact that when we arrived here he was waiting for us at the door?'

'I accept your apology, officer,' replied Jeffrey.

'Yes. It is something that will play on my conscience,' said Justin, letting the words hang in the air. 'That reminds me actually, there was another gentleman who used to work here, wasn't there?'

'If I could have been certain that he was a gentleman, he would probably still be here,' said Jeffrey.

'Did something happen, sir?'

'No, nothing really,' he replied after a moment's reflection, taking on a surprisingly modest tone.

'Could you elaborate on that, sir?' said Justin. Again, there was a moment of quiet.

'Oh, very well,' he said, inspecting the burning end of the cigarette he had just lit. 'I suppose I can be somewhat of a jealous husband at times. This fellow was much closer to my wife's age than I am, and I just didn't trust him. I didn't want him hanging around, what with my being out of the house so much of the time.'

'And was there anything at all untoward going on?' Jeffrey's face softened into a slightly embarrassed smile.

'No, of course there wasn't,' he said. 'I'm aware of the fact that it can sometimes be a bit of a problem of mine.'

'Your wife *is* a lot younger than you though, isn't she, sir?' said Cameron. Jeffrey looked up.

'And what's so wrong about that?' he said, the abrasive edge instantly returning to his manner. 'God knows I spent the best part of my youth in bloody Africa, and there's nothing much worth pursuing down that way, I can tell you!' he snapped.

'Let's just keep to the point, shall we?' said Justin, addressing them both. 'When we spoke to your staff they told us that Stephen had also left your service on one previous occasion, but that he then returned shortly after. Why was that, sir?'

'He decided he didn't want to be here anymore, so he left. Then he realised that he had made a mistake, and so he returned,' replied Jeffrey.

'Did you feel affronted at all by the fact that he had left your service so abruptly then changed his mind and walked straight back in? Did you take him straight back, sir?'

'He was always a good servant, so I didn't see any reason not to.'

'Do you know why he decided to leave, sir, when he was, by this time, already quite deeply involved with Miss Smith? It seems a little odd that he would just up and leave her, seemingly on a whim.'

'You would have to ask him that. I don't know the details of their relationship; it all happens below stairs.'

'But, you do have quite a high turnover of staff, don't you, sir?' said Justin, 'particularly amongst the female members. I would assume that you do have some involvement in what goes on.'

'They come and go as they please,' said Jeffrey, brushing the insinuation aside, his tone becoming increasingly flat and defensive.

'Why is it that the women tend to leave more often than the men? Apart from Stephen Hollis and the other gentleman, of course.'

'I don't appreciate where this is going,' he replied.

'We're nearly finished, sir,' said Justin. 'The high turnover of girls…so to speak?'

Rolling his eyes in annoyance, Jeffrey replied, 'They're just not as reliable – all those hormones flying about – it probably makes it hard for them to keep any job down. If they wish to leave, it is up to them. And if they're no good then, of course, I let them go.'

'How difficult can the job be?' said Cameron.

'Are you quite done?' said Jeffrey, moving to get up again. 'Some are cut out for it and some are not. It's as simple as that,' he said. 'Maybe other employers have lower standards than my own, but that's really none of my concern. I expect the best.'

'Like young Catherine?' said Justin.

'Yes, like young Catherine,' replied Jeffrey. 'She will be sorely missed.'

Justin looked down at his watch.

'I think we've taken up enough of your time today, Lord Keating,' he said.

'Don't we all.'

'We would just like to have another quick chat with young Sandra, and then I think we'll be off.'

'Thank you most kindly, officer,' said Jeffrey, shooting daggers at him as he got up and left. He slammed the door shut behind him.

'I think I'll do the talking from now on thank you, Constable,' said Justin.

'Of course, sir.'

The door opened and in came the girl.

'Shut the door please and have a seat,' said Justin, 'we'd just like to have a quick word about a couple of things we'd like to clear up.'

Sandra sat down opposite them, exhibiting the same nervous look as on the previous occasion.

'Now, Miss MacGuire,' Justin began, 'why did you lie to us before about being asked to swap shifts with Catherine?'

'I didn't,' she replied, looking panicked.

'So, are you calling your employer a liar? Lord Keating told us that Catherine had asked him on the Wednesday afternoon if the two of you could swap shifts.'

'Maybe she did, I don't know. It was Lord Keating who asked me.'

'And he asked you on Wednesday afternoon?'

She nodded.

'But I thought you told us that he asked you at the weekend.'

'I can't remember now. Everything's all mixed up.'

'Well, that's all right. Everyone's allowed a memory lapse from time to time,' he said, looking across at Cameron. 'Let's try and do a little bit better from now on, shall we?'

Sandra looked at him nervously, not wanting to give anything else away.

'You've been working here for nearly two years now, so you will have seen a fair number of girls come and go in that time. Do you have any idea why that might be?'

Sandra was already shaking her head, long before he had finished asking the question.

'No,' she said, her eyes darted towards the door momentarily.

'I see,' said Justin, writing something down on his notepad. 'So, you were here when Stephen left and then later returned. Do you know why he did so?'

'I don't know,' she replied, 'nothing I was told about.' Justin passed the pad across the table so that she could read it. She looked down at the words: *Does Lord Keating force you or any of the other girls into sexual relations?*

Sandra gave him a look as though he were pointing a gun at her.

'So, you don't know why Stephen came back to re-take his old position? Yes or no?' he said, pointing at the note. 'This is quite important.'

The girl stared at him for a moment, looked at the door again and then back down at the note in front of her. Justin tapped it with his finger. Seconds passed as she sat looking back at him blankly, indicating neither answer.

'Very well,' said Justin. 'That will be all then, thank you for your time.'

'So, you think he does then?' said Cameron as they drove back towards London.

'Probably. But I would appreciate it if you would stay quiet during the interviews, if you don't mind,' said Justin.

'Of course, sir. Sorry, sir.'

'I'm the one in charge of this investigation.'

'I apologise, sir.'

'I don't like him any more than you do, but you need to take care with people like him, Constable.'

'Yes, sir.'

'None of them seem too sure about who asked who to swap shifts, or even when it actually happened for that matter. But I think Lord Keating's lying. I can see him arranging the swap so that he could play out his little joke involving Sandra, but I don't yet see why Catherine would want to be in the apartment alone. We can press Jeffrey on this and we'll also check with Stephen. I'm sure Catherine would have said something to the man she was about to marry.'

'You'd expect so, sir.'

'But regardless of that, something tells me Lord Jeffrey Keating's up to something. I hope I made it clear to him that he won't be getting any special treatment.'

'Oh, I think he understood that very well, sir.'

'Good. He'll be used to getting his own way.'

'We don't know for certain that he has been up to anything with the female staff though, sir.'

'So why didn't she deny it? When we get back, I think I'll post a constable to the manor house to keep an eye on him. I don't think it would do us any harm to have him observed, at least until we can speak to Mr Hollis again.'

Ten o'clock was the strict cut-off point for visiting Lord Henry. By the time Justin had climbed the steps and knocked on the red door, it was already a quarter-to.

He sat down on the sofa in the drawing-room, feeling exhausted now that the prescription had worn off. The door glided open.

'Darling, what a pleasant surprise,' said Lord Henry. 'How are you?' He was dressed in a velvet smoking jacket, cocktail in hand, and wore a navy-blue cravat in his open shirt collar. 'Take this away will you,' he said, passing his glass to his servant, 'and bring us some whisky.' He sat down on the sofa opposite Justin, crossed his legs and lit a cigarette.

'So, Sergeant, how has life been treating you of late?'

'I'm completely exhausted,' replied Justin.

'Marvellous. I saw some terrible business in the papers this morning. I hope it's not one of yours.'

'If you mean the Green Park case then yes, it is.'

The servant returned, placing a decanter and two glasses on the table.

'That will be all for now,' said Lord Henry, watching him leave the room. He poured two large whiskies and passed

one of them to Justin. 'To think of that kind of obnox-
iousness happening right on your own doorstep,' he said,
shaking his head. 'Well, it shouldn't surprise me these days, I
suppose.'

'It happens all the time,' said Justin with a shrug, 'it always
has.'

'Well, I shouldn't work myself too hard if I were in your
position; there are bags underneath your eyes. I hope you
realise that you owe it to your friends to preserve the last
meagre remnants of your youthful good-looks. Anyway, I'm
having a little gathering here on Saturday evening with some
rather special friends of mine, and if you refuse to come I
assure you I shall never speak to you again. I'm afraid Noel is
currently out of town – New York as a matter of fact – but
I'm simply dying for you to meet him. Nevertheless, you will
find yourself in the most extraordinary company if you do
decide to grace us with your presence.'

'Yes. Why not?' said Justin with a shrug.

'Of course, some of the guests won't be special at all – so
do remember to keep your guard up! Needless to say, I shall
be getting rid of them before the *jazz* begins.'

'I won't be in the mood for jazz, Henry.'

'No, and more's the pity,' he replied.

'Anyway, I came here for a reason,' said Justin. 'This Green
Park case: the flat belongs to one of your acquaintances –
Lord Jeffrey Keating. I interviewed his servants a couple of
days ago – one of whom I recognised, much to my
embarrassment. He worked for you until very recently and
he recognised me immediately.'

'Oh yes,' he said, 'that'll be young Samuel. Lovely fellow.
Nothing for you to worry about there; he's very much a
member of the club. How's she doing?'

'*He's* doing well,' said Justin. 'Sends his regards. A little too
obviously for my liking.'

'Oh yes, he is one to play games, that boy. I hope he put on
a good show.'

'A little too good. But I don't think my colleague noticed.' Henry rolled back on the couch with laughter.

'Oh, I shouldn't worry,' he said. 'Innocent until proven otherwise, don't they say? I can't imagine working for Jeffrey has the same perks as being in my service. If it gets too much for him, you can remind him that there's always an opening here,' said Henry, his eyebrow arching.

'He doesn't seem to have forgotten,' replied Justin. 'But anyway, about the case.'

'Oh, of course – that poor girl. Who was she?'

'She was another of Lord Jeffrey's maids, I'm afraid. She was using the flat on her day off, as they all do, apparently. It was the nature of the killing that I find troubling.'

'Oh, you mean?'

'No, nothing like that. Everything but. Though it seems there's a lot more to it. It wasn't a robbery, and no-one seems to have witnessed anything untoward, but it does seem as though it must have been planned rather meticulously. Only the other members of the household seem to have known she was there,' said Justin, remembering his whisky and pausing to take a large sip. 'Lord Keating changed her work schedule, either that day or at the weekend prior to it, no-body seems to quite remember when. Otherwise, she wouldn't have been there at all.'

'Oh.' Henry sounded intrigued.

'I was wondering if you could fill me in as to Lord Jeffrey's background. He's been a little difficult in his own kind of way, and I must say, I don't particularly like him.'

'Jeffrey Keating? Oh, I would make him your first line of enquiry! Lord knows what goes on in that house; enough to keep Hieronymus Bosch awake at night, one would think!'

'Really?'

'Good God, no,' laughed Henry. 'One would think he was well past it by now. But then…there are always rumours of course; you know how it is.'

'Not really, Henry.'

'Oh, you know what it's like; Chinese Whispers, that's all. It's always like that at The House. Shall we get some soda?'

Henry rang the bell and the servant appeared. Flexing his index finger twice, he made a 'chh, chh' sound, and the servant left the room. He returned a few moments later with the soda siphon.

'No, I imagine Jeffrey takes advantage where he can,' he continued, again eyeing the servant, 'but then he's entitled to a trip downstairs once in a while.'

'Downstairs?'

'Yes. To the servants' quarters, so to speak.'

'I see.'

'I think he has a tendency to get rid of any young girls who aren't accommodating enough, but I very much doubt there's much more to it than that. So long as he's cock-of-the-walk in his own house, I imagine he's perfectly happy.'

'Get rid of the girls how?' said Justin.

'Oh, I don't know…theft, laziness I suppose. Accusations. Nothing they can do anything about, of course. They just have to pack their bags and get out,' he said, looking pointedly at the servant, who then promptly left the room. 'Oh yes, and he's probably a naturist – a surprising number of them are, you know. Soda?' He offered Justin the siphon. Justin declined. 'Mind you, we all have our peccadillos,' continued Henry. 'Speaking of which, has your little problem been bothering you any more lately?'

Justin sat back, covering his eyes with the palm of his hand.

'I haven't received anything more in the post,' he said, 'though the last lot was sent from outside London, so there's not much I can do about it anyway. I don't suppose you've heard anything?'

'Give me a chance, dear boy, it's only been a couple of days. Now let me think. Windsor…royalty…well, of course! It must surely be the work a queen!' he said, laughing alone at his little joke. 'Actually,' he continued, 'I do know a man in Windsor. Are you having the post office watched?'

'Like I say, it's not my patch,' said Justin. 'I can't post someone all the way out there. And besides, I don't think it would be much help.'

Lord Henry put down his glass.

'Still, I think it's worth doing. I just happen to have a *very* special friend high up in the Berkshire Constabulary, who just might be able to help in some way.'

'Really?'

'Of course, dear. You didn't think you were the only officer of the law concealing mauve drawers? Our people are everywhere, you know.'

'No, of course not,' said Justin, but the smile on his face was one of defeat.

'Other than that, I would advise you to hire a private detective.'

'If you know someone who could help me out, it would be far better. I would appreciate the help.'

'Of course you would. I said I would sort out your problem for you and indeed, I shall!'

Five

It was coming up to five o'clock in the morning. A second car pulled up behind the first. An officer got out, approached the vehicle in front and opened the door.

'Any action?' he said.

'None whatsoever,' said the constable, his eyes half closed.

'You'd better get off then, you look knackered.'

'Did you bring coffee?'

'Yeah, why, do you want some?'

'No. You're going to need it.' He started the engine and drove off into the grey half-light of the country lane.

The second officer got back into his car, moved into the vacant space just across from the oak archway, and pulled out a newspaper and his flask of coffee. He turned to the sport section and folded the sheet over, resting it on the steering wheel, trying to make the best of the dull light. The figure of a journalist appeared at the passenger door next to him. The officer leaned over and lowered the window.

'Police, you idiot! Get lost!' he said, as the window pane rose back up. The man lowered his camera and shrank away.

At ten o'clock there was movement. A work van came up the lane and turned in under the oak arch. The officer picked up his notepad and pencil and took down the registration while the reporters rather helpfully blocked the van's way. Peppering the air with an impressive range of expletives, the driver finally managed to lurch the vehicle past them. At the top of the drive, two men in grey overalls got out and disappeared into the house.

They reappeared at eleven o'clock, got back into their van and left the grounds. As they reached the reporters there was a hollow thump, followed by more swearing as the van picked up speed and swerved off up the lane.

By half-past two, his patience was starting to wear thin. He got out of the car to stretch his legs and smoke a cigarette in the fresh air. Blowing smoke up towards the clouds, he watched to see how far it would go before it dissipated into nothing. Then, as he lit a second cigarette, he heard feet shifting in the gravel nearby, the sound of a car door slamming and an engine turning over.

He climbed back into the car as the vehicle coming down the gravel path picked up speed. As the group of reporters spilled out onto the road, a window flashed past, giving him the briefest glimpse of Lord Keating at the wheel. He started his engine, nudged the car through the crowd and followed the silver Citroen.

The two cars headed north through the village of Warnham and then onto Oxshott, before edging along Richmond Park. At a quarter-past three, Jeffrey pulled up outside an antiques shop in Acton and got out of his car. He was holding a large brown envelope in his hand. The officer pulled up some distance behind him and watched as he knocked on the side door of the shop, set-back from the street, probably leading up to the property above. On the fourth knock, Jeffrey was let in and did not reappear until over an hour later. Thankful for some action at last, the officer followed him back to the manor house.

Andrews sat forward, his forearms resting on his desk. 'So, where are we?' he said.

'I don't have a lot to go on so far, sir,' said Lisson. 'I've been trying to trace two cars that were spotted in the area, but no luck yet. For the most part I'm waiting on Inspector Lamoureaux.'

'I thought you might be,' said Justin, his eyes scouring the wall of Chief Inspector Andrews' office.

'So, what have you got then, Fauntleroy?' said Andrews turning to him.

'I'm concentrating on the motive, sir,' replied Justin. 'There's something not quite right going on at the house.'

'What do you mean?'

'Well, it seems like quite a complicated arrangement there. I think with a bit of digging around, someone's going to tell us what we need to know.'

'All right,' said Andrews turning back to Lisson, 'if you're done at the Green Park property for the time being, maybe you can join him out there.'

'Actually, sir,' said Justin, before Lisson was able to reply, 'it's a bit delicate at the moment. I think it's better if I handle this personally for now. I have some personal contacts who might be able to open some doors and get me the information I need. I'm going to have to tread carefully though.' Andrews sat back and crossed his arms.

'Personal contacts, eh? In those circles? Christ, you really are one of them, aren't you?'

'I just need a bit more time.'

'Are you sure you're definitely onto something? It'd better be more than just whispers on the fucking croquet lawn.'

'Someone in that house must know something, but I don't think they're about to just come out and tell us. And with all due respect, sir, I think we might progress a bit more quickly with Inspector Lisson concentrating his energies elsewhere for the time being.' Andrews sighed.

'All right then,' he said. 'I'll give you a few more days to dig up a lead and then I want the pair of you down there, you got that? It's all over the fucking papers already, and if it goes on for too long I'll be getting called down there myself. And you don't want that!'

'No, sir,' said Justin.

'All right, I've heard enough. Now just bugger off the pair of you.'

They left the office and Justin went back to his desk. Cameron came over.

'Sir, there's a call for you from DC Perry,' he said.

'Any movement?' Justin replied.

'Yes, he says it might not be important, but he followed Keating to an address in Acton.'

'All right, get the details from him, will you? Get the address and I'll see if it's worth following up.'

'Right, sir.'

Cameron went back over to the phone. Lisson passed him on his way over.

'So, what's going on then?' he said, leaning on the edge of Justin's desk. 'You're gonna need to get me up to speed unless you make some arrests in the next forty-eight hours.'

'Like I said, I'll involve you when I need you,' said Justin. He looked down at his work then noticed that Lisson was still standing by his desk. 'I don't want you cocking things up and blaming the rest of us,' he continued, 'I'll call you when I have to.'

Just then, Cameron reappeared holding a sheet of hand-written paper.

'Got the address, sir,' he said, handing Justin the sheet. Lisson snatched it from mid-air.

'What's this then?' he said.

Launching himself out of his chair, Justin tore the sheet back out of Lisson's hand.

'Quick, isn't he,' said Lisson. He turned to Cameron, 'Have you seen him box yet?'

Justin sat back down, quickly read the sheet and then reached for his hat.

'I'm going out,' he said, looking up at Cameron. 'Be ready to take any more messages if they come in.'

Justin took one of the newer cars and drove down to Harrow Road. He parked up outside an unremarkable black door, set within the parade of shops, and gave it a loud knock. There was the sound of footsteps and then the door opened.

'Good afternoon, sir,' said the proprietor, recognizing Justin at once – his face breaking into a practiced smile. He let Justin in then followed him through the whitewashed brick passageway to the bathhouses out back.

They stopped at the reception room. The Moorish tiles, and the scent of the incense and tobacco mixing with the clammy air, lent the place a hint of the exotic. The proprietor moved behind the desk.

'Do you require the use of the steam room, sir?' he said.

'Not at the moment. I'm afraid I'm here on a matter of some delicacy.' The proprietor looked confused. Justin showed him his identity card. 'We've had a complaint about some photographs being taken on the premises,' he continued.

'Photographs?' said the proprietor.

'Photographs of your clientele; unwanted attention, shall we say? The images are somewhat compromising and have been used to threaten the individual. I need to have a look around the premises – discreetly of course.'

'Well, I can't think what you mean, sir,' said the proprietor, shaking his head. 'Why would anybody wish to do a thing like that?' A certain detached coolness had now come over him. Justin knew that he had recognised him instantly, but his tone no longer betrayed their familiarity.

'Obviously I'm on your side – for now – with regards to what goes on here, so I don't want the vice squad getting in-volved. That wouldn't be very good for business now, would it? But I need your cooperation, otherwise I might not be able to help matters,' said Justin. The proprietor's expression remained static.

'I don't know exactly what it is you think goes on here, sir, but I'm afraid we have clients in at the moment,' he said after a short pause. 'I can't let you in without good reason and without the right authority.' The line seemed well rehearsed.

'Look, I know the position from where the pictures were taken. It will only take a few minutes and then I'll be gone.'

'And what exactly do you expect to find there, sir?'

'I don't know until I look. That's why I need to see it.'

'I've already told you, sir, we have people in. If you wish to come back with the court's authority, then I shall not stand in your way.' He spoke the words as though it were a dare. Justin leaned over the counter.

'Listen to me, you know who I am, and I know all about you. Who do you think sends you the anonymous warnings when there have been complaints made to the police, or when the next raid's coming? If you want to keep this business open then you need to help me out a little. I'm not asking a lot.' The proprietor cleared his throat.

'Now you listen to me, sir,' he began. 'Many gentlemen come here – and some ladies too for that matter – from all walks of life, and to enjoy the use of our facilities. If some of them feel that they have information which is relevant to us – as they often do – and which they wish to inform us of, then I'm sure it is much appreciated. But as far as I'm concerned, their business is their business and none of mine.' He leaned in towards Justin. 'And I don't know exactly what you are referring to with regards what goes on here, *sir*, but I can assure you that there is nothing illicit taking place on these premises, and that is a fact.'

Justin stared at him, taken aback by the man's ability to double-cross.

'I can make things very difficult for you,' said Justin finally, hoping to have concealed the impotence of the threat.

'There is no impropriety here, sir,' he replied, taking on a slightly bored tone, 'I can assure you of that. Now, if you don't mind, sir,' he said, pointing towards the exit.

Justin found himself out on the street with the door slammed shut behind him. He cursed himself for not maintaining his anonymity as he paced over to the car.

He picked up speed as he navigated the narrow roads, still reeling from the bathhouse owner's deceit. Determined now to uncover some evidence against Lord Keating, he drove out to the address in Acton to which Jeffrey Keating had been followed.

The bell rang above the door of the antiques shop. Justin went up to the counter. An elderly gentleman introduced himself as Simon Elliot; the man whose name it was above the door. Justin showed him his identification and noticed the old man's eyes flutter.

'Could you please tell me where that side door leads to?' said Justin.

'Yes, of course, officer,' he replied under Justin's suspicious gaze. 'It leads to the flats upstairs. My wife and I are directly above,' he said, nodding towards the ceiling. 'At the very top is a photographer who rents the garret rooms from us.'

'What kind of photographer?' said Justin. He could feel his heart skip at the mention of it.

'He takes family portraits mostly, I believe,' he said, averting his eyes. 'But his business really has nothing to do with us. He just rents the rooms from us.'

Justin thought for a moment and looked around at the shop under the weak electric light.

'Are your taxes up to date?' he said, 'including earnings from the rental property?'

'Of course, officer,' he said.

Justin pretended to take a closer look at some of the stock, most of which seemed to have been stashed haphazardly in the dark little shop. Pathways of wooden flooring meandered between the polished furniture and some rather suspect looking pieces of objet d'art.

'I need some information,' said Justin. 'I believe a Lord Jeffrey Keating is a customer of yours; is that correct?'

The antiques dealer thought for a moment then shook his head.

'No, I don't believe so. I've not heard the name before.'

'He must be a client of the photographer's upstairs then,' replied Justin. He looked down at the floor, the feeling of alarm now growing inside of him. 'He was here yesterday afternoon and he entered by the side door, I believe. He was carrying a large brown envelope.'

'I did have a visit from a client yesterday – a Mister Edward something – let me just check.' He went over to the counter, pulled a folder out from underneath it and sifted through some papers.

'Yes, this is it,' he said pulling out a sheet. 'Mr Edward Collins, lives out in Ascot. He's a client of Mr Turner's – oh, he's the photographer upstairs.'

'Go on,' said Justin.

'He visited Mr Turner first and then came downstairs and knocked on the door to my flat – I'm at home most afternoons you see; we have an assistant who fills in down here. I'm getting on in years, I'm sure you understand, so I can't be here all the time and on the odd occasion–'

'What did Mr Collins want?'

'Ah, well, Mr Collins was looking to sell some African pieces, a few French items as well; some of which I was rather interested in. He had a number of items from Tanganyika to sell. I asked him how he came across them and he said that he enjoys stealing from the Germans – though not literally, of course. I seem to remember that he was also carrying an envelope, probably of photographic prints.'

'Did you see the images?'

'No, the photographs are nothing at all to do with me,' said the dealer insistently.

'What kind of thing do you specialise in?' said Justin taking another look around.

'I don't really specialise in anything as such, only what happens to be popular at the time. Continental pieces are of course very good sellers for us at present. I myself am looking to expand my collection.'

'I see. Do you know what Mr Collins' business was with the photographer upstairs? It seems like quite a detour from Ascot just to get some photographs printed.'

The antiques dealer shuffled slightly and looked down at the floor.

'Oh…I couldn't really say.'

'Couldn't or won't?'

Mr Elliot put the sheet of paper back in its folder. He seemed to be stalling.

'What is there to be so coy about?' said Justin.

'Well, I have caught a glimpse of some of Mr Turner's work and some of it is… how should I put it? I'm fairly certain it wasn't meant for my eyes.'

'Meaning?'

Mr Elliot shuffled again, looking increasingly uncomfortable.

'Well…I've only ever caught the very briefest of glimpses. Maybe it would be better if you were to discuss this with Mr Turner himself. I'm not sure if he's in, but you are of course welcome to go up. I'll leave the side door open for you,' he said quietly. 'As I say, his business has absolutely nothing to do with mine.'

Justin climbed the stairs to the top floor, feeling somewhat agitated after what he had just heard. He knocked on the door and waited for an answer, but sensing the emptiness of the apartment, he knew that no-one was coming. He gave the thin pine door a push and it bowed slightly. With only a single mortise lock to secure it, he knew that he could easily kick it in. Under normal circumstances he probably would. He decided to leave it for another time.

He took one of the photographer's cards from the shop downstairs: *Malcolm Turner, Photography*.

'I'll need to speak to you again,' he said as he left the shop.

He sat in the car and pondered the significance of Jeffrey's use of an assumed name. It seemed implausible, but he couldn't stop thinking about the unlikely link between Lord Keating's movements, his photographic prints and the package that had been sent to his desk. Keating had given his address as being in Ascot – just a short drive from Windsor. So far, it seemed to fit. But why would Keating want to have something over him? How would he even know that Justin would be on the case – if, of course, Jeffrey had anything to do with it? The package would have had to have been sent shortly before the murder had even taken place. I'm just being paranoid, he thought, as he stubbed out his cigarette and started the engine.

Back at The Yard, he phoned the tradesmen who had been seen visiting the manor house, but there was no-one available to take his call. It was now half-past five. He picked up his hat and reached up to the peg for his jacket, just as a uniformed officer came striding in.

'I've a message for you from DC Dawkins, sir,' he said, a little out of breath. 'He says that he followed the mark into Soho and to tell you he's now parked up in Wardour Street. He followed the suspect on foot to Berwick Street and he says you should meet him on the corner of Berwick and Broadwick, and to get there immediately if you can.'

'How long has he been there?'

'Ten minutes perhaps.'

Justin ran for the door.

Taking one of the new Crossleys, he headed north into Soho. DC Dawkins was waiting for him on the corner as he said he would be, smoking a cigarette behind a parked meat truck.

'Where did he go?' said Justin, moving under the market canopies to give himself more cover. Dawkins smiled.

'The one on the left, sir,' he replied, indicating two adjacent doors in the parade of shops. 'He must be after a new suit.'

Above the brass numbers on the smart black door was a plaque which read: Milliner and Keats, Gentleman's Tailors. But the address was infamous – at least amongst those of a certain set. From morning until lunch, it operated just as the brass plaque claimed, but from mid-afternoon to the early hours, it catered solely to an entirely different set of needs.

'I can't say I'm surprised,' said Justin. 'How long has he been in there?'

'About twenty-five minutes, sir. He parked up in Wardour Street and I followed him here on foot.'

'Did he see you park-up?'

'No, there were too many vans in the street. He was probably more worried about pick-pockets.'

'Well done, Constable. Go back to your car and whenever he comes out, follow him to wherever he goes next. Call a message into the station as soon as you can.'

'Sir,' he nodded and set off back towards his car.

The market traders were beginning to pack up. Justin lit a cigarette and moved behind a collapsed canopy next to a wall. He pulled down the brim of his Homburg in an attempt to further conceal his identity, and kept an eye on the shiny black door as he waited for it to open.

A few more minutes passed before Lord Keating stepped out, head down, being careful to avoid making eye contact with anyone in the street. Justin followed him, watching from the other pavement as he set off then cut back onto Peter Street and headed towards his car.

Justin dropped his cigarette into the gutter as soon as he was out of sight then crossed over and knocked on the door. Footsteps descended the staircase and a man appeared in the hallway.

'Good evening,' said Justin, and waited for a reply.

The man looked him up and down, trying to decide whether to trust the lived-in suit or the polished accent. Fingering the measuring tape around his neck, he finally chose the latter and let Justin in.

At the top of the stairs was a reception area and a crescent shaped desk. A rail of newly tailored suits sat behind it, awaiting collection. Justin could hear the mechanical tapping of sewing machines behind one of the doors and he caught a glimpse of some industrious movement through the mottled glass.

Facing the desk, reclining on a chaise-longue, sat a young woman smoking a cigarette through an elegant hand-painted holder. With her unlined face and her boyish frame – and despite the artful makeup and the sophisticated couture – Justin placed her age somewhere well short of twenty. He tipped his hat to her as she turned to face him, smiling sweetly at him before raising an eyebrow to the man with the tape around his neck.

A door opened at the end of the room and another, even younger-looking girl appeared. She seemed surprised to see him standing there at first, as she self-consciously ran her palms down her thighs to flatten her dress. She took a seat next to the other girl.

'How much?' said Justin to the man with the measuring tape, motioning towards the girl who had just entered the room. With a slight bow of the head that bordered on facetiousness, he silently passed Justin a leather-bound menu.

'You can discuss that with the lady, sir,' he said.

'Thank you,' replied Justin, moving towards the girl. The man nodded to her and she got up, took Justin's hand and led him into the adjoining room.

Justin shut the door behind him, making sure that it was latched before casting his eye over the room. The sound of the market outside could still be heard, smothered though it was by the thick, heavy curtains, as the carts were loaded-up and the debris swept into the gutters. Standing in the semi-darkness, with the candlelight flickering onto the burnt ochre walls, they could have been anywhere in the world: the effect being heightened by the fact that the decorators seemed to have raided a Moroccan bazaar.

Opposite the bed, on top of the mantelpiece, sat a large bronze reticulated clock; a further attempt, no doubt, to evoke a sense of the continental. The girl went over to it and made a note of the time on a piece of paper, disturbing as she did so, the ribbons of smoke that were twisting up from a small incense burner placed below it. An art deco wall sconce dully lit the cornice and the ceiling over the head of the bed, leaving the exotic pattern of the bedsheets mostly in shadow.

Justin felt a sudden revulsion at the thought of Jeffrey lying on top of them mere minutes before, especially seeing that they were still a little crumpled. In an instant, the air seemed tainted and the sounds from outside had become less exotic, infecting the room with the seamy grime of a London market.

The girl sat on the bed in front of him and started to pull down the top of her dress.

'What can I do for you, sir?' she said, looking up at him. She was the picture of innocence.

Justin pulled out his ID and showed it to her. Her shouldders dropped.

'I would like some information about your previous client,' he whispered, slipping the card back into his pocket.

'We don't give information about any of our clients,' she said, reaching forward to undo his belt. Justin put his finger to his lips then grabbed her wrists, squeezing them in a way that threatened to break them.

'How often does he come here?' he said quietly.

Twisting her wrists upwards and outwards, the girl freed her hands, surprising him with the proficiency of her technique.

'I thought you were here for something else, sir,' she replied, leaning her head to one side. He lowered his face to hers.

'I don't go with whores and I've got more important things to do than go around arresting them,' he whispered. 'The man who was here before me; do you know who he was?'

'I don't know who you're talking about, sir,' she replied.

'Don't play dumb with me you little tart. I'll take you in if needs be! Just tell me what you know about him,' he said, clutching her wrists again, holding them together this time to prevent her from freeing them.

She sat still for a moment, looking up at him as though judging whether or not she could trust him. Finally, she whispered: 'There's a peephole in the door.' Pulling her wrists towards her, she drew him down onto the bed and then knelt down on the floor in front of him. His grip loosened.

'What difference does it make if I know him or not?' she said quietly, as she went back to manipulating his belt buckle.

'You won't be implicated in anything,' said Justin. He stopped her just short of undoing his top trouser button then leaned forward and cradled her head. He looked up towards the door and saw light appear through a crack in one of the panels. 'There's nobody at the door now,' he said. 'We've been tracing your previous client as part of a murder investigation. Now tell me, how often does he come here?'

He could see the fear in her eyes as she raised her head and looked up at him, and she paused for a moment, unsure as to whether or not she should continue.

'What is it?' he said.

She seemed to hesitate again, then said, 'Are you here because of Emma?'

She bent her neck forward and started moving her head in a gentle rhythm.

'Who's Emma?' he said.

He waited for her reply, but none came. He was starting to get annoyed. Justin pulled her up on top of him and, as he did so, felt moistness on her cheek. He wiped the tear track away with his thumb.

'What is it?' he said.

'We saw the photographs.'

'What photographs? Was it your previous client?' She was now clearly struggling to keep from crying.

'No, it was Jack,' she eventually said, nodding towards the door. She knelt back down and lowered her head into his lap.

'What were the photographs of?' he whispered, leaning down and stroking the back of her neck. It was a while before she could answer. Finally, she pushed him back onto the bed, lifted her dress and moved on top of him.

'They were photographs of Emma. We saw them on Friday…Saturday morning after the shift. Mr Vardy was here too.'

Justin pulled her closer to him so that her face met his.

'Who the fuck is Emma?'

Again, she took some time to reply. When she did so, her voice cracked.

'She used to be here,' she said, finally getting the words out, 'one of the younger ones.'

'I don't understand what you're talking about,' he said.

The girl started to move more vigorously, just enough so that the bed creaked a little louder and covered both their voices.

'She was one of the girls here. Same age as me, but she'd been here a lot longer.'

Justin pulled her back down towards him and all movement between them stopped.

'When did she leave?'

Through her tears, the young girl almost broke into a smile.

'Nobody *leaves*,' she said. 'She just disappeared a year or so ago.'

'What were the photographs of?'

'Jack said this is what happens if we give him any grief. Her throat had been cut and her face was…' she tailed off.

Justin pushed her gently as a reminder to keep up the pretence and she resumed a slow, rocking motion.

'Are you sure it was her?' he said.

'We all recognised her.'

'Listen to me, your last client was Lord Jeffrey Keating. A murder took place at his apartment. What else was in the photographs? Did you notice where they might have been taken?'

'There was just blood everywhere and some sort of pattern behind her. A rug or something.'

The girl wiped her eyes as they continued putting on the act in silence. Once enough time had passed, Justin gently lifted her up off of him.

'That's enough. Get yourself together,' he said.

He got up and fastened his belt buckle, being careful to block the view of her through the crack in the door panel as she wiped her eyes.

'How much do I owe you?' he said.

'Call it eight,' she said, readjusting her dress and starting to look a lot more composed.

He took the notes from his pocket, counted them out and put them in her hand.

'I'll make sure we protect you,' he whispered, and made his way over to the door.

Six

It was ten o'clock in the morning. Justin was sitting in the Detective Chief Inspector's office.

'I think we're on the verge of something, sir. That high-class brothel in Berwick Street, Milliner and Keats–'

'The tailors? What about it?' said Inspector Andrews, sitting up in his chair at the mention of it.

'Lord Jeffrey Keating has been acting a little suspiciously, so I had him observed and followed, and he led us there. I paid them a visit to see if I could get some more information on him.'

'Did you speak to the brothel owners directly?' said Andrews looking alarmed.

'No, sir, but I spoke to one of the girls.'

'And do they know you were there – the owners I mean?'

'Not unless the girl told them, and I don't think she would have. I think she'd be risking her life, sir.' Andrews leaned forward on the desk.

'What do you think you're doing, Inspector, messing about in brothels?' he said.

'The girl I spoke to yesterday, sir, told me they'd seen photographs of a bloodied corpse early one morning. The way she described it, I'd be amazed if it wasn't Catherine Smith.'

'Jesus. Are you sure of that?'

'From what she said, sir, it was just how Catherine had looked, and they would have been about the same age. She said the photographs were of a girl who used to work there – one who'd been working there for some time. She called her "Emma" and said that she had gone missing over a year ago. That would have been around the time Catherine started working for Lord Keating.'

'But you haven't seen the photographs?'

'No, sir, but it's a hell of a coincidence isn't it? It must have been her. Either way there's a body involved so it'll need investigating. The place is one of the Sabini's. I've checked the file, but I'll need further clearance before we raid it. The sooner we do it the better, I'd say.'

The Chief Inspector leaned back in his chair and rubbed his palms on his waistcoat.

'Son…if you already know that we have all this information about the place on file, why do you think we've done nothing before now to shut the place down?' Andrews reached for his packet of cigarettes, lit one and offered the packet to Justin. He declined. 'There'll be no raid on that place,' he continued, 'there'll be no such thing.'

'Why not, sir?'

'Christ, do you really need to ask?' he replied.

'I don't see how we can avoid going in there.'

'Well…there's the clientele for one thing, you know what I mean? And then there's the blokes who run it, for another. Do you understand that? As far as that brothel's concerned, neither you nor I can do a thing about it.'

'But we need to get in there and search the place, at least. Even if we can't shut them down, it's still a murder investigation. It doesn't matter who's involved.'

'I know what you're saying, and I agree – it shouldn't matter – but you're not *that* naïve, son. The investigation cannot go onto those premises. Not this time.'

'I have no choice. I still need to get in there,' Justin insisted.

'You'll do no such thing, Inspector,' he replied, rising from his seat. 'You'll not go anywhere near that fucking brothel! Do I make myself clear?' Having made his point, he took a long drag from his cigarette and sat back down. 'You've not had your stripes long, Inspector, but I put you on this case for a good reason. Even before we knew just how high profile it was going to be, I knew that it needed to be treated with some delicacy. I should have you taken off it right now for going in there without my say-so. Why didn't you check if it was all right first?'

'There was no time, sir. Keating had just left the place and I needed to know which girl he'd just been with.'

'We may've had other operations going on – you could've compromised them. Or what if you'd been caught – how do you think that would that have made us look?'

'To whom, sir?'

Andrews smiled at him as though he thought he were simple.

'There's one thing you need to understand,' he began, 'and being from the sort of background you are, you should already know this anyway. There are some places that are simply off limits – I know it's not right, but it's just the way it is. It's never been any different,' he said shaking his head. 'If you go about creating trouble, you could be stepping on some very expensively shod toes, do you catch my drift?'

'The law's the law, sir.'

'No, Lamoureaux, it's not. The law's the law for the likes of you and I, but not if you happen to be the ones making those fucking laws; that puts you in a slightly different position. You and I don't live in the same world as they do – you should know that, you're not a bloody civvie. Now, I'm happy for you to do whatever you need to do with regards to the murder case, but you will not go anywhere near that fucking brothel!' he said, prodding the desk with his index finger. 'Do I make myself clear?'

'Perfectly, sir.'

'If I catch you there again, you'll be straight off this case and that'll be the least of your worries, I can assure you.'

'Bloody typical,' said Justin, dumping himself down in the chair at his desk. He looked up at Cameron. 'Is it too early for a drink?'

'Even for a Scot,' he replied. 'Did he not get you the clearance?' He pulled up a chair.

'"It's one law for us and another for them," or some such nonsense,' said Justin.

'But that's shite! The courts won't see it like that; we can bring in whoever we like,' he replied.

'I'm not so sure. You know, sometimes I think it would be better if we could act above the law.'

'Aye. You do wonder what the hell's going on sometimes.' Cameron leaned back, putting his hands behind his head.

'We can still make the arrests, but we can't go anywhere near the brothel. Outside of it we can do what we want, but if they know that – as I'm sure they must do – then I'd expect them to be keeping the evidence we need safely hidden away where they know we can't get to it.'

'What if I needed a new suit, sir? Couldn't we get someone inside that way?' Justin looked around to check that no-one else was listening.

'How we get in isn't the problem – it's the fact of us getting in. But that's an idea. Obviously, we'd have to do it on the quiet. Even then, I'm not sure we could get much from it.' He thought for a moment, then said, 'We could always just go in there anyway.'

'What, not even on the quiet? I'm not sure I fancy that, sir,' said Cameron.

'We'd both be in civvie jobs if we got caught. Or worse. But it's worth some consideration. In the meantime, I still think we should put the squeeze on old Jeffrey. If what I've been told is true, it puts our honourable friend right in the frame. He'll swing for it if the court finds him guilty on common purpose.'

'Is that what you want to see, sir?'

'It'll free up Lady Keating, if you're still interested? No, I just don't like the man. We need to speak to Mr Hollis again. Why didn't he just take Catherine with him and then they would both be free of him?'

'It's beyond me, sir. Maybe it was because of money. I bet he's regretting not having done so now.'

'Yes, I should think he is.'

'But what if it was a different girl in the photographs, sir? What if we're barking up the wrong tree?'

'It's possible, I suppose. But then Keating just happens to turn up at the brothel? It's too much of a coincidence. The dates match, the method matches–'

'But wouldn't he stay clear of the place so soon after the murder?'

'He doesn't know he's being watched.'

'Other than by the press outside his house.'

'Even if they followed him, they'd only see him going to his tailors. Catherine's lack of history I also find very interesting.'

'Aye, but do you think he'd want a former prostitute as a housemaid?'

'Who's to say that he knew at the time? Maybe he only found out later…And come to think of it, yes, I think that's exactly the type of girl he would want at his beck and call.'

'Aye,' said Cameron, 'there's a lot of coincidences.'

'Too many coincidences. My guess is that he knew all along. Say, for example, Catherine wouldn't give Jeffrey what he wanted; I'm sure he's used to making the odd trip downstairs.'

'How do you mean, sir?'

'Oh…it's a friend of mine's saying. It means getting *involved* with the staff. So, say she refused him – would you put it past him to tip-off her former employers as to her whereabouts? How else would they know where she was and when she would be at the apartment alone?'

'Mr Hollis also knew.'

'Yes, and we may find that he's also no longer above suspicion. Maybe she told him about her past. I wouldn't put anything past anyone when they feel betrayed. Or maybe he knew about it all anyway. Maybe that's how he met her. Who knows? I need to get back inside that brothel.'

Justin pulled out a sheet of paper from a file on his desk. 'According to this, the place is run on behalf of the Sabinis by one George Vardy. He's the big shot who also owns the jazz club around the corner. We could probably pick him up there if we needed to – but it's best if we don't do it just yet.

There's another man who goes by the name of Jack Gormally. He's small fry. We'd be better off bringing him in first for something, so long as we do it away from the brothel. He basically runs the girls; probably the suited henchman who let me into the building yesterday. If I can get the vice squad involved, we should at least be able to offer them some kind of protection. I suggest we take an early one this afternoon and get out there for around five-thirty tomorrow morning. I'll square it with Lisson, as much as I hate having to involve him. We can follow whoever emerges straight from Berwick Street.'

The sky steadily brightened as the dullness of dawn gave way to a familiar smothering white mass that reached right down to the Macadam. Justin and Cameron had been waiting patiently in the car while the market traders set up, gradually blocking their view of the tailors shop.

Forced out onto the pavement, Justin sat down in a grimy doorway and smoked away quietly, hidden from view. DC Cameron stood just a few feet away reading a newspaper and keeping an eye out for the first sign of movement. The nascent aroma of a nearby fish stall had begun to invade the air.

'It's nearly seven,' said Cameron, checking his watch. 'It'll be bloody annoying if he's left by some other way.'

'There's no back access to these buildings,' replied Justin. He cast his eye along the pavement and got to his feet. 'Hold on, something's happening.' Justin knelt down behind a timber cart and watched as a man stepped out of the building and went over to one of the market traders. Doffing his cap apologetically, the trader jumped-to-it and moved his cart out of the way of the man's car as quickly as he could.

'That's him,' said Justin. 'That's Mr Measuring Tape.'

Two young women appeared, following him out to the car and climbing into the back of it. The engine started. Justin and Cameron walked swiftly back to their unmarked police car.

'Brazen, isn't he?' said Cameron. He started the engine. 'I'm half-surprised he doesn't lock the girls in the cellar or something.'

'He can be as brazen as he likes,' said Justin. 'We've given him no reason not to be. Quick, he's moving off.'

The car pulled out, did a u-turn and then drove straight past them. Cameron waited a few moments before following.

Justin checked that the two accompanying officers were close behind them. The sight of Lisson being driven by Bennet in the car behind was far from ideal, he thought, but it would have to do.

'Don't let anyone get in front of us until the roads open up a bit,' he said.

They turned right along Oxford Street and followed on through the smart terraces of Fitzrovia. As they headed north-east, the polished brass door-knobs gradually gave way to exhaust tinged windows and worn netting. The scent of the factories filled the air, indiscriminately stifling the neighbourhoods they relied upon.

At Newington Green, they turned east and continued towards the slums of Stoke Newington. A few more turns and the car pulled up outside a house half-way down one of the more neglected terraces. The front door opened as if someone had been waiting for the girls. They got out of the motorcar and moved towards it.

'They're different girls,' said Justin, catching a proper glimpse of them as Cameron pulled up further down the street. He leaned across to get a better view as they walked up the short path. 'Yes, they're definitely different girls.'

Another man appeared in the doorway, nonchalantly ushering them in, while Jack Gormally — minus the tape this time — got out of the car. Lisson appeared at Justin's window.

'That him?' he said, leaning in.

'Of course it is,' replied Justin. Lisson motioned to Bennet to follow him. 'I'll stay low,' said Justin, 'I might need to get into the tailors shop again.'

Cameron got out, joining DS Bennet and DI Lisson as they approached Jack Gormally.

'Mr Gormally, sir?' said Lisson.

'Says who?' came Gormally's disarmingly well-spoken reply. He looked towards the house.

'I'm Detective Inspector Lisson, this is DS Bennet, DC Cameron,' he nodded. 'I'd like to have a word with you, if you don't mind.'

The man at the door suddenly jumped-to and went back into the house, bolting the door behind him.

'Am I under arrest?' said Gormally, sounding disinterested.

'Not as such–' began Lisson, his words breaking off as he watched Bennet walk over to the car and open the boot.

'You can't just go in there,' said Gormally.

Reaching inside, Bennet pulled out two suits wrapped in plastic. He held them up and then dropped them onto tarmac in front of him.

'Do you mind!' said Gormally. Bennet reached further into the boot, lifted something up and then pulled out a weighty looking rubber cosh.

'Ah, well then, sir,' said Lisson, 'it looks like you *are* under arrest.'

'That thing's not mine!' said Gormally.

'We can discuss that at the station, sir,' said Lisson.

'Oh, I see,' he replied. 'And to think, it's not even my car.'

'We're not too worried about the car, sir,' said Lisson. 'Let's take him in, lads.' Gormally looked back towards the house.

'I won't be long, girls, don't you worry,' he said. Cameron and Bennet put him in handcuffs.

'I wouldn't bet on that, son,' said Cameron, 'you've got a long day ahead of you.'

'We'll see about that,' he replied.

Justin ducked his head down onto the driver's seat until the car had pulled away. Cameron walked slowly back and got in.

'Did anyone see me?' said Justin.

'No chance,' said Cameron, 'but I'd still keep your head down for a bit, sir.'

'At least we know where the girls are now. We'll have to wait to get in there. Like Andrews says, we can't be seen standing on too many toes just yet.'

Cameron emptied Gormally's pockets at the reception desk and then led him downstairs to an interview room.

'The inspector will be in shortly,' he said, sliding an ashtray across the table before leaving the room. Lisson and Bennet descended the stairs.

'We'll give him a going over for an hour or two,' said Lisson. 'I don't expect he'll say much if he's got any sense.'

Down in the garage, Justin was sitting in the driver's seat of the car with the engine running. Cameron came running down the stairs.

'I've got his keys,' said Cameron, holding them up.

'Good man. Let's try and be quick about it, shall we?' he replied.

They headed north and then sped through the narrow streets of Soho, pulling up outside the tailors shop on Berwick Street. Justin did his best to block the view of the market traders, standing behind Cameron as the constable worked his way through the set of keys.

'Bingo,' he said, pushing the door open wide and then shutting it firmly on the street behind them. An old man was passing at the top of the stairs and looked down to see them standing at the foot of it.

'We're not open yet,' he called out moodily. Justin and Cameron started up the stairs as the tailor looked down at them over his half-moon glasses. 'I said, we are not open yet.'

Justin held up his ID, making sure that the tailor did not have time to read the name.

'Open that door,' he said, pushing past him and heading straight for what looked like the office.

'You can't just barge in,' said the tailor. Cameron again produced the set of keys and started to try each of them in the lock.

'What's in here?' said Justin. The door swung open. 'Never mind,' he said. Cameron went over to the window and opened the Venetian blinds. Now they could see the row of black steel cabinets along the back wall and the square black door of the safe, just above them.

'Fuck, I hope they're not in there,' said Cameron. The tailor watched from the doorway, unsure of what to do, while Justin and Cameron started searching through the drawers.

'Sod it, just tip 'em,' said Justin, turning over the first drawer and scattering the contents all over the floor. In less than a minute, the entire row of cabinets had been turned out into one big pile. The tailor stepped out into the hallway.

'You stay there!' shouted Justin. The man froze. Perhaps another time, when his blood was not up, Justin might have felt sorry for him. But this was different.

'Find me the combination to this safe!' he said to him, as he and Cameron started pawing through the mass of papers.

'I've never been in here before,' he replied, the sags under his chin shaking as he stammered. 'This is Mr Gormally's office, it has nothing to do with Milliner and Keats.'

'And which one are you, Milliner or Keats?' said Justin.

'Neither. My name's Thomas Samuels,' he replied. 'Both Milliner and Keats are deceased, I'm afraid.'

'Good. You stay where you are – stay where I can see you!'

Cameron bent down behind the desk and tried each of the keys in the locks of the drawers. Unlocking one of them, he tipped it out onto the floor, picked up a large manila envelope from the pile and tore it open. He looked down at the contents and smiled.

'Got him,' he said, as he held the photographs up to show Justin. An appalled groan came from the doorway.

'Now you understand, sir,' said Justin, turning to the tailor behind him.

As Cameron looked again at the images, his smile faded. The roughly-shot photographs had rendered the scene in explicit detail. Even though he had seen the corpse in the flesh when they had inspected the apartment, the camera had captured something quite different. The fresh, glistening blood gave a presence of life to the images. He could see terror in the girl's eyes.

Lisson stepped out of the interview room and shut the door.

'Nothing so far,' he said, shaking his head, 'but we haven't been trying very hard to convince him…yet.'

'He might talk to us,' said Justin. He took the photographs from Cameron's hand and held them up for Lisson to see.

'And what have we got here then?' Lisson flicked through the images, exhaling deeply with disgust. Two uniformed constables appeared, shifting themselves up against the wall as they shuffled past in the narrow hallway.

'They were at the "tailors shop."'

'Looks like she could do with a few stitches,' said Lisson.

'Christ…listen, I don't want Andrews to know about them just yet, so you'd better keep this to yourself.'

'Will do. I'm impressed,' he said, passing the images back to him. 'I've had the car brought in, so we can take a closer look at it when it gets here. I'll get someone from forensics onto it – check for bloodstains.'

'Good idea.' Justin looked down at the photographs. 'We'll see what he has to say about these.'

He opened the door, and he and Cameron stepped into the cavernous, subterranean interview room.

'Mr Gormally, sir, how are we doing?' said Justin, as he and Cameron sat down at the table. He could see that Gormally recognised him. Gormally smiled and stubbed out his cigarette amongst the butts in the ashtray.

'We've got something for you.' Justin spread the photographs out on the table under the light of the electric bulb. Gormally looked down at the images and sat back in his chair.

'What are these?' he said with a shrug.

'You really don't know?' said Justin. Gormally shook his head.

'They've got nothing to do with me,' he replied. He reached for his cigarette box then leaned forward and let Cameron light his cigarette for him.

'You don't seem shocked at all by these photographs,' said Cameron, putting the lighter back in his pocket. He picked one of them up. 'Maybe you can't quite see what it is,' he said, shifting his chair round closer to Gormally. 'This one here shows a young woman – probably only about nineteen or twenty – and it looks as though she's had her throat cut. Do you not find that disturbing at all, sir?' Gormally took a long drag on his cigarette and blew the smoke straight at Cameron.

'It's not very nice, I'll admit,' said Gormally, 'but it's got nothing to do with me.'

'Let's start at the beginning, shall we?' said Justin. 'What exactly is your role in the business – the tailors shop, I mean? You report to…George Vardy, is that correct?' he said, checking what he had written in his notebook.

'I believe you already know that, officer,' he said, smirking back at him, 'I deal with the accounts. I seem to remember you came in looking for a new suit the other day, unless I'm mistaken?'

'We're not too worried about what goes on there,' said Justin.

'So I gathered.'

'But we *are* very interested in where you were last Wednesday night.'

'I've no idea where I was,' said Gormally.

'Oh, I think you do.' Justin fanned the images out on the desk. 'How did you get into the apartment?'

'You're not making any sense, officer,' said Gormally.

'It was you and someone else, wasn't it?'

'I don't know what you're talking about, I'm afraid.'

'Someone's been telling tales on you,' said Cameron.

'Have they really?'

'Yes, they have.'

'Well, they must be lying. I shall have to have words with them.'

'You aren't leaving here any time soon, I assure you of that, Mr Gormally,' said Justin.

'We'll see about that,' he replied.

There was a knock at the door and Lisson appeared.

'Can I borrow Cameron for a minute?' he said to Justin.

'What for?' he replied.

'The car's in. Bennet's out somewhere. I just need a witness.'

'All right, fine. You go with him,' said Justin turning to Cameron. 'We're nearly done for the moment here anyway.'

'Sir,' nodded Cameron as he got up and left the room. Justin waited for him to shut the door behind him.

'Was that your car you were driving this morning?' said Justin, turning back to Gormally.

'No.'

'So, whose is it then?'

'It belongs to Mr Vardy.'

'Were you in that car on Wednesday night?'

'I don't know.' Gormally shook his head. 'I can't think where I was Wednesday night.' Justin lit himself a cigarette and leaned over the desk.

'Look, why don't you just tell me what's going on…while they're both out of the room,' he said, adopting a friendlier tone. 'Whatever's happened, I know full-well that the order came from above.'

'I don't know what you mean,' said Gormally.

'Look again at these photographs,' he said sitting back and pushing the images towards him. 'You know as well as I do where these came from. It's not looking very good for you, Jack.'

'I don't know what you mean,' he said again.

'It means that my colleagues are going to check that car and if they find even the slightest piece of evidence linking you to this, you're going to swing. That is, unless you start helping us.'

Gormally took another silent puff on his cigarette.

'All right then,' said Justin. 'Does anyone else use that car?'

'A lot of people use that car.'

'Like who?'

'I don't remember. It's not my car.'

'So, you didn't use it on Wednesday night?'

'I'd have to check who's been using it and when.'

'That would be very helpful if you could do that,' said Justin. 'Would Mr Vardy have been using it, do you think?' Gormally smiled.

'I doubt it very much. Mr Vardy drives a Bugatti.'

'Don't they all,' said Justin to himself. 'I shouldn't think he'd be seen dead driving that old Austin then?' Gormally shook his head.

'All right then,' said Justin standing up. 'Make yourself comfortable, Mr Gormally; you're not going anywhere soon. I'll be back in a short while.'

Justin made his way up to the office, meeting Cameron halfway on the stairs.

'We've got him, sir,' said Cameron looking pleased with himself.

'Got who?'

'The knife, the murder weapon; it was hidden in Gormally's car.'

'The knife was in the car?' said Justin, looking and sounding incredulous.

'It was shoved down the back of the seats,' replied Cameron.

'Why would he have the knife in the car?'

Cameron paused for a moment, looking about as if searching for the answer.

'I don't know, sir, but there it was.' Justin turned to head up the stairs. 'It was obviously him, sir. We've got the weapon…the photographs–' Cameron called out after him.

'It's Vardy's car, not Gormally's,' replied Justin.

'That doesn't really matter though does it, sir?' Justin turned to face him.

'You don't think?' He stepped back down, pulling Cameron over to one side of the hallway and looking around. 'Who found it, you or Lisson?'

'I did, sir. I was searching the back seat.'

'Listen to me, you need to watch it with him,' said Justin speaking in a low voice. 'It's usually his underlings who manage to find the "evidence". He's done it before.' He let out a long sigh. 'Where's the knife now?'

'With forensics, sir. They've found bloodstains in the car as well.'

'All right, well at least that's something. Come upstairs with me and we can do the paperwork.'

Just then, Lisson appeared in the hallway, passing them on his way to the reception area.

'Vardy's in, come on,' he said. He stopped to wait for them by the door at the end of the hall. 'I take it he's told you then?' he said to Justin.

'Yes, he has,' he replied flatly.

'It's amazing what turns up down the backs of sofas, isn't it?' said Lisson. Justin and Cameron followed him out to the front desk.

'Mr George Vardy?' said Lisson, before he had even made it fully through the door. Vardy turned to him, his face red and bloated beneath his Fedora.

'I'm arresting you on suspicion of the murder of Catherine Smith,' continued Lisson before he could say anything. Vardy's mouth dropped open. Lisson smiled. 'If you'd like to step this way, sir,' he added.

Chief Inspector Andrews emerged from the office behind the desk.

'Hold on, hold on,' he said. Justin held up the photographs for both Vardy and Andrews to see.

'We've got the murder weapon as well, sir,' said Lisson. Justin placed the photographs in the hands of the chief inspector who then started flicking through them. He turned to George Vardy.

'Empty your pockets please, sir, and we'll go into one of the interview rooms,' he said, still grimacing from what he had seen of the photographs. 'We're going to have to clear this up.'

'I'd like to speak to my solicitor,' came Vardy's calm reply.

'All in good time, sir,' said Andrews. A constable took him down. Andrews turned to Justin and Lisson.

'I need a word with you in my office, both of you!' he said, and they followed him upstairs.

Justin shut the office door.

'You'd better have some bloody watertight evidence, or you've got yourself right in the shit with this one,' said Andrews, his face was just inches away from Lisson's. 'Don't you know who he is?'

'Yes, sir, we all do. But we've found what looks like the murder weapon in the back of Vardy's car.'

'In the back of his car?' said Andrews, sounding just as incredulous as Justin had shortly before. 'That's strange, you would have thought he'd have gotten rid of it by now, wouldn't you, Inspector Lisson?' He turned towards Justin who could sense his breath on his face, and with it the stench of stale coffee and cigarettes. 'You two are telling me that you found these photographs *and* the murder weapon, purely by chance, hidden in the back of one of his cars?'

'Just the weapon, sir,' said Lisson. 'The knife and a length of ligature.'

'What ligature?' said Justin, 'she wasn't even tied up.' Lisson's eyes narrowed.

'The photographs are from elsewhere, sir,' he said, 'Inspector Lamoureaux'll tell you.' Andrews turned to face him again.

'Are you gonna explain?' he said, as Justin quickly tried to think of an answer. 'Where did you get these photographs?' said Andrews, holding them up in front of him. He took another step closer towards him. 'What did I say to you about going near that fucking brothel?'

'We haven't been anywhere near it, sir,' replied Justin.

'Don't fucking lie to me, son.' He dropped the photographs onto the desk and rubbed his eyes.

'I visited the place during the daytime, sir. It's a tailors shop.' Andrews cursed him under his breath.

'I'd take you straight off this case and drop the whole thing if there was any evidence I'd personally authorised any of it,' he said. 'I'll be out of here soon, remember. Don't expect me to take the blame for any of your actions.'

'We've got enough to make it stick, sir,' said Lisson, butting in. 'I'm sure you don't want to see those two walk, sir.'

'That's beside the point,' he replied. 'What happens when the evidence isn't accepted in court because it was illegally obtained?'

'We can cross that bridge later, sir,' said Justin. 'No-one can prove that we were at the tailors shop, sir.'

'So nobody saw you?'

'Well, obviously the tailor, but it's his word against ours. Besides, sir, forensics have also found bloodstains in the car.'

'That could be from anything,' said Andrews sighing deeply. 'So how are you going to explain the evidence?'

'I'll find a way to bring the girl in, sir,' said Justin. 'She's scared enough to say what I tell her to.'

'I'm telling you now,' said Andrews, 'both of you – that you're in way over your heads on this one.' He turned to face the wall. 'Fuck it,' he said, waving them both away. 'You'll be answering for it yourselves. Find an explanation for the photographs, make it stick and get the fuck out of my office.'

'Thank you, sir,' said Justin. They turned and left.

Justin turned to Lisson outside in the hallway.

'I take it the weapon's a plant?'

'I take it you have an explanation for those photographs,' he replied.

'I'll find one.'

'Never mind,' said Lisson. 'He could be right, we could be dealing with something much bigger than we both realise. We're going to have to work together on this or we're both gonna be in the shit.'

'All right then,' said Justin after a few moments' reflection, though he looked defeated. 'Keep your enemies close, hey?'

'No need for that, Inspector,' said Lisson, and they went downstairs to the interview rooms.

'Mr Vardy – the man himself,' said Lisson, pulling up a chair at the table. Justin shut the door. 'How's business?' The buttons of George Vardy's waistcoat almost popped open as he sat back in his chair.

'So-so,' he replied.

'Looks like you've got some explaining to do,' said Justin. He lit a cigarette and offered one to Vardy, who answered by taking a puff on his fat cigar.

'Is that suit a bit tight, sir?' enquired Lisson. Vardy had loosened his tie and put his hat down on the table in front of him, revealing an indentation all the way round his head from where the rim had pressed into his greased back hair. 'You should find yourself a decent tailor.'

'PC Fields, is it?' came his raspy voice. 'Get a move on, son, I've got things to do.'

'Haven't we all,' said Lisson.

'I thought Fedoras were women's hats,' said Justin.

Vardy picked up the hat, pinched the crease and turned it over, displaying the high quality of the workmanship.

'Prince Edward don't think so. Fashions change, my son,' he said, eyeing Justin's worn-in suit. 'Are we here just to talk about hats?'

Justin placed the photographs face down on the table.

'We know all about your links to the Sabinis,' he began, 'it's hardly a secret. We also know about the drugs, the prostitution–'

'Calm it down, son,' replied Vardy.

'We're not interested in any of that for now…luckily for you.' Justin sat back in his chair. 'Can you tell us where you were last Wednesday night?'

'At my club, I should think. All night long.'

'Can anyone verify that?'

'There was plenty of staff on.'

'Anyone whose wages you're not paying?' said Lisson.

'Well, I don't know. Customers, I suppose. I'm sure I could dig out a few witnesses.'

'I'm sure you could,' said Justin. He turned the photographs over and slid them across the table.

'Who's that then?' said Vardy, leaning forward to inspect the pictures. He puffed on his cigar.

'We were hoping you could tell us,' said Justin.

'Never seen her before in my life. What are you showing me this for anyway, it's disgusting.' He pushed them over towards Justin and leaned back in his chair.

'Yeah, we're sorry to have to show you these just before lunchtime, sir,' said Lisson, 'although you don't seem too affected by them, I must say.'

'Oh, I'm deeply shocked, I'm sure' he said, his cheeks inflating with more tobacco smoke.

'Was that your car Jack Gormally was driving this morning when we pulled him in?' said Justin.

'Probably. What car was it?'

'It's an Austin Twenty, dark green,' said Lisson.

'Yeah that's one of mine. Everyone uses that car.'

'What's that got to do with it?' said Justin.

'Just everyone uses it, that's all. It's a sort of company car.'

'We found something quite interesting hidden in the back of it,' said Justin. Vardy shrugged and pursed his lips.

'Ain't got nothing to do with me, son.'

'So, you don't recognise these photographs?' said Justin.

'Nah,' replied Vardy.

'We found them this morning stuffed down the back seat of your car,' said Lisson. Justin looked across at him and then back at Vardy.

'That's right,' added Justin, clearing his throat.

'Course you did, son,' laughed Vardy, 'course you did.'

'They were concealed with the murder weapon,' said Lisson. Vardy laughed even louder.

'That's a bit careless, isn't it?' said Vardy, looking at one detective, then the other. 'Ain't got nothing to do with me,' he said, shaking his head.

'See, personally I'd be really quite shocked if they turned up in my car,' said Lisson, 'especially if I trusted the people who'd been using it.'

'Yes, it is quite shocking,' he replied, 'I shall have to have words.'

'It's all a bit amateurish, don't you think?' said Justin. 'It puts you in a tight spot. We're hoping Mr Gormally might be able to shed some light on the matter. That way, you would be in the clear.' Vardy's smile faded.

'I'm never out of the clear, son,' he replied then sat quietly, as though considering his options. 'Well, I don't know,' he said eventually. 'Everyone uses that car. You can ask Gentleman Jack if you like, but I don't think he'll be much help, do you?'

'We'll give it a try, sir,' replied Lisson. 'But it would save us all a lot of time if we knew which of your employees was responsible. As it stands, what with it being your car…' He gave a wince and a tut. Vardy stared back at him with a blank expression.

'Ain't got nothing to do with me,' he said again.

'We'll be back in a short while,' said Justin, as he and Lisson got up and left the room.

The door to the other room opened.

'Mr Gormally,' said Justin as he stepped inside. 'Your boss isn't too happy with you.' Lisson placed an open packet of cigarettes on the table, lit one and sat down.

'I don't suppose you're a member of a union, are you?' said Justin, lighting his own cigarette.

'I don't know what you're talking about, officer,' replied Gormally.

'Well, you've just been implicated in a murder and, personally, I don't think you did it. Sounds like one for the tribunal, don't you think, Inspector Lisson?'

'Yeah, it does sound like a bit of a pickle,' he replied. 'I'd take strike action if I were you.' Gormally looked at him in silence.

'He does have a point though, your boss,' said Justin. 'He wasn't driving the car, so we can't pin anything on him. He told us we should come and have a little chat with you. That was helpful of him, wasn't it, Jack?' Again, there was no reply.

'So, what we have here is you…then we have your boss…although I think he's pretty safe,' said Lisson, 'then we have the car, a concealed murder weapon and the photographic evidence.'

Justin spread the photographs out, once again, on top of the table for him to see.

'Are you going to tell me where these are from?' said Gormally.

'The back of your boss's car,' said Lisson.

'Oh, they were, were they?' Gormally laughed. 'That's funny, I didn't see them there. Neither did you mention it earlier. Who in the world's going to believe that?'

'It's like I said to you earlier, Jack,' said Justin. 'I can only help you if you help us. It's Vardy's car, not yours, and that's pretty much the only thing you've got going for you. Whatever happened, I know it was on his orders. I'd believe your word against his.'

'How was the service we provided the other night, officer?' he replied, hoping to waylay the conversation, 'I hope she lived up to your expectations?' Lisson turned to Justin.

'Were you round there the other night?' he said in mock outrage. 'That's not a new suit you've got on is it, Inspector?'

'I can't think what he means, Inspector,' replied Justin.

'You two should be on the stage,' said Gormally.

'It's the scaffold you're going to be on if you're not careful, Jack,' replied Justin.

'I think you're making a terrible mistake,' said Gormally, leaning across the desk towards him.

'What I think, Jack,' said Justin, 'is that you are going to swing. That is, unless you help us pin it on the man who gave the orders.'

'Have a think about it, Jack,' said Lisson, as he and Justin got up to leave the room. As he reached the door, Lisson turned and brought his hand up to his neck to make the sign of a noose. They went back to the other room.

'How did you get into the flat?' demanded Justin. Vardy's eyes remained fixed on the wall. He took a deep breath then shrugged and shook his head.

'Gormally reckons you had the keys,' said Lisson. Justin looked at his partner angrily, but he knew he had to go along with it.

'Now I know you're talking rubbish,' replied Vardy as he pulled another cigar out of his pocket, bit off the tip and lit it. 'My solicitor here yet?'

'What do you need one of them for? You guilty or something?' said Lisson.

'Call my solicitor, please,' he replied.

'I don't think I have his number,' said Justin, pretending to feel in his pockets. 'Do you have it, Inspector Lisson?'

'No, I did have it on me. I think I must have left it in the motorcar.'

'I'll come with you and help you look for it,' said Justin, getting up. They moved towards the door. 'We shouldn't be too long, Mr Vardy. I'll bring you back a telephone.'

'Right double-act you've got going on,' said Vardy, as they left the room.

Standing outside in the hall, they each smoked a cigarette.

'We're going to need to protect the girl so she can help us,' said Justin.

'We can easily bring her in if we can find her,' replied Lisson.

'Yes, but we can't keep her. We need to get into that safe house as soon as possible, then maybe Andrews can do something about it.'

'I'm going to stay here and work on these two,' said Lisson. 'I'm quite enjoying this.'

'All right,' said Justin, 'just don't get too creative. We've got enough tracks to cover as it is.'

Justin left him in the hallway and knocked on the door of the Chief Inspector's office.

'What do you want?' came the angry voice from inside.

'We need to bring one of the girls in,' said Justin, poking his head around the door.

Andrews looked up at him angrily.

'Where are they?'

'They're in a safe house in Stoke Newington. We need them for evidence.'

'Ah, for fuck sake…Fine. You can bring them in and then let those other two go,' said Andrews. 'I told you already that the evidence so far is all circumstantial.'

'One of the girls could be a key witness if we can make her testify, but we'll have to offer her protection first.'

'Fine, do what you want,' he said, sounding bored with the conversation. He looked down at the papers on his desk. 'Take Cameron with you and don't get yourselves shot!'

The two cars sped north towards Newington Green – Justin and Cameron leading, two uniformed officers following; each of them carrying the weight of a Webley Revolver in their inside pockets.

They turned into the street and crawled to a stop on the curb some distance short of the house. The two uniformed officers took the alleyway alongside the property, creeping behind the fence with their guns drawn. Justin and Cameron ducked down as they passed the closed curtains of the bay windows at the front of the house. Justin stood under the arch of the recessed front door and gave it a loud knock.

The door rattled loosely in its frame as he struck it, giving way to a disappointing, bodiless echo. Cursing under his breath, he leaned around the corner into the alleyway and signalled to the other officers to force entry.

Hearing the thud and recoil of the back door, along with the shouts of the other officers, he drew the gun from his waistband and swung his full weight against the front door.

'Police!' he and Cameron shouted. The door slammed into the adjacent wall as they burst into the hallway. A picture frame fell from a wall upstairs, smashing at the top of the staircase. Justin raised his gun to it, then drew it back as he and Cameron moved into the front of the house.

A thick cloud of dust blew up into the half-light of the bay windows as the door to the front room swung open. The room was empty.

They climbed the stairs to the first floor and searched each of the rooms while the other two officers worked their way along the downstairs hall. Justin kicked a blanket across the floor in one of the bedrooms where it had been lying, twisted and swiftly abandoned. It landed against the side of a single bed next to the window. He pulled open the curtains, letting the mid-day light shine in through the fetid air.

'We should have brought them in earlier,' he said, as he sat down on the edge of the bed. He looked over the mess of the bedroom. The wardrobe doors swung lightly in the air. Next to that was another bed and a cheap vanity chest with a three-piece mirror. A single red lipstick lay on the floor underneath it amid the cracks of the exposed floorboards, adding to the derelict impression. Justin kicked the blanket away from his feet.

'You don't think they could be at the brothel, sir?' said Cameron. Justin shook his head and checked his watch. Standing up, he fiddled with the catch on his gun and put the piece back in his waistband.

'That's the last place they'll be. They must have been taken to another safe house somewhere.'

'We can't be sure your girl was here anyway, sir.'

One of the uniformed constables came into the room.

'All empty, sir,' he said.

'Yes, I can see that, thank-you,' replied Justin. 'Stay with us for a while, I think we might still need you.'

'Sir,' he nodded and left the room. Justin turned to Cameron.

'I suppose we're going to have to check out the place in Soho anyway,' he said. 'Have you still got the keys?'

Cameron took them out of his pocket and held them up in the light.

'God help us if anyone catches us this time,' said Justin.

Half an hour later they were back in Berwick Street. Justin walked over to the other car and the uniformed constable opened his window.

'Just knock on that door and if anyone answers, tell them you've got the wrong address. Then head straight back to the station. Knock a couple of times to make sure. If there's no answer, just go. We'll do the rest.'

'Will do, sir,' he replied.

Justin watched from the car as he approached the door to the tailors shop, knocked repeatedly then went back to his vehicle and drove away.

'Do you remember which key it was?' said Justin, as they sat and waited a few moments in the car.

'This one here, sir,' said Cameron, separating it from the bunch. 'Shall I go on ahead?'

'No, I'll go. I'll let myself in and you can knock after a minute or two, just in case it's being watched. Keep your gun where you can reach it.'

'Sir.' Cameron quickly checked the weapon and replaced it in his inside pocket while Justin did the same.

'See you shortly,' he said, putting on his Homburg and stepping out onto the pavement.

A few seconds later, he was inside. Cameron looked at his watch and, hearing no gunshots, went and knocked at the door.

'It's no good,' said Justin, letting him in. 'They've tidied the place up – strangely enough – and buggered off. It's like they were never here.'

They climbed the stairs and looked around the office. Every bit of the mess they had left had been cleared away.

'The tailor must have done it,' said Justin. 'They must have given him orders to call them in and to clear the place out.'

'We couldn't do much about that, sir. Have you looked in the other rooms?'

'No, not yet.'

Cameron opened the door to the tailor's rooms. The hat stand was bare, and the two rows of Singers had been left unattended. He opened the next two doors where the girls plied their trade. Both rooms were pristine and empty.

'It's just like a posh hotel,' said Cameron, stepping into one of the rooms. He nodded towards the bed. 'How was she, sir?' he said with a smile.

'Not to my taste, Constable,' said Justin, as he turned back towards the stairs.

'Come in, Lamoureaux,' said Andrews. Justin opened the door.

'This is Mr Martin; Mr Vardy's solicitor,' said Andrews. Justin closed the door and sat down.

'This is the officer in charge of the case,' said Andrews. The bespectacled man sitting across the desk turned to Justin and said, 'I'm afraid you're going to have to release my client immediately. I'm sure I don't have to tell you this,' he said looking at him sceptically, 'but the evidence against my client – if you can call it evidence – is purely circumstantial. It does not warrant his further detention.'

Justin looked across at Andrews and thought he detected a smirk behind the blankness of his expression.

'Do you have any evidence directly linking Mr Vardy, Inspector?' said Andrews. Justin shifted in his chair.

'I need to speak to you in private, if you don't mind, sir,' he replied.

'Excuse us one moment,' said Andrews to the solicitor, as he and Justin stepped outside. He shut the door. 'What is it, Justin?'

'The girls weren't at the safe house, sir. If we let Vardy go, I think they'll be in danger, and we're going to need their evidence.'

'What do you want me to do about it?' said Andrews. 'Do you have anything on Vardy or not?'

'Not directly, sir.'

'Well, that's that then. We don't have much leeway with people like him, you know that. If you've got nothing on him then there's no point keeping the gentleman waiting,' he said turning back towards the door.

'Gormally has to stay in though, sir.'

'We can keep Gormally in for now. That's Vardy's solicitor in there remember; you can do what the fuck you like with the other one…for now. I reckon we could have enough on him to make it stick anyway, despite the mess you've created. Now, I'm gonna go and have a little chat myself with Mr Vardy and see if I can get him to help us out a bit – though I'm not too optimistic about it. I want Lisson to work on Gormally over the weekend, and, as it's yours and Cameron's day off tomorrow, if you've got no leads on the girls, I'd advise you both to bloody well take it. Leave this to Lisson.'

'Have Gormally and Vardy spoken to each other, sir?' said Justin.

'Of course not. What do you think this is, a bloody tavern?' he replied. 'Listen, I want you to take a break and come back fresh to work on Gormally. I need to have a think about all this anyway. Don't let me see you here tomorrow!' he said and disappeared back inside his office.

The horn of the gramophone crackled as the familiar con-coction began to take effect. Justin sank into the comfort of his chair and into the music. As he let himself drift, caught in the swirl of his senses, he looked at the rain tapping and dripping intermittently on the window. He rested his feet on the coffee table and swallowed another pill, washing it back with another large swig of whisky.

His breath seemed to come out of his body in one slow, deep motion, as the next comfortable wave drifted through him. He perched the small bottle between his index finger and thumb, and held it up to the light so that the ceiling rose caught its rounded nape, giving it a yellowish glint.

Through the gap in the curtains, he could see individual round blots where rain drops were being driven against the glass. Then the marks would dissipate into first long, then clear, and then finally invisible streaks as the wind let off again. He thought of Cameron and how drunk he had looked when they both left the office, and shook his head in pity.

He took out a pill, turned it over and gave his attention to the small V that was embossed on one side of it. In his altered state it seemed to fascinate him, and it was quite some time before he realised that the music had stopped and that the record was still spinning.

Another sip from his glass and again it was empty. He looked over at the gramophone; it would need cranking this time, he thought. In his mind he got up and replaced the needle on the record, and heard the sounds emanating from the machine. Still sitting in his chair, he reached for the whisky bottle and refilled his glass.

Holding the pill up to the light again, he wondered if it would be enough to kill him. There was comfort in knowing that you could choose when to die, if you wanted to. He held it up to his lips as if to tempt himself, then dropped it back into the bottle and lit another cigarette.

Over the continued crackle of the gramophone, he heard a dull thud, as something dropped onto the hallway rug. Levering himself out of his chair, he went out, switched on the light and saw a rain splashed manila envelope lying flat on the doormat. He came back into the living room and tore it open then looked at the photographs and found that he again was the subject of the images. Sobriety struck him instantly.

He switched off the lights in the room then pulled open a drawer in his bureau, took out his revolver and returned to the hallway.

He stood in the darkness. The glow of a single lamp out in the street came in through the fanlight, making everything look rounded and indistinct. In one swift movement he pulled the door open and ran out into the rain, and across to the edge of the lawn, where he ducked down behind the hedgerow. The back wing of a dark saloon turned the corner, rocking a little in the glistening street as it sped off behind the end terrace.

Justin went back into the house and took the photographs into the bedroom, where he could turn on the light and look at them properly.

There were four of them in total this time: one taken as he exited Westminster Underground Station, two of him driving a car through what looked like the streets of West London, and one more as he walked along some unidentifiable street. He flicked through the images again, each of them adding to his confusion.

The one of him alone in the street seemed fairly incongruous with the rest of the set. He tried to picture the location, but the background was blurred and there was nothing to say how recently it had been taken.

He opened the drawer next to his bed and loaded the empty gun from a brand-new box of ammunition. Turning out the light again, he went back into the front room with the photographs in his hand and poured himself another whisky by the light of his Parker Beacon.

The rain had now stopped, he saw, as he closed the gap in the curtains. There would be no more music tonight. He sat back in his chair in the dark, drained his glass and refilled it again, then flicked out his lighter.

Seven

Cameron finally woke-up at the sound of a passing car horn. Even as he lay in bed he could already feel the heat of the morning. A steady stream of sunlight cut into the room through a gap in the curtains. He checked his watch and saw that it was already a quarter-past ten, and only then did it occur to him that it must be Saturday.

He must have had a few by the time he left Scotland Yard the previous evening. As far as Cameron was concerned, it had already been a heavy night on the whisky, making sure they had not missed anything that might lead them to the girls. He got the impression, however, that the inspector's night was only just beginning. 'Sod it, it's only a job,' he remembered Inspector Lamoureaux saying, and they had left it at that. At the chief inspector's insistence, both he and Justin would get the weekend off.

He had given in to temptation this time and chatted up the pretty barmaid at a pub on the way home. For a split second, as he lay in bed now, he thought to check that he had not brought her back with him. If he had, he would have known it by now. He could just imagine the scene. Luckily, the room was empty, and he could hear the reassuring sounds of voices on the wireless, and plates clattering in the kitchen.

He pushed the covers back and swung his feet over the edge of the bed, surprised to find he was not feeling too bad. He put on his dressing gown and opened the curtains. There were a few hefty clouds hanging about, threatening to make it one of those days that flits between dullness and light. But for now, the sun was shining. He rubbed his temples and forehead with the tips of his fingers then opened the bedroom door and stepped out into the dining room.

William, his youngest, was playing with some wooden blocks on the rug in front of the unlit fire. He ruffled the boy's hair as he walked past then sat down at the table and poured himself a cup of black coffee. The lingering aroma of the bacon and eggs he had just missed out on did little to rouse his appetite.

'Morning,' came his wife's voice from somewhere in the kitchen. Cameron understood the tone. She carried on washing the dishes.

'Where's Andrew?' he said, taking a cigarette out of a box on the mantelpiece and lighting it with a match.

'Paper round,' she replied. 'He won't be back till this afternoon.'

Something moved at his leg. Cameron looked down to see William holding up a green wooden block, trying clumsily to put it into his father's hand. Cameron reached down and took it.

'Thanks,' he said, sitting down again, pulling the ashtray towards him and propping his cigarette up against its inside edge. He lifted the boy up onto his lap. The first few puffs of tobacco seemed to have formed a poisonous cloud inside his head. He took another swig of hot coffee.

'Have you had your breakfast yet, wee man?' he sighed. He was starting to feel a bit sick. William smiled back at him, not comprehending.

'No, he hasn't,' said Maggie, coming in from the kitchen, carrying a bowl of mushy cereal and some buttered toast. She picked William up and put him in his highchair.

'Can you give it him?' she said, turning and heading back into the kitchen.

'Aye.'

Cameron reached for his cigarette and took one final drag then grimaced as he extinguished it. He picked up the buttered toast and tore it into several pieces then placed them on the little tray in front of William.

The boy grasped at the soggy bread, squashing a piece of it in his fingers and holding it up to Cameron's mouth.

'No, son' he groaned, 'that's for you.' He pushed the toast further across the tray towards the boy. He took another sip of coffee then picked up the bowl, scooped up some of the porridge and spooned it into young William's mouth.

Outside, the sun had slipped behind a large cloud that now cast a pallid, depressing shade into the room. Memories of the previous evening's conversation were now flowing back to him. If they were not able to track down those girls pretty soon then chances are, they'd had it. But how do you go about doing your job with your hands tied behind your back? In the hours that had passed, they could have been moved anywhere. Or perhaps far worse. He angled the spoon back into the porridge and aimed it once again at William's open mouth.

'Could you cover the dinner up next time?' he called out to Maggie in the kitchen. 'You keep doing it. It was all dried-out by the time I got home.' He could see her through the doorway, intermittently visible as she moved around the kitchen.

'Aye then. You should come back earlier,' came the voice from the kitchen. 'No-one else complained. It's not easy with a toddler and those two, you know.'

'Aye, I know,' he called back to her then turned to his son. 'And it's an easy life in the CID,' he muttered. But he was in no mood for an argument.

He lifted the spoon back up to William's lips, but before he could get it into his mouth, a soft little hand shot up and stuffed in a piece of toast. The porridge smeared down the boy's cheek.

'Ah, for f…' Cameron put down the bowl and looked for a cloth but got side-tracked by his developing headache. Finding a dishcloth on the back of his chair, he wiped William's face then gave him some water from the bottle and picked up the bowl.

'Let's try that again, shall we?' he said, piling up the spoon this time, reasoning that it would be quicker and easier if he could get it all into his mouth in one go.

As soon as the spoon touched the little boy's lips, William turned his head again and the porridge smeared down the same cheek just as before, dripping down and completely missing his bib.

'Ah, ya wee f…' said Cameron.

'Don't swear in front of William,' came the stern admonishment from the kitchen.

'Ears like a bat, that one,' Cameron whispered to his son. William swallowed another small piece of toast.

Cameron reached for the cloth again and wiped up the mess. Then, in what he considered to be an impressively cunning attempt, he clicked his fingers in front of the boy's face while grabbing the spoon, dipping it into the porridge and aiming it at the boy's mouth.

Still, William was quicker. Almost as though he had sensed it coming, the boy seized a piece of toast and stuffed it into his mouth, causing the porridge to spill all down the front of him, yet again.

'Ya bastard,' said Cameron under his breath. Resignedly, he put down the bowl and felt a bolt of pain shoot through his head. 'Ah, just have your toast then,' he said. William smiled at him again with his usual innocent expression, as the half-chewed ball of toast fell out of his mouth and rolled down the front of him onto the rug.

'Is he eating?' Maggie called out.

'Yes, yes,' replied Cameron, his patience beginning to fail him. He picked up a new piece of toast and put it decisively into William's mouth then swallowed the rest of his coffee and again eyed the cigarette packet.

William sat forward and coughed a little. Then, with the beginnings of a cry, he started to move and writhe about in his chair. Cameron looked on, alarmed, as the boy began to struggle.

'You all right?' he said. The little boy's mouth was wide open now, but Cameron could see that the toast was not there. He was starting to wheeze.

'Maggie!' shouted Cameron, half frozen as he rose from his chair. 'Maggie! Get in here!' William started to rock his small body as he struggled to breathe. 'Shit!' shouted Cameron.

Not knowing what else to do, he started to push upwards on the child's chest with the tips of his fingers. Maggie arrived from the kitchen.

'What is it?' she said urgently.

'He's choking!'

Grabbing William under the arms, Maggie turned him upside down and slapped him hard across his back. The wheezing continued. The boy's face was reddening. Maggie turned him over and started to shake him over the tray of his highchair, while Cameron stood helplessly looking on.

Then, from inside the boy's chest, there came the sound of a muffled cough. Then a stream of vomit shot out of him and he let out a cry. Cameron looked down at the tray and the slimy piece of half-chewed toast which had just landed on it with a gentle splat. Maggie turned the boy upright and held him close to her, rocking him gently as he started to bawl.

'Fuck,' said Cameron drawing out the word.

'You've got to watch him when he's eating!' said Maggie.

'I was. He just–' Cameron stalled, not knowing what else to say. He sat back down, filled with relief now, and reached for the packet of cigarettes.

Gradually William's sobs became quieter and more muffled as Maggie clutched him to the nape of her neck. Cameron picked up the boy's water bottle and passed it to her as she wiped her own eyes with the back of her hand.

'Is there anything I can do?' he said timidly.

'You've been out boozing,' she said, with real anger now. 'Go and take a bath!'

'I was late at work. I had a few with the inspector while we discussed a case,' he said, but her back was already turned.

By now William's cries had settled into moans as he looked at Cameron accusingly over Maggie's shoulder, sucking his thumb.

'It wasn't my fault,' he mouthed to the boy, taking a puff on his cigarette before shaking his head in disgust at it and stubbing it out.

Maggie put William back into his high chair and sat down to feed him, and the room was calm once again.

'Right. I'll draw a bath then,' he said, feeling strangely betrayed given his honest intentions and the physical state he was in. Maggie ignored him. Quietly, he sloped off towards the safety of the bathroom with the intention of staying there until shortly before lunch.

William was on the floor of the dining room, sitting on the rug in front of the fire grate, pushing a wooden toy around and following it wherever it happened to go. As he came back past, Cameron pushed the wooden blocks into a slightly neater pile in the middle of the floor and sat down next to his son.

Thoughts of the earlier incident still haunted him, though by now the boy seemed to have long forgotten it. William crawled up to him and he suddenly felt himself filled with a mixture of guilt and fear as he leant down and gave the boy a hug.

His wife came into the room then remembered something she needed to do in the kitchen and left again without making a sound. He could sense her presence. Cameron and Maggie seemed to have the ability to irritate each other these days without either of them needing to utter a word. It was a skill they had both nurtured and developed, though neither one of them could say exactly what it was that annoyed them so much. Ever more frequently these days there would be hard words or looks, long silences and tension, followed by mutual confusion.

Cameron looked down at the round cheeks and big eyes of his son as the boy crawled across the rug, squealing and chasing an inanimate block towards the fire grate. Once he had reached it, and after momentarily focusing all of his innocent attention on the piece of wood, he shifted over to a book that was lying on the floor nearby and started crumpling the pages with uninhibited carelessness. As Cameron sat there, he wondered what they had brought him into; what he and his wife had saddled him with. He was shocked, all of a sudden, at their irresponsibility.

Just then the door opened and his daughter came into the room. At eight years of age, she already seemed to have matured uncomfortably beyond the need for his protection. She came over and kissed him on the cheek.

'Morning sweetheart,' he said.

'It's afternoon, Dad,' she replied as she made her way into the kitchen, her English accent seeming even more pronounced for the fact that he rarely saw her these days. Both of the older children looked and sounded like Londoners, and he fully expected William to one day be just the same. It was as if all three of them were adopted.

He heard his wife in the kitchen telling Charlotte to lay the table for lunch, and he decided to help her.

'Could you help, Dad?' said Charlotte, coming back into the room.

'Aye,' he said, smiling.

'Are you feeling unwell today?' she said looking up at his darkly ringed eyes. He could sense Maggie's presence in the kitchen nearby.

'No. Just a bit tired, love,' he said, avoiding her gaze as they set out the places.

Maggie came in from the kitchen carrying a plate of corned beef with bread and butter, and they all sat down at the table. Cameron left it to her this time to put William into his high chair and make him eat.

'Where's Andy?' said Charlotte. She had set out a place for her older brother.

'He's out on his round,' said Maggie, cutting up thin pieces of meat and putting them onto a plate for William. 'He'll be back later this afternoon.'

'Why can't I get a paper round too?' said Charlotte, renewing the old discussion.

'You'll not be doing any paper round,' said Cameron.

'But why not?' she replied.

'Because you're too young,' he said, 'and it's a job for boys, not little girls.'

'We've spoken about this before, Charlotte,' said Maggie. 'You're too young and your father says no. Here, give this to your brother.' She passed Charlotte the small plate on which she had put William's food. 'Are those shoes still pinching you, love?'

'Yes, Mum,' replied Charlotte. 'I've been wearing plimsolls in class.'

'Plimsolls?' Maggie turned to Cameron. 'Your daughter needs some new shoes. If she gets caught with those on, she'll get the cane!'

'Well, get her some then,' he said. It was the first time they had made eye contact that afternoon.

'I will, I'll take her out this afternoon…if we've got the money left that is,' she replied.

She knew how unlikely it was that he would have spent it. They could afford them, even if it was at a stretch. Cameron kept his eyes on his plate.

'Andrew's going through his pretty fast as well,' said Maggie.

'We'll get one pair this week and another the next,' he replied. 'It's not winter, you know.'

The front door went, and the sound of the passing traffic came in briefly up the stairway. Andrew walked in, a little out of breath.

'Afternoon,' said Cameron.

'Afternoon, Dad,' he replied, going straight up to the table, taking a slice of bread and starting to butter it.

'I thought you weren't back until later,' said Maggie.

'I won't be, but I was starving,' he said, taking a bite and turning away again. 'I'll be back later,' he mumbled over his mouthful of food as he went back out.

Cameron felt as though he hardly knew the boy these days, having been missing from his upbringing for far too long. When he had finally been demobbed, there was an under-staffed police force only too happy to take up the role of putting the squeeze on his finances and time. The story was all too common. Now that Andrew was old enough to be out of the house by himself, Cameron had become slightly envious of the young lad's freedom. Guiltily, he looked across at little William as the boy sat innocently chewing his food – guilty because, as he did so, he was also thanking the Lord that this would be his last weekend at home for a while.

'My mother's coming over in an hour or so,' said Maggie, without looking up from her plate.

'I'll nip out for a pint then,' he replied.

'You're going back there again?' She looked up at him.

'Aye,' he said putting down his knife and fork. 'I told you already, I wasn't at the bloody pub last night.'

Charlotte giggled.

'Don't swear at the table – not in front of the children!' said Maggie.

'We had a couple of drinks at work. Do I constantly have to repeat myself?' he said.

'Aye, at the office, of course…It's a wonder any cases ever get solved at that place. All too inebriated. I don't know where you get the money.'

'I'm going to go out for just one pint – just to catch last orders before closing. All right?'

'Aye, suit yourself,' she sighed.

The two of them ate without another word between them while Charlotte tried her hardest to stop giggling.

It was already past two by the time Cameron got to the pub. Standing amongst the regulars, he looked around for anyone he might know. Eventually he saw one of his neighbours sitting on a stool at the far corner of the bar and went over to stand in the empty spot beside him.

'Afternoon Marty,' he said.

'Oh, afternoon Cam. You're just in time.'

'Last orders at the bar,' the barman called out. Several sets of hands shot up into the air. Cameron ordered a pint of mild and a light ale for his neighbour.

'Very good of you, sir,' said Marty, taking the drink. 'How've you been?'

'Ah, the usual,' he sighed. 'Busy. Thought I'd get out of the house while I still had the chance.'

'Yes, it's a working man's prerogative, I reckon.'

'Aye, it is that. Cheers.' They both drank.

'And yourself?' said Cameron.

'Can't complain. The sciatica's a bit of a pain in the backside.'

'Boom, boom.'

'I know, I thought that was a good one,' he said.

The two of them drank in silence then Marty said, 'Have you been following the cricket?'

'Nah, it's not really a Scot's game,' replied Cameron.

'South Africa have been abominable,' continued Marty. 'England had them on the ropes within the first hour earlier in the week.'

'Is that so?' said Cameron, trying to feign interest, but only succeeding in sounding a little sarcastic.

'Dreadful performance,' said Marty, seeming not to notice.

'I might try and keep an eye on The Open,' said Cameron.

'Ah, yes, of course. That'll be more up your street. There's that American to look out for. I don't suppose you're a betting man at all?' said Marty, reaching into his inside pocket. Cameron smiled.

'No, I can't say I am,' he said. 'Why, do you know of any illegal betting rings you think I should hear about?'

'No, no,' stuttered Marty. 'I meant on the horses…down at the races, of course.' Cameron laughed.

'It's all right Marty, there's no harm in organising a little wager here and there,' he said. 'Just as long as the old plod doesn't find out, hey?'

'That's the spirit, son.' Marty looked noticeably relieved. He reached inside his jacket again and pulled out a pouch of tobacco. 'Yes, well it's not really my kind of thing anyway,' he said, finishing his drink and lighting his pipe. The bell went for the close of bar.

'I must nip to the loo,' said Marty, 'same old trouble again, son. I'll still be standing at the urinal by late opening at this rate. You've got all this to look forward to.' He tapped Cameron on the arm and disappeared.

Cameron finished his pint then opened his wallet and saw that it was almost empty.

'Christ,' he said to himself, drawing out the word in a long sigh. Even if the bar had not been closing, he would barely have been able to afford another pint.

The door swung open and one-by-one the men started to leave. Some of them were his neighbours, people he vaguely knew by name. Others were not the type to be seen dead having a conversation with a copper in public. Even though his wife knew some of their wives – and was even quite good friends with some of them – for him, things were different. There was always the stigma that inevitably went with the job.

He made his way towards the exit and held the door open for an old man as he shuffled out.

'Thank you, son.'

'My pleasure,' he replied, and followed him out into the street.

Her mother would still be round there, he thought to himself. Cameron looked up and saw that the sky had clouded over. Doesn't look like rain, he thought, and he decided to take a walk along Holloway Road.

The exodus from the pubs had now scattered, merging into the side streets down towards Highbury Fields, or up the other way towards the Archway. He stood at the junction, having not yet decided which way he wanted to go, and nodded to a policeman who was standing in the street, directing the traffic. There was little to sway his decision. In the end he headed south towards Highbury Corner.

His eyes barely left the pavement as he dawdled along. Only after some time did he come out of his daydream and finally glance up.

Waiting at the tram stop straight ahead of him was a young woman, her straight dark hair neatly framing her features and splaying at the ends where it met her collar. There was nothing particularly extraordinary about her, but nevertheless, the sight of her was enough to arouse his interest. Noticing her slightly heavy jaw and the almost unhealthy whiteness of her skin, he was taken with her all the same.

She turned and looked at him as he passed, as though she could sense his eyes on her. Cameron looked away, turning his attention back to the paving stones and the worn brown leather of his cap-toe shoes.

He seemed to be noticing more and more of them lately; it was as though they were everywhere. Women seemed to have multiplied, still vastly outnumbering the men after the years of conscripted barbarity.

His brother wouldn't have been so shy, he thought to himself, as he continued on, smiling at his memory. Tommy would have strolled right up to her, wife or no wife. He had always gone for the real beauties, the real stunners that everyone else was afraid of. But that was all over now. Just like one of Cameron's old pals had once said to him, 'One minute you're laughing and singing and joking, and then suddenly, in the wink of an eye, you're the only one left.' Now he knew what that meant.

He had repeated the same quote to Inspector Lamoureaux the night before, while they were drinking. Christ, that bloke can put them away, thought Cameron, picturing the inspector. Perhaps that was the answer, he said, speaking his thoughts aloud to himself like a madman as he walked along the street. With all that whisky the previous night, they had spoken a lot about the past.

'Tommy got the Chlorine,' he had told Justin, while the latter poured two more overly generous measures. There were no complaints. 'Probably thought it was tear gas because apparently he kept moving…horrible. He wasn't with my battalion.'

'Life will shock you at times,' came the disarmingly truthful reply.

Too right, Cameron thought now, as a familiar empty feeling came over him. It was one that always seemed to accompany the memories of people and things he could never get back.

He continued on past the tram stop, stealing another quick glimpse of the girl as he moved off along the pavement. With a feeling of unexplainable poignancy, he turned to look at her one final time, knowing he would never see her again. She had a certain poise about her, he thought, as she reached into her handbag for something. Reminiscent of Lady Keating, perhaps? They had one thing in common, regardless of anything else; he knew that both of these women were well beyond his reach.

He stopped to light a cigarette as a tram pulled up at the stop. Then, as he put away his lighter, he looked up to see the vehicle moving away, taking the lady with it.

How on earth did she end up with someone like him? he thought, as he carried on walking. It was Lady Keating on his mind now; he had already forgotten about the girl. He continued blindly along the pavement, imagining himself combing Lady Joanna's hair away from her face with the palm of his hand. He turned the corner at the tube station. A man and his dog passed by, but he barely saw them, feeling the smoothness of her skin and her fingers pressing gently into the small of his back. The pavement ahead of him was deserted and the sky above was threatening rain. As his hands moved down to her hips, he felt a burning sensation between his index and middle finger. He flicked the remnants of his cigarette out into the street.

She had trapped him and let him down – that was how he saw it. It was back to his wife now. He tried to calculate how long it had been since they had last been *together*. It was almost criminal, he thought. They must be in contravention of their wedding vows, at least. Was it the same for all couples?' he wondered, and wished he had done a lot more research.

They must have been in love at the beginning – he was sure of it. At one time they had worried about not seeing each other while he was away; worried perhaps that in being apart, their feelings for each other might change.

When he thought of her now it was like watching an image being played back on film; the cool air of the auditorium, the distance between them. Flat images comprised of whites and greys. Through the prism of hindsight, their early worries seemed to have been a warning to them right from the start.

He stopped half way along the street and looked around, wondering where, if anywhere, he had intended to go.

One advantage of being a copper was that you knew the whereabouts of most of the local brothels. And there were several nearby. Only once had he ever been to one; a youthful mistake on a few days leave somewhere outside of Toulouse. It was still a mystery to him how anyone could enjoy the experience. But as he reached into his pocket now and felt the thick role of rubber, he wondered if the time had come to give it another try.

Only after his wife had questioned him about their money problems had he gone into the bedroom, slid the drawer open, reached to the back of it and put the thing in his jacket pocket. It would only serve her right if he were to use it now, not that she would ever know it. If only he could remember an address…

He carried on walking. The excuse he gave himself was the lack of money, though he knew it was not the actual reason. He could always find a few bob, if he really needed it. In his mind he could see his hand knocking on the door, see himself being led up the staircase then going into the room and seeing the ideal girl. That was how it would be.

Maybe this is what people do, he thought. Maybe they just flit from one fantasy to another, pretending to themselves they're not lost.

His eyes were drawn to the windows of the lifeless pub
across the road and he saw a flick of its grimy curtains. Who
am I kidding? he finally thought, then turned around and
headed back the way he came.

The children were all in bed. Cameron and Maggie sat
together in the living room; him reading a book, while she
got stuck into her knitting. His eyelids were drooping now
due to the inexplicable tiredness that had steadily come over
him.

He looked at his watch and was amazed to see that it was
only eight o'clock. He had been doing his best to concentrate
on the book in front of him, but for some time now the
words had seemed flat and his attention had been drifting.
At the end of a paragraph he would suddenly realise that he
could not remember a single thing he had just read. Going
back to the start, he would then read it over again and
invariably the words would be familiar. He was getting sick
of the endless cycle. Finally, he gave up and rested the book
on his knee.

'How about some tea?' he said, looking across at his wife.

'No thanks,' she said, her eyes fixed on the rhythmic flick
of the needles in front of her.

During the war he had pictured how he would spend his
Saturday nights; a few pints at the local, a game of darts
perhaps. Amongst other things, these were the thoughts that
had kept him going.

'What are you reading?' she said. He picked up the book
and glanced at the cover, as though having already forgotten.

'Crime theory,' he said.

'What are you reading that for?'

'It's for work.'

'I know it's for work,' she said shortly. 'Are you on a
training course or something?'

There she goes again, he thought. Always badgering him
about the same old shite.

'No,' he replied. He knew that he should expand on the answer, if only for the sake of good manners. But it felt good when the words did not come.

'Oh,' she said, disinterestedly. He fiddled with the pages of the book on his lap.

There should be a five-year trial in every marriage, he thought, then you can either carry on or cash your chips and try something new. That could be us.

The image of the girl he had seen waiting at the tram stop that afternoon popped into his head.

'Christ,' he said under his breath.

'What was that?' said Maggie.

'Nothing,' he replied, and made some vague indication towards the book lying face down on his knee. He looked at his watch again and shook his head. It was now four minutes past eight.

Eight

Justin went back into the front room, drying his face with a towel. He went to open the curtains but then stopped midway, thinking better of it. The corona of light around the edges was enough for him to see around the room and know that he was not being spied on from outside.

If this is how I must live for the time being, then so be it, he thought, still shivering deeply from the cold.

Next to the chair he had woken up in this morning, too cold to dare move, lay his Colt Revolver and the whisky bottle – almost empty now – lying on its side on the rug. The alarm clock in the bedroom had eventually woken him up, having first shaken itself off the side table and then landed face down on the floor. Twenty minutes had passed before he had managed to struggle out of his chair and switch it off.

He picked up the gun and emptied the chambers into the palm of his hand, dropping all six rounds into the draw of the side-table. He looked around for an empty glass and poured himself the last inch of whisky from the bottle, mixed in some water from the siphon and took the drink with him into the bathroom.

He lay in the bath for some time, letting the heat soak deep into his bones and getting goose pimples each time he emerged from the steaming water. He slid down, fully emerging himself in an attempt to thaw out his sinuses, then came back up, took a sip of the whisky and water, and shivered.

Draining the rest of the glass, he cursed himself for not having a second bottle in reserve. But it was probably for the best, he thought; he needed to get out of the house today if he was to preserve whatever sanity he had left.

So long as he kept to places where he was beyond reproach, it should be all right. Thinking through his options, he eventually decided that the pub and then the race track would be the safest places to go.

The uppers had started to kick in by the time he had dried and dressed himself. He brewed some coffee in the kitchen, swallowed it steaming hot then lit a cigarette and went into the hallway to get the morning paper.

His feeling of trepidation dissipated as he approached the front door and saw only the newspaper waiting for him on the mat. Much more of this can't be good for the nerves, he thought, as he went back into the safety of the kitchen.

He sat down at the table and turned to the racing section to see what was on the roster at Alexandra Park. Folding the paper open at the relevant section, he sat there for some time and drank more coffee. As he finished his second cup, he realised that the kitchen blind was open and that someone could potentially be looking in. He went over and pulled it down violently. That was enough. Slamming the paper down onto the kitchen table, he threw on his jacket and hat, and left the house.

The omnibus had been almost empty when he had got on at Bayswater Road, but had gradually accumulated more passengers en route to Chalk Farm. Justin could feel himself slouching in his seat as he looked out from the top deck. Fighting off the nausea, he sat up and lit a cigarette, feeling around for the empty hipflask in his pocket.

His heart was pumping hard now but his head was still cloudy, as he gazed out at the pedestrians, streaming and congregating around each parade of shops.

The coffee and whisky and uppers had combined to create a burning sensation in his empty stomach. But in spite of this, by the time the bus came to its final stop, he was beginning to feel a slight hunger.

He got off and bought a sandwich at a coffee shop, barely eating any of it, as he stood and waited for the pub next door to open. When at last it did, he bought a smallish bottle and filled up his hipflask, quickly swallowing the rest of it in two drafts.

He bought himself another newspaper and went into the ground. Once inside, he nudged his way through the thickening crowd towards the racetrack, where he could get a clearer view of the tote boards.

'Come along please,' said the bookmaker. 'Yes, sir,' he said to Justin. The look on the bookie's face was one of both boredom and poorly-concealed contempt. He knew where the balance of power lay. Justin thought how odd it was that the law banning off-course gambling had forced him to do business with a probable member of the Sabini gang.

'Yes, sir – you, sir,' said the bookie, pointing right at him now.

I've just finished dealing with one of your lot, thought Justin, as he was suddenly reminded of Catherine and the girl at the brothel.

'Come on, son, we ain't got all day,' came the voice of a punter beside him. It was all too repellent. Justin turned and nudged his way back through the crowd.

He took a swig from his hipflask and checked his watch. The race was drawing near. If he did not put a bet on soon, it would have been pointless coming. He went over to another bookie – one that looked equally shifty – and handed him the money. Then he moved out towards the front of the stand.

As he looked out over the horizon of gentlemen's hats, his mind turned back to the question of whether or not he might have been followed. But what did it matter? It was only a bloody racecourse. They could take all the pictures they liked while he stood blamelessly watching the race. He reached into his pocket for his hip flask and took another swig.

There was a surge towards the front as the horses lined up and everyone waited for the gun. Then a quietness came to the crowd.

The crack of the gun shuddered through the air and a unanimous bawl burst from the spectators as they moved forward together. It was as if a hurricane had swept through behind them.

The horses' hooves rumbled against the turf, growing louder as the jockeys approached, beating out a familiar tattoo. Justin kept his eyes on the riders as they turned into the first bend. The calls from the crowd were becoming increasingly aggressive. The air was electric. It surrounded him and swallowed him up.

As the caps and colours shrank from view, he could see that his horse was already slipping off the pace. What did it matter? Justin looked on as the first few disgruntled faces turned and headed back in the direction of the bookies.

Turning into the far straight, there was now half a length between the leader and the rest of the pack. The horse matching the name on Justin's ticket had fallen even further behind. As they turned the bend into the home straight, the fate of Justin's horse was already sealed. He took another quick nip from his hipflask. It's just a game, he thought. By the time it crossed the line he had already torn up his ticket and was reaching into his pocket for his pencil and the newspaper.

'No luck?' said a man standing next to him, as he too screwed his ticket up and let it drop to the ground.

'Some way behind,' replied Justin, shaking his head as he went back to studying the newspaper.

'John Parker,' said the man, holding out his hand. There was something about the name that was not quite right.

'Richard Cameron,' said Justin, as he shook his hand.

'Shame about the weather,' said Mr Parker, 'I thought it was supposed to be sunny. It keeps threatening to lighten up though. Are you staying the whole day?'

'I don't know,' said Justin. He looked out towards the course and found himself scanning the crowd for any sign of a camera.

'Any tips for the hurdles?' said Parker with a friendly smile. 'You look like you know your stuff.'

'I'm willing to do a trade,' said Justin.

'That for the two-thirty?'

'Done.'

Justin would have said anything just to get rid of the man. Holding his newspaper out at arms-length to make sure there was space between them, Justin pointed to the name of the horse he had ringed. Parker took a step closer towards him.

'How sure are you?' said Parker.

'It's reliable,' said Justin shortly, stepping away. 'What about the two-thirty?'

'I'll have to get back to you on that,' replied Parker, tapping his right nostril with his index finger as he turned away. 'Good day,' he said, and moved off into the crowd.

I've just been had, thought Justin with a smile. Notoriously tight were some of these gamblers. Normally that kind of hustle would have made him livid – the sheer audacity – but now he just felt relieved. He reached into his pocket, took another large gulp of whisky from the flask and calmed down.

I'm becoming paranoid, he thought to himself as he approached the bookies to place his next bet. From now on, for the rest of the day, I'll simply ignore anyone who attempts to speak to me.

He placed two more bets on a couple more races and by the end had almost managed to come out even. But the money was immaterial. He had gotten rid of some time. Checking his watch and seeing that it was approaching quarter-to-two, he decided to catch last orders at the pub on the corner.

He ordered a pint of ale and a large scotch then sat down on a barstool. It was surprising to see so few people in the bar, but he was not complaining. When the door of the pub opened and closed somewhere behind him, he did not look up, but kept his eyes fixed on the drinks in front of him. Even when he heard a familiar voice, he tried his best to ignore it. Then a hand dropped heavily onto his shoulder.

'A'ternoon Inspector.'

Justin looked up to see the face of George Evans, an inspector in the vice squad over at Vine Street Station. It was not a welcome sight.

'Afternoon George,' he replied, trying to keep the irritation out of his voice.

'You want another one?' said Evans, pointing to the half empty pint glass in front of him.

'Yeah, I'll have the same,' he replied. The barman nodded. 'What are you doing round here,' said Justin, 'you live here?'

'No, the old man lives down the road, so I pop-in sometimes,' he replied.

There was a rivalry between the two teams of officers, same as there was just about everywhere in the force. To Justin it was just more pettiness and it grated, but he put up with it because the information they could inadvertently provide him with was of a particularly personal relevance.

Nowhere was the rivalry more obvious than when they met for the annual charity boxing event, at which Justin was relied upon to uphold the honour of the team at Scotland Yard. The respect he had gained from it meant that he could usually glean from them whatever he needed to know.

'You look a bit worse for wear,' said Evans, glancing at the empty whisky tumbler in front of Justin. 'You been at the races?'

'Yes, I'm afraid so,' he replied, sipping his pint.

'Lost?'

'About even.'

'Don't mind lining the Sabinis' pockets then?' he said with a smile.

'I was rather hoping they'd be lining mine,' said Justin.

'You wouldn't be the first on the force, either way,' replied George.

Justin looked at the beer in his glass and wondered how quickly he could get it down without seeming rude.

'You been busy?' he eventually said.

'Same as always,' said Evans. 'Same shortage. We need more officers over at ours, and the ones we've got are talking about striking again.'

'It's the same everywhere.'

'Our governor says yours is off soon, back to Ireland.'

'He told you that?'

'That's what he reckons. You heard anything?'

'Nothing much. But there's always talk,' said Justin, taking another large gulp of beer.

'I wouldn't fancy it,' said Evans.

'His job?'

'No, Ireland.'

'He's still on the reserves. It doesn't sound like he has much choice in the matter,' said Justin.

'So, you *have* heard then?' Justin shook his head in reply.

'Are you off all weekend?' said Justin, just to change the subject.

'Yeah, then back on for the next three,' said Evans.

Justin took another large gulp just as the barman called last orders.

'I'll have to get you one next time,' he said, 'I've a lady waiting.'

'Cor…she'll change her mind when she sees you in that state!' said Evans. 'Are you sure?'

'I'll have a walk and sober up a bit first,' said Justin.

'You do that, Inspector,' said Evans, laughing now. 'Don't drive there for gould-sake, you might run yourself over!'

Justin nodded goodbye.

Bloody typical, he thought, as he waited at the bus stop. Justin had planned on having another large scotch in the pub to calm himself down before the journey home. His hipflask was empty, and he was faced with a choice: go home and wait until evening opening or find some other way of killing the rest of the afternoon. The bus pulled up and he got on then went upstairs and smoked a cigarette.

The rocking of the bus brought back his nausea and helped him make his decision. He alighted near Regent's Park. His watch said a quarter-past three. Already deep in the ditch, he knew that he either needed to find more alcohol or face-out the discomfort. He could always chance some more uppers. With the pubs now closed, he decided that it would be best to go for a walk.

The people in the street seemed to be moving at an entirely different pace. He could sense his mood darkening. The shabbiness that Inspector Evans had so easily detected in his semi-drunken state, and the messiness of his mind and body, only added to his rising self-consciousness. Justin knew himself well enough to know that he should head for somewhere safe – the park perhaps – where he could remain hidden.

He kept his eyes down and walked on, but the people kept coming. Men going about their business, couples, lone women going only God knows where. Every variety of civilian passed him by. They were only too happy to exclude him; these people he could easily find fault with, pull rank on, take into custody if and whenever he felt the need. It would not be too difficult to invent some story or to be the sole witness of some minor misdemeanour which would allow him to exert his power. He could show them how it feels.

He passed the barred cellar windows of an underground club: one that was underground in more than just the literal sense. The name of the place escaped him now. One evening he had been down there shortly before the plod had arrived. It had been yet another near miss. That was one night for which he had not heard of any plans, nor picked anything up from the blokes in vice. They had been unusually tight-lipped that week, and that alone should have raised his suspicions.

That night he had been lucky enough to leave the club just half an hour or so before the police had arrived. A chance encounter had saved him from a far less fortunate one and he had unwittingly avoided the raid.

Some big names had been taken in that night; powerful ones, though most of their cases would soon be dropped. Some of the other clients were fully aware of Justin's occupation and he had worried that they may have said something, having thought his behaviour suspicious. But not one of them had mentioned his being there. It was something for which he remained grateful.

He passed through the wrought iron gates of the park and continued along the path, reminded of all the times he had passed them heading out in the motorcar on some mindless, unavoidable errand. He had dreamt about having the free time to do what he wanted, but whenever he actually had it, reality never quite measured up. He had overlooked the boredom and quiet loneliness that plagued his leisure time, while fantasising about it, trapped in the confines of the working week.

He set-off along the meandering pathway towards the lake, lighting a cigarette and drawing the smoke deep into his lungs. The clouds had come over now, robbing the park of the verdant hues of summer, its luminosity and the crystal-line glints the sun lent to the water.

Looking ahead, it suddenly struck him that the path he was on would take him past the public toilets. If photographs were being taken, then this was not the place to be. He smiled at the ridiculousness of the situation. As the white hut with its green tiled roof came into view, it occurred to him that he actually did need to use the toilet. Yet again, it was typical. Knowing that he was now not far from Bayswater, he decided to hold on for the safety of home.

A lone man exited the building, his back to Justin, a bowler hat on his head, and a cane swinging in his left hand. Justin couldn't help but wonder.

This is how normal people must feel, he thought, as they try to distinguish between an incorrigible pervert and a gentleman every time they come by a public convenience.

Just one look was usually enough to tell him who was 'in' and who was not. It was an instinct he had developed over time, forged in situations where the prospect of getting caught-out was particularly daunting.

This one's a doctor, Justin decided, turning it into a game as he so often did. He followed the man along the tarmac. His senses had been refined over the years to equip him with an unerring intuition. The man turned onto the grass and made his way over to what looked likely to be his wife and child.

Right again, thought Justin, smiling to himself. You can always spot a good doctor.

The psychiatrist he had consulted about his condition, he now remembered, had also had a bowler hat, hanging up on a hook by the door. The series of consultations had come after he had heard about the possibility of using hypnotism to cure his particular kind of madness.

Though it had been nothing extraordinary in the boarding school dormitory – not even considered abnormal behaviour – as he had grown older, the attitude of the other boys had changed. What had once simply been light-hearted play now seemed to have been re-classified as something to be regarded with the greatest contempt.

Most of the other boys had adapted to the presence of women in their lives with a deep and vibrant enthusiasm. He had wondered how long it might be before he too would experience the same tingling rush when in close proximity to the opposite sex. Even now, a part of him still waited.

The psychiatrist's treatment had failed and, had it not been for the intervention of the war, he may have looked for another doctor. But on returning to England, he had found that society had shifted again, as though the evident fragility of life had caused it to revaluate what was really important. Men of his type, so long as they had served their country, were now considered at least a little less bestial. Or that was how it had seemed. And besides, the secret he kept weighed less on him now. What troubled him these days was far more distressing.

His new doctor had prescribed him barbiturates to stop the
dreams that affected him night after night. He was told to
smoke more tobacco. For his other problem – the minor one
as it had now become – he could always escape to France, or
Italy perhaps; places that were far more forgiving. By
remaining in England, and in the police force, in particular,
he had created for himself the worst of all possible
situations. At times, he almost envied the men for whom his
own thoughtless actions had resulted in their deaths.

He stopped at the lake and looked out. Last night at the
office, Cameron had asked him whether or not he actually
liked people. Christ, was it really that obvious? In reply, he
had said that he liked those who were vulnerable; he had said
it without even thinking. He liked to try and help people, is
what he had really meant to say.

What I would give to be surrounded by people I could
trust, he now thought.

Two drakes and a hen made circular patterns on the water,
as both of the males tried to guard her from the attentions of
the other.

Across the lake, Justin spotted a man standing alone in the
bandstand, looking out across the park, taking pictures with
his camera. He started to feel uncomfortable.

Back at home he could drink some water before pro-
gressing to more whisky if, of course, he could get hold of it.
It would help to kill the time safely while he smartened up in
preparation for the evening.

Henry's parties had a tendency to plummet from the height
of sophistication to the depths of vulgarity, as they pro-
gressed towards the sybaritic wee hours. Much depended on
the class of company he had chosen, which itself depended
on the degree to which he had indulged his penchant for
concocting volatile social mixtures.

Justin knew well enough to dress up for the occasion and to
splash on some aftershave to help cover up the smell of
whisky. Once before, he had turned up in his double-

breasted suit half-drunk, and had counted himself lucky not to have been escorted from the premises. It was the first impressions that counted with Henry, and certainly not the last as, by the time he left the next morning, he found himself facing the cool autumn breeze without his tie, with his shirt flecked grey with cigarette ash, and with a half empty bottle of Jonnie Walker in his left hand.

Having almost been picked up by the police on that occasion, it was not a mistake he wished to make twice, and so he dusted off his dinner jacket and promised himself that he would leave before things got too out of hand.

Whether it be high or low, Justin never felt daunted by the type of company Henry kept. On the one hand, Justin's family's minor aristocratic connections had taught him how to conduct himself in civilised company, while on the other, his job had taught him how to deal with the rest. And as for the other guests, it was sometimes evident that there was very little that differed between them: it always amused him to see how an excess of drink could be such a social leveller.

Among many of Henry's friends, however, Justin's choice of profession was considered somewhat of a weakness; a social faux pas, in fact. It sometimes seemed to him that his position commanded the respect of no-body at all. For this reason, or at least in part, it had become a habit of his to consume large amounts of his favourite spirit shortly before leaving the flat. This evening was no different. Pacing his drinking was never a problem for Justin; it was the pace he selected that invariably let him down.

Justin paid the cab as it pulled up in Bloomsbury, then climbed out and knocked on the familiar red door. From inside, he could at first hear only a woman's laughter. Then came the rumble of a seasoned baritone, footsteps coming along the hallway, and the click of the latch.

'Good evening, sir.'

'Good evening, Peter.' Bowing slightly, Peter let him into the hallway.

Despite their familiarity, Peter always put on an impeccable show of formality. No outsider would have ever suspected a thing.

'I'm not too late, I hope,' said Justin.

'Not at all, sir. The guests are still on champagne and cocktails,' he said, leading him down the hall. 'May I bring you something?'

'Just the usual champagne,' said Justin. 'Make it a double.'

'Certainly, sir.'

Peter opened the door to the drawing room which now seemed tiny, given the number of bodies that were crammed into it. Above the din of the conversations and the sound of Pulcinella playing lightly in the background, Justin could make out the gruff proclamations of the host in his more formal mode.

Justin discreetly scanned the room for someone he recognized, but in failing to do so, he took out a cigarette and lit it, just to keep himself occupied.

A servant came into the room, carrying a tray of hors d'oeuvres, and Justin slipped in behind him as he negotiated his way across the room. Justin felt a tap on his shoulder.

'So glad you could make it, dear man,' said Lord Henry. It seemed odd to be faced with his public persona. 'I have here an acquaintance I would like you to meet.'

Peter reappeared next to Justin carrying a silver tray and his whisky and soda.

'Thank you,' he said, and followed Henry across the room.

'Justin, this is Lionel Balfour, MP for Richmond and very soon to be Foreign Secretary unless I am very much mistaken.'

'I sincerely hope you are not,' replied Lionel.

'Indeed. And this here is Mr Justin Lamoureaux — a *very* good friend of mine indeed and one of the most unimpeachable characters you are ever likely to meet,' said Henry.

'Very pleased to meet you,' said Lionel, offering his hand. 'That's quite an introduction.'

'I'm afraid our mutual friend here flatters me,' said Justin.

'Honestly, Lionel,' said Henry, 'his military honours don't do him justice.' He turned to Justin. 'Mr Balfour and I had been discussing the problems in the Ruhr before I so rudely abandoned him, but I'm sure we won't bore you with that,' he said with a patronising look. Despite the impeccable show he put on there was always something of the real Henry lurking within the ex-major general. 'Anyway, I must leave you two for a short while. You must get to know each other. Please excuse me,' he added, waving to a new arrival in the room as he moved away.

'So, you're confident about the Secretary position then?' said Justin.

'As one can be at present,' said Balfour. He leaned closer. 'To be honest, I think the general public is getting fed-up with such total incompetence.'

'Is that anything new?' said Justin.

'I wish I could say it was. It's the fallout from the European problem of course; it's not an easy situation. But it is to be expected when the French and the Germans are involved, I'm afraid. The whole continent's a bloody mess. I take it you're with us?'

'I prefer to stay out of it if I can,' said Justin.

'A wise choice,' smiled Lionel. 'So, we shouldn't expect your vote?'

'Well…I was really more of a Liberal – before the split, that is.'

'Oh, I see. And which side do you come down on?'

'Well, I can't stand Asquith.'

Balfour smiled.

'No, and you're not the only one. I suppose that decides it then.' Balfour took a sip of his champagne. 'And what exactly is it that you do, if you don't mind me asking?'

'I'm a detective inspector,' he replied.

'Oh,' said Balfour, with an interested, if slightly confused look on his face. His eyes shimmered as he made calculations in his head. 'I had you down as…well…something a little different,' he said, sipping his drink. Justin smiled.

'Yes, well. I suppose life presents each and every one of us with a set of challenges that is somewhat unique.'

'Quite.'

Just then one of the servants came into the room.

'Ladies and Gentlemen, if you would like to come through. Dinner is about to be served.'

Justin felt somewhat surprised and flattered, as they sat down at the table, to find himself sitting within shouting distance of Lord Henry. To the left of him sat a rather overweight, middle-aged gentleman whom Justin thought he should recognise, while to his right was a leading actress in one of the local theatre's most recent hit shows. Justin smiled at her as she took her seat.

'Justin Lamoureaux,' he said as they shook hands.

'Beryl Thorndon,' they both said in unison. She smiled.

'I recognised you from the posters,' said Justin.

'Yes, I'm afraid they're everywhere,' she replied.

Her light-brown, voluminous hair was cut short at the chin and curved in over the large flat plains of her cheeks. There was a stillness in her eyes which seemed to lend her an air of patience and compassion, and which immediately put Justin at ease.

'Have you seen the show?' she said, loosening her shawl at the shoulders.

'I'd be surprised if I could get tickets at the moment,' he said, a little embarrassed to have to admit that he had not.

'That's really very flattering,' she replied, 'but I always have tickets for friends of Henry's. You shall be my guest.'

'Thank you, I would like that,' he replied.

'This is my husband, Leonard,' she said, patting the arm of the man at her side.

'How do you do,' he said as he and Justin shook hands.

'He is currently also my director,' she added.

'Sounds complicated,' smiled Justin.

'Oh, I wouldn't wish for any other,' she said. 'And what is it that you do, if you don't mind me asking?'

'Oh, I'm a detective inspector,' said Justin a little shyly.

'With the Metropolitan Police?'

'Yes, I'm afraid so.'

'Well then, I shall have to watch my p's and q's this evening,' she said smiling.

'Not for a second.'

The champagne was served, fostering a natural break in the conversation. To the left of Justin, a heated conversation had already begun between the man next to him and a neighbour further along. He turned to Justin.

'What do you think?' he said, tacitly demanding his support. 'Shouldn't there be a guaranteed minimum five-year term for whoever is the victor in this coming election? Three elections in two years? It's gone backwards and forwards like a bloody tennis ball!'

Without waiting to hear Justin's reply, he returned to his conversation.

The soup was served. Justin took alternate sips from his whisky glass and from the fresh glass of champagne that had been placed in front of him. As the conversations began to settle, the man to his left turned to him again, sighing as though the previous conversation had worn his patience almost to the point of capitulation.

'And what is it that you do, may I ask?'

Justin looked down at the man's place card and read the name, Sir Reginald Burfield. Oh God, he thought to himself, now recognising the frequently bellicose MP. Looking up, he saw Henry's mischievous smile directed towards him from across the table.

'I'm a police officer,' replied Justin.

'A policeman? Good God, I thought you were some kind of actor.'

Beryl, sitting to the right of him, looked up.

'Well, I expect you missed out on all the action then,' continued Burfield.

'No, I was in France.' replied Justin flatly, already becoming annoyed.

'Oh, well that's all right then,' replied Burfield, taken aback. 'Managed to send some Krauts back in a box, I hope. Very admirable. I thought your lot were exempt from service.'

'Not all of us. And not if you chose to go in. I was in for all of it.'

'Good man. Must have put a hole in your career plans though. You must be very well connected to be an inspector at your age, in spite of it.'

Ignoring him, Justin finished his whisky and looked out across the table in search of any conversation that might save him. To his right, Beryl was talking to one of the young wives sitting across from her.

'Yes, but it's not as glamourous as all that,' he heard her say.

'Not at all,' added her husband.

'But we did open first in New York. George wanted to test it away from home before opening at The New.'

'Oh, I see,' replied the young woman, looking a little starstruck.

There seemed little Justin could add to the conversations in the room. But at least he had successfully shaken off Burfield, who was already busy looking for trouble elsewhere.

'Civilian deaths will never go down well with the British public, be they German or otherwise,' came a voice from somewhere in the room.

Justin drained his whisky tumbler. Sitting across the table from him was a rather irritable looking, corpulent, middle-aged gentleman and his wife. He also had a face Justin thought he should recognise, but as he did not, he looked to the man's wife for clues.

The blue of her eyes hinted at her having once possessed some rather striking good looks, and the two of them had an air about them that suggested they expected a certain standard of service. Momentarily free of conversation, the lady adjusted the ermine stole that she kept draped around her shoulders, arranging it to sit just so over the delicate black lace of her dress.

I've seen rats that size, thought Justin with a smile.

Above them, the waving glint of the chandeliers shone onto the gilt mirror frame, swayed by the breath and movement of the guests below.

'…I can understand Poincaré's position though; he never wanted troops in there in the first place.'

Having slipped himself another upper while waiting for his cab to arrive, Justin had emerged from his earlier consumption in a far better mood than he otherwise might have. As he sat on his quiet island now, looking out to sea, he felt for a moment almost perfectly content.

The woman sitting across from him had a rather timid pose, almost apologetic, as she took neat little nips of soup from her spoon whenever the conversation would allow it. In fact, the wives' words were mostly inaudible, adding only a faint background treble to the bass tones as they battled it out for centre stage.

'…it's Baldwin's hubris which brought all of this about in the first place anyway…'

Hubris…yes that's the word, Justin thought to himself.

'…Poincaré's bloody lucky if you ask me – he can just stick to the plan and completely save face.'

'…and maintain the *entente*…'

The tablecloth seemed almost luminous with its impossible whiteness. Justin watched the waiter as he continued to pour the champagne with slow swooping movements and a look of intense concentration.

'…sit tight a while and stick to the terms of the Dawes plan…'

'…they can't even eat, let alone anything else…'

'Yes, she's playing Joan of Arc…' came a muffled whisper.

Justin had forgotten to ask what was for dinner. Anything but pork, he now hoped. The screams of one of the young men, as Justin had dragged him a full twenty yards back to the safety of the trench, was something he could do with forgetting about this evening. The wire had been cut, of course, but under heavy fire he was unable to steer him around the sharp twisted barbs which poked themselves deep into the young soldier's chemically stripped skin.

God, he hoped it would be game or roast beef, quail, anything…anything other than roast pork. It was the colour and consistency that did it.

'…I'd have them all shot…' came another voice from across the table.

The waiter came over and topped up Justin's champagne flute.

'Would you mind getting me a large scotch?' said Justin, turning to him. The waiter hesitated.

'Spirits will be served after supper, sir,' he replied apologetically. 'But I could bring you a cocktail, if you wish?'

'A cocktail?' said Justin, unimpressed. 'Whisky and soda's a cocktail. Bring me an extremely large one – and go easy on the soda.'

'Certainly, sir,' said the waiter with a hint of displeasure.

The corpulent gentleman sitting across from Justin clicked his fingers to summon one of the waiters as Justin looked on.

How many of these *gentlefolk* have stood on the slippery duckboards with sodden, rotting feet? thought Justin. How many have smelt chloride of lime as it drifts across the shell-pitted ground?

The man gave the waiter an order, then, as he moved away, turned to his wife and shook his head impatiently. The woman seemed to gather herself up as she sat back in her chair and looked around the table, aggrieved.

Which of these people had felt the strange mixture of fear and temerarious impatience in the minutes leading up to a daylight attack?

The waiter placed Justin's drink down in front of him.

'Thank you,' said Justin, with a feeling of remorse for the way he had previously spoken to him. 'I appreciate it.'

'My pleasure, sir,' replied the waiter with a look that told him all was forgiven. Justin's neighbour turned to him again.

'So, I suppose you were in support of the strike, were you?' he said.

'Pardon?'

'The police strikes. You were all for them, I suppose,' said Sir Burfield.

'I wasn't involved at the time. But I would have been in support of them, yes.'

Beryl had by now finished her conversation and was listening in from the other side.

'Too right,' she added. 'And there'll be more of them where they came from.'

'I presume the two of you have met,' said Justin, sitting back in his chair so that they could view and assess each other.

'Once or twice,' said Beryl. 'We've had our little spats haven't we, Sir Reginald?'

'So I presume you condone dereliction of duty, Mrs Thorndon,' replied Sir Burfield, adding, 'and putting the general public at risk?'

'And I presume you condone the families of public servants being raised on poverty wages, Sir Burfield,' she said in reply.

'Public duty is too important for strike action,' he said. 'Lives would be at stake.'

'Yes, quite. And what came first; the strikes or wages that were below that of an unskilled labourer? How's the Champagne, by the way?' she said.

Sir Burfield swallowed a mouthful and took the glass away from his lips.

'Exquisite, thank-you, Mrs Thorndon. And I expect to face the guillotine for it later on this evening.'

'Vive la France,' she muttered audibly, adjusting her shawl.

Justin looked up and saw Lord Henry smirking at him from across the table. Justin grimaced back at him. Lord Henry got up from his seat.

Over the years, Henry had made it a custom to do the rounds at the table, speaking to each of his guests in turn. He would usually start with whoever was nearest to him and then move round in whichever direction he had chosen, but this time he headed straight over to where Justin was sitting.

'And how are we doing over here?' said Henry, leaning in between Justin and Sir Burfield. 'I hope you two have made each other's acquaintance.'

'Yes, a very good chap,' said Sir Burfield, nodding towards Justin.

'Oh, he's more than that,' replied Henry, 'his gallantry at the Somme has seen him decorated, but I shouldn't think he told you that, as of course a true gentleman wouldn't.'

'It's lucky I didn't then,' said Justin.

'Good man,' said Sir Burfield, raising his glass and taking a sip, though he seemed disinterested.

'Anyway, I must move on. The second course will be arriving before I make it round,' said Henry, turning away. 'Berrryyylll,' he almost sang, moving off to the other side of Justin.

Sir Burfield returned to his conversation with the gentleman to the other side of him and made no further attempt to engage Justin in conversation.

As Lord Henry moved away, both Beryl and her husband leaned in towards Justin.

'I hope you don't mind, but I couldn't help overhearing your conversation. Henry said you were decorated after the Somme,' she said.

'Yes, that's correct. I was given the M.C.'

'Oh, nobody's simply given it,' she said. 'My husband was also decorated. He was invalided at Ypres.'

'Yes, I decided to get out early,' added Leonard rather modestly. Justin smiled.

'I'll drink to that,' he said, raising his glass.

After dinner the guests retreated into the drawing room. Justin stuck to whisky while the brandy and cigars were passed around. From across the room, Justin made eye contact with Lionel Balfour, which was enough to make him quickly catch hold of Beryl and engage her in conversation, just as she and her husband were leaving.

'Ah, you must meet Mr Lamoureaux,' she said to the man with whom she was just ending her conversation. 'This is Lord Aston,' she said, turning to Justin. 'We have something of a war hero here in Mr Lamoureaux, I believe,' she added, as the two men shook hands. 'He has, of course, suffered abominably at the hands of Sir Burfield throughout the entire dinner.'

'Oh, I shouldn't worry about him,' said Lord Aston to Justin. 'He's always been the same: completely and utterly mad!'

'Well, that's something of a relief,' said Beryl. 'Anyway, I'm afraid we must be off.' She turned to Justin. 'Mr Lamoureaux, I shall be in touch with Henry about getting you those tickets. I hope very much you'll be able to come.'

'That would be wonderful. I would love to,' he said. Then Beryl and her husband left, much to Justin's disappointment, leaving him alone with Lord Aston.

'So, a war hero,' said Lord Aston.

'Well…not really,' said Justin.

'And what is your occupation nowadays?'

'I'm a detective inspector,' he replied. Lord Aston's head rocked backwards as though he had just taken a jab to the chin.

'A police officer? What in the world would make an educated man want to do a thing like that?'

'Well–' he began, but before he could continue, Lord Aston's attention had been siphoned off by someone more important.

Justin stepped back in order to separate himself from a group that was beginning to form around Lord Aston. Standing alone again, he looked at the room and felt some relief in being spared the boring conversations. The only source of colour amongst them was the material of some of the women's dresses. Looking at the crowd now, in their blacks and dark greys, he could see how reined-in they all were; how far their behaviour was from their true nature. They were obviously playing the long game. His resentment of them had steadily increased over the years, and his tendency to class men as those who had fought in the war and those who had not, only served to pique his hatred of them.

This was what it had all been for; all the murder and savagery, he thought. There seemed almost nothing about them that was not calculated, their having perfected the art of jostling for social position. Every one of them was telling a lie. It all seemed so predictable.

So, this is the sum of human existence, he thought to himself. It seemed that Lord Henry alone still had the ability to surprise him.

Out in the hallway, Henry was busy whispering something to one of his servants when Justin came in. He turned around.

'Ah, Justin, my good man,' came the voice of the old soldier. 'How the devil are you? Enjoying the evening?'

'I'm afraid I must be off, Henry. It's been a long day and I've had more than my fill,' he said raising his empty tumbler.

'Yes, you are looking a little worse for wear,' he said, grabbing Justin's arm. 'Still, that's nothing a good deal of water and some more coffee won't sort out.' Justin moved towards him and lowered his voice.

'The truth is, I really can't stand these dreadful people much longer, Henry.'

'Beryl? But she's a dear!'

'Yes, I know she is. I don't mean Beryl. Anyway, she left a short while ago and I–'

'Oh, come now,' said Henry, his voice softening into the more familiar tone, 'there are several guests I think you should meet,' he said, with a knowing glint in his eye.

'No, Henry. Really, I must go,' he insisted. Henry looked around to make sure that the two of them were alone.

'Listen, my dear,' he purred, 'I must apologise for putting you next to that dreadful Burfield…but you must admit it was rather amusing.'

'Yes, well, it was probably a wise move to put a police officer between him and Beryl.'

'Exactly. Your services were needed,' he said flatteringly. 'Speaking of which–' he broke off and let go of Justin's arm just as someone came out of the drawing room. Then, seeing that it was only one of his servants, Henry replaced his hand and continued, '…speaking of which, you can't leave yet, I have a jazz quartet starting a little later and I am expecting some of my more *special* acquaintances to stay on.'

'That's not really my kind of thing, Henry, you know that. But thanks anyway. I really must be leaving.'

'I hope you are referring to the music!' said Henry, feigning having taken offence.

'Really, Henry, have a good night,' said Justin turning towards the door.

'Suit yourself,' came the gruff voice of the old soldier as he turned and re-entered the drawing room.

Justin stepped out into the fresh air and, as he lit another cigarette, all of the day's alcohol seemed to hit him in one go. He looked along the road for a cab then decided that it would be a better idea to walk off some of the booze. Looking towards the lights, he headed off towards Soho.

Many of the first-floor windows were lit red along the street; some with their curtains closed, others left open, some with the women inside brazenly leaning out.

A woman appeared at one of the windows as Justin passed by. Underneath it, a man came out of a doorway, pulling the door shut behind him as he exited the building. Hiding his face behind his collar, he hurried off along the street.

There were women standing about on the pavement as well, more discreet than the ones upstairs, yet still remarkably obvious.

'Evenin' darlin',' said one of them as Justin passed.

Men of his kind had to stay hidden; there could be no open secrets like this, he thought. Even behind closed doors, you had to be careful. Sometimes especially when the doors were closed.

He came off of Poland Street, swaying a little as he walked, then took a couple more turns and stopped outside the gentleman's tailor shop in Berwick Street. The lights were off.

The red windows dotted along the street showed which properties were in use. Vardy's girls could be in any one of them right this minute, he thought. They could be just yards away from where he was standing, and he would never even know it. There was little he could do.

For a moment the street was quiet. Justin headed towards Oxford Street to get a cab home. He took a pill out of his pocket, put it into his mouth and crushed it between his teeth. The bitter, chemical taste of it struck him. He tried to move it to the back of his mouth with his tongue, which only seemed to spread it further. His mouth was filled with it.

Nine

'Has anyone checked on Stephen?' said Samuel, as he, Sandra and Betty dried the breakfast utensils in the kitchen.

'You're offering, I suppose?' said Sandra, with a sly wink. Samuel closed his eyes in disapproval.

'I'll go if nobody else has,' he said.

'Poor lad, God help him,' said Betty, shaking her head. 'It's the ones left behind who suffer.' Samuel looked at her blankly.

'Yes, well…I shall go and check on him anyhow,' he said.

Sandra winked again at him as he passed, and again he ignored her.

He turned onto the hallway at the top of the grand double staircase then looked up and stopped mid-step. Lady Keating was standing at the end of the hall with her back to him and was knocking gently on the door to Stephen's room. Carefully, Samuel crept back around the corner to where he could listen in, intrigued and relieved that Lady Keating had not seen him.

Stephen had tried his best to escape into sleep the previous night, but he had found it impossible. Several times he had almost dropped off and experienced a falling sensation that had instantly shaken him awake. With his thoughts subsequently filled with the abstract horrors of semi-consciousness, he had eventually stopped trying.

The ashtray next to his bed was now full of butts, and his sheets ash-smeared from the cigarettes he had been chain smoking in order to stay awake. The packet lay empty on the floor.

He ignored the knocking at first, hoping that the visitor would go away. The stream of sunlight coming in through the crack in the curtains had gradually made its way across the room to his bedside table and was now shining onto the glass tumbler, refracting through it and highlighting its brittleness. Having been lying in the same position for what seemed an interminable amount of time, he found himself staring at the glass and the water jug sitting next to it, picturing the jagged edges that would appear the moment he smashed it. The uneven shards merged in his mind with the stream of red that would pour down his neck from his jugular vein, as he drove them deep into the skin and then slowly across it.

The door clicked open and Lady Keating appeared. For the first time in hours, Stephen looked up. Seeing her pale face, and the sensitive expression painted on it, he felt he could not simply lie there ignoring her. With what seemed an incredible effort, he summoned all his strength and forced himself to sit up in bed.

'I'm sorry to bother you, Stephen,' she said, looking around the heavily shaded room. 'Do you mind if I open the curtains?'

'Go ahead, M'Lady,' he heard himself say.

She crossed the room and drew the curtains back gently then turned to face him. His eyes were heavily ringed from lack of sleep and all the nicotine, and his face was unshaven. As he looked up at her, the sunlight shone down through her golden hair giving it a near transparency.

'I just wanted to say how sorry I am,' she said after some moments. 'I can't help but feel guilty about it; she shouldn't have been at our apartment. It must be a terrible shock to you.' Stephen stared at the oak door standing ajar at the far end of the bedroom.

'One of many shocks, I'm afraid,' he replied, looking down at the silvery ash flakes on the bedsheets. 'Anyway, it wasn't your fault,' he added quietly.

'If there's anything I can do — anything I can arrange for you,' she said. 'Even just for someone to talk to.' Her eyes moved towards the door. 'I can't stay long…'

'Of course not,' he shrugged. They were both well aware of Jeffrey's pathological jealousy.

'I appreciate your concern,' he said. Every word seemed to drain more of his energy.

'You don't have to return to work tomorrow if you aren't up to it,' she said. 'I'll talk to Jeffrey.'

'No…tomorrow's fine. I can't stay here forever,' he said stroking the bedsheet and leaving black smudges across it.

'Well, it's up to you,' she said.

Feeling that there was nothing more she could say, she made her way towards the door.

'Thank you again,' said Stephen. She smiled briefly and nodded in reply as she left.

Lady Keating walked along the hallway, smoothing her skirt, then turned the corner and continued onward. Samuel watched her from around the opposite corner, holding his breath and hoping she would not turn around and see him. His concentration was such that he did not notice Sandra appear at his side, holding a basket of bed linen, having come up the stairs from behind. She startled him. Fearing that Lady Keating might turn around and see him, Samuel leapt around the corner, scowling at Sandra as he went and knocked on the door to Stephen's bedroom. Sandra let out a giggle.

Lady Keating turned around.

'Would you mind changing the sheets and airing out Stephen's room if he comes out at all?' she called to Sandra from along the hallway.

'Of course, M'Lady,' she replied. 'I was just on my way to your room to do the same.'

'Good. Thank you, Sandra,' she said. 'Oh, but don't disturb Stephen if he stays in there, will you?'

'Of course not, M'Lady.'

Lady Keating thanked her again and carried on down the hall, while Sandra, behind her, stuck out her tongue with as much spite as she could muster. Opening the door to the master bedroom, Sandra went in and threw the bedsheets onto a chair next to the bed.

There was another knock at the door. Stephen sat up straight and brushed the hair back from his face.

'Come in,' he said, half-hoping to see the return of the beautiful blonde apparition. Samuel peered round the edge of the door.

'Oh. Come in,' said Stephen. Samuel closed the door behind him, pulled up a chair and sat down next to the bed.

'How are you feeling?' he said gently. Stephen looked at him, searching for the right words.

'Excellent,' he replied flatly.

Samuel patted the bedsheets, ignoring the sarcasm, then got up and went over to the wardrobe and opened the doors.

'Now, I think it's about time you got dressed,' he said pointing at Stephen, '…and that you had something to eat.'

'I don't think so,' he replied, dropping his head back against the head-rest.

'Well, I do. You can't stay in here all day feeling sorry for yourself.' He pulled out a shirt and jacket on the same hanger, along with a pair of neatly pressed trousers. 'Come on, you're getting up.'

Despite himself, the feeling of warmth and of being looked-after made Stephen listen to Samuel. No-one else had made such an effort to look after him, just when he really needed it.

'Thank you,' said Stephen, as Samuel placed the clothes over the back of a chair, '…for all you've done for me.'

'Not at all. Now, up you get, and I'll run you a bath,' he said, leaving the room.

Samuel waited while Stephen soaked himself in the water. He had taken the key to the bathroom and was holding it in his hand so that Stephen could not lock the door and try to drown himself. Afterwards, he took Stephen downstairs to the empty kitchen and gave him a plate of leftovers from breakfast, which he then forced him to eat. The cook was due back within the hour to begin preparing the Sunday lunch. Not wanting to be dragged into it, he made sure they moved quickly.

Lord Jeffrey sat back in his leather chair in the library, lit a cigar and spread out the Sunday paper across his lap. The headlines once again fulminated over the occupation of the Ruhr and he shook his head as he let his eyes scan over them, before moving on to something more interesting. There was a knock at the door.

'Yes. What is it?' he said. He never liked being disturbed on Sunday mornings. The door swung open and Lady Keating appeared.

'Ah, come in, dear,' he said, closing the paper and patting the chair next to him. Though relations between them had been quick to cool during their five-year marriage, he had always considered it a gentleman's duty to show his wife the utmost respect.

'I shan't keep you long,' she said, closing the door behind her. She remained standing. Jeffrey recognized the look of some kind of heightened emotion on her face, though he could not say which one it might be. Nevertheless, it always surprised him how even the merest hint of her suffering was still enough to make him feel protective of her.

'What is it, my dear?' he said.

'I was just thinking, I'm not sure if I would feel comfortable with Stephen starting back again tomorrow – not if he's not feeling up to it.'

'Oh?'

'It must have been such a terrible shock to him – all that's happened. I would prefer it if things remained calm and quiet for a while. It would put me on edge to have him around, unless I could be sure that he was feeling better.' Jeffrey lent forward and balanced his cigar on the edge of the ashtray.

'I see what you mean,' he said, 'and I do understand how awful it must have been for you. But he must start back some time.'

'Yes, I know. And if he's in a fit state then I am perfectly fine with that. I just don't want any more distressing scenes, that's all.' Jeffrey picked up his cigar.

'I shall have a word with him and if he needs more time, then so be it,' he said gently.

'Thank you, Jeffrey,' she said.

'Not at all. We'll manage somehow.' Lady Keating quietly left the room.

As soon as the door was pulled to, Jeffrey rolled his eyes. Then, as he picked up the paper, he looked up at the clock on the wall and saw that it was coming up to a quarter-to eleven.

'Ah,' he said, as he put the paper back down and crept over to the door to make sure Lady Keating was out of sight. He listened for a moment then stubbed his cigar out in the ashtray and quietly left the room.

The door to the Keatings' bedroom opened silently, just as Sandra was smoothing out the fresh bed sheets with the palm of her hand. Sunlight from the window out in the hallway drifted across the floorboards, catching her attention. Jeffrey closed the door gently behind him then came over to where she was standing and put his arms around her.

'And how's my little model?' he said smiling, as his hands slid down her back to rest on her behind. She yelped as he gave her a squeeze.

'Shh,' said Jeffrey, 'someone might hear.'

'What someone might that be?' she replied. Jeffrey smiled then went back over to the door to make sure it was shut.

'Have you seen Stephen today?' he said.

'No, I 'ain't,' she replied, moving back into his arms. 'Sam has though. He seems pretty eager to take care of him,' she said with a laugh.

'Yes, I bet he is. Listen, can you check on him later and see what kind of mood he's in? She doesn't want him hanging around all maudlin, and come to think of it, neither do I.'

'Of course, M'Lord,' she said in her most seductive manner.

'You can report back to me a little later; say around nine o'clock, down in the wine cellar? It's been far too long.'

'Not down there,' she whined, 'it's too bloody cold. Can't we do it in the summer house?'

Jeffrey thought for a moment. 'All right,' he said. 'But bring some candles – we don't want anyone else catching us. I know the poor girl's no longer with us, but we can't risk being seen from the kitchen, and we don't want to give that bloody cook any cheap thrills either.'

'Chance would be a fine thing,' said Sandra. 'Candles sound good to me.'

As Jeffrey turned to leave, Sandra remembered something.

'Oh, yeah,' she said, 'have there been any more *developments*?' Jeffrey smiled back at her.

'No, not just yet. I shall drop by the photographer's again early this week and pick them up.'

'Should be some money in it soon then, I hope.'

'Very soon, my dear.'

'Though I'd do it anyway,' she added, coming up to him and kissing him. Jeffrey pushed her away gently.

'Remember, nine o' clock,' he said, then turned and left the room.

Sandra glanced down at the bed sheets she had just flatten-ed out then, making sure that the door was closed, she lay back on the bed as if she were the lady of the house.

Samuel and Stephen were out walking in the grounds of the house. The sun's warmth felt almost oppressive as they strolled out across the neatly kept lawn but was lightened somewhat as they stepped under the thin shade of the Birch trees. Neither of them had spoken for some time, the only sounds being those of the birdsong overhead and their woollen trouser legs swishing in the long grass.

'I find it lovely and quiet out here,' said Samuel, as they stopped and looked around, trying to decide which direction

to take next. Stephen remained mute. 'It's good to get out of
the house. I thought it would be good for you to get out of
that dull little room.'

'Yes. You were right,' Stephen replied, taking a deep breath
of the fresh morning air.

They continued onward under the trees, neither of them
having consciously chosen a direction to go in. The
undergrowth continued to thicken beneath their feet until
they eventually crossed the unspoken boundary of what was
acceptable for them to walk through. Silently, they turned
back towards the house and emerged from under the trees,
half-way between the main property and the white pavilion
of the summer house.

The sprinklers, which at this time of day were never on, had
left the grass soft and bouncy under foot. They skirted the
lawn then climbed the stairs up to the veranda and sat down
on the deck of the summer house, facing out across the
garden towards the main house.

'Thank you, Samuel…for everything you've done for me,'
said Stephen once again, his eyes fixed straight ahead of him.
'It hasn't been easy.'

'There's no need to thank me. Anyway, you've already said
that. I'm just glad I can be of help.'

'But why have you done so?'

'I'll do anything to help out an old friend,' he replied.

'We're hardly old friends,' replied Stephen. 'We hardly even
knew each other…'

Samuel waved the comment away.

'Everyone needs a sympathetic ear once in a while,' he said.
'Anyone with a heart in their chest could see that you needed
that.'

'Yes…well. Your ears have heard a little too much from me
over the past few days, I fear.' Samuel turned to him and
smiled.

'It's been a pleasure to get to know you better,' he said. 'We
were like ships that passed in the night at the house in
Brighton.'

'Well, I hope you're good at keeping secrets,' said Stephen.

'Everybody has secrets,' he replied gently. 'I always wondered if our paths might cross again.' He turned back to face the main house.

Through the window, Stephen could see Betty moving about in the kitchen and he suddenly started to feel uncomfortable. In the two weeks that Samuel had been working at the house, Stephen had been too wrapped up in his plans for himself and Catherine to give him a second thought. Then, since the tragedy, his mind had been scrambled by the shock and his suffering. It was only now, in a moment of calm, that he gave him any deeper consideration.

'I think we should return to the house,' said Stephen, getting up, his manner having become instantly more guarded. He descended the staircase.

'Oh…yes…of course,' said Samuel, getting up after him. He followed Stephen down the steps and across the lawn, falling behind at a much slower pace. On reaching the back of the house, Stephen stopped at the door and waited for him to catch up.

'Thank you again, Samuel,' he said, speaking with far greater formality than he ever had done before.

'My pleasure,' said Samuel with a smile, trying not to let his expression betray his true feelings.

'I'm going up to my room now. Please tell the others I'll be down a little later.'

'Of course.'

Samuel watched Stephen pace quickly away from him up the stairs then made his way to the kitchen.

Jeffrey picked up the telephone in the living room and ordered the switchboard operator to connect him to the workmen's number. Having specifically made it clear that they only wished to be contacted at the weekend if it was absolutely necessary, it was with an audible sigh that a man's voice came on at the other end of the line.

'Ar'ternoon.'

'Yes, good afternoon. Is that Mr Peters?' said Jeffrey.

'Yes, that's him. Who am I speaking to?'

'Jeffrey Keating. I need to speak to you about the work you were supposed to be starting at my house in Horsham tomorrow.'

'Ah yes, sir,' he said, sounding a little suspicious. 'What was it, sir?'

'Well, it can't commence tomorrow I'm afraid. It shall have to wait.' There was a pause on the line.

'Oh…and for how long will that be, sir?'

'Indefinitely, I'm afraid. It's just not required at the moment.'

'Well, that's no problem, sir,' he replied, trying to keep the sound of immense irritation out of his voice. 'Obviously the contract is already signed, sir, so a fixed proportion of the overall cost will still have to be paid by the due date.'

'I don't think I can manage that just at the moment, I'm afraid. You see we've suffered a rather tragic event – a murder in fact. I'm afraid there's going to be a delay while we all try to get our heads around what's happened; we're all very heartbroken. I shall have to see about settling that fee at a later date.' There was another pause.

'I'm very sorry to hear that, sir, but a contract is still a contract. If you like we could re-arrange for the work to be carried out at a later date, but obviously we've had to put off other work to do your work, so we have costs that need to be met within the agreed time.'

There was another pause.

'I'm afraid it's just not possible at the moment. I'm sure you can see to giving us a little bit of leeway. It would be the gentlemanly thing to do.'

Yet again there was silence on the line. Mr Peters cleared his throat.

'Have you no heart, man?' said Jeffrey in a sudden burst of temper. 'We have had a tragedy come upon us which has left us all completely bereft. I'm sure we can come to some amicable agreement.'

'This is an amicable agreement, sir, it's set out in the contract. Now I can speak to my brother but–'

'Yes, and you can tell your brother exactly what I am telling you. I do not appreciate your callousness at a time like this and so you can tell your brother that Lord Jeffrey Keating will not be paying a penny.'

Another pause.

'We can involve the courts if we really need to, sir.'

'Yes, and I look forward to it. I look forward to seeing what results from *Lord* Jeffrey Keating versus *Misters Nobody* bloody Peters. Is that what you want? Right then. Good day.'

He jammed the receiver back into its cradle, missing the catch the first time and violently forcing it in on the second attempt.

'Dreadful man,' he muttered as he went over to the drinks cabinet and broke one of his own house rules by pouring himself a pre-lunch sherry.

Samuel opened the door to the kitchen and let himself in with a deep sigh. The smell of roast beef filled the air as Betty took it out of the oven and laid it to rest on the table. Sandra looked up from the glass she was polishing.

'You took your time, didn't you? We need to get table ready. What did you do, slip under the bedsheets with 'im?' she said.

Again, Samuel closed his eyes to the vulgarity.

'Actually, I made sure that he got up and got himself dressed. Then I gave him breakfast and we took a turn in the garden so that he could clear his head. A *turn*, in your parlance,' he added, 'means a *walk*, before you commence with the innuendos.' He turned to Betty. 'Stephen won't be down for lunch, I'm afraid. But maybe later on.'

Betty nodded.

'Already eaten, has he?' laughed Sandra.

Betty's top lip curled up in an expression of disgust.

'Here,' she said, passing a small plate of Yorkshire puddings across to Sandra. '*You* take this up to him,' she said rather pointedly, 'and get yourself back down here sharpish.'

Sandra put down the glass she was holding and looked up at Samuel in a way that told him to take over the polishing of it. Then, she took the plate of food with her out of the kitchen.

There was a knock on the door just as Stephen was on the verge of falling asleep. He had thought about wedging a chair up against the door handle and now he regretted not having done so. Every time he had tried to fall asleep, a man had appeared, holding a knife. But he was too tired to put it off any longer. He had almost made it, just as the second knock at the door brought him back to being fully awake. He sat up in the bed.

'Come in.'

The door opened and Sandra appeared.

'Just brought you some lunch,' she said, walking over to the table and laying the plate down on top of it.

'Thank you,' he said, trying not to sound impolite.

Sandra had a coarseness and stupidity about her that never failed to irritate him. He could read her thoughts, they were so simple, probably before she had even had them herself. She looked down at him; his nearness to sleep had made his eyes puffy and brought a slight oiliness to the surface of his skin.

'Sorry to hear about what happened,' she said quietly.

'Thanks,' he said, without looking up at her.

'I mean, I know what she was, but still–'

'Yes, thank you Sandra,' he snapped. 'Was there anything else you wanted?' She glanced at the table and the untouched water jug.

'I see Samuel's been looking after you. You been out earlier?'

'Yes. And what of it?'

'Nothing. It's just he 'ain't been here long. You can always talk to me if you like. We don't want you turning funny or nothing.' Her hips swayed almost imperceptibly.

'Thanks…I'll keep that in mind,' he said, rubbing his forehead.

There was a moment of silence during which he expected her to leave.

'I wouldn't rush back to work if I were you,' she said. 'You're not missing much.'

'Good. Listen Sandra, I just really want to be left alone at the moment. Thank you for bringing the food, but really I just want to be left in peace.'

'All right. Well, you know where I'll be.'

'Yes…yes I imagine I do,' he said pointedly. She turned and left the room.

Sandra went back down to the kitchen, giggling silently to herself all the way. The kitchen door opened and Samuel appeared in the hallway, carrying a tray of glasses towards the dining room.

'I reckon you might have turned him,' she said, laughing fully now as she entered the kitchen. Samuel tried, but failed this time, to ignore the comment.

Lunch was served at three o'clock. Samuel poured the Claret for Lord Keating and the usual iced water for Lady Keating, while Sandra dished out the roast beef and vegetables along with the trimmings. The two of them bowed and curtsied, and then left the long oak panelled dining room.

A large expanse of leaded glass gave a generous view across the lawn at one end of the room, but in spite of this, the sun's light never quite seemed to enter it. This, along with the dark oak panelling and the green canopy just above the windows outside, made the room seem cavernous.

Jeffrey had purposely parked his blue Bugatti in a spot where he could see it while he ate Sunday lunch. Next to the door at one end of the room was the old grandfather clock, the sound of its ticking filling the air during the numerous gaps in the couple's fragmented conversation.

'He seems to have settled in well,' said Lady Keating, meaning Samuel.

'Yes,' replied Jeffrey, his sigh elongating the word. 'I shall be having a word or two with my friend Henry Cunningham about his choice of recommendations.'

'Why? Whatever do you mean?' she replied. Jeffrey smiled.

'You really mean that you haven't noticed?'

'Noticed what?'

Jeffrey went back to cutting up the meat on his plate.

'Let's just say I think Lord Cunningham was playing a little trick on me, knowing my values the way he does. It's probably in retaliation for my stance on article forty-three. I suppose it's quite amusing really.'

'I don't know what you mean, Jeffrey,' said his wife, in a tone that seemed to lend finality to the conversation. He smiled at her as though at a child.

The ticking of the clock and the tapping of cutlery filled a gap of some minutes.

'Mrs Hawtrey has been in touch again about the Summer Fete,' said Lady Keating.

'Oh yes,' he replied disinterestedly.

'I don't mind helping out, but I hope she doesn't try to drag me along to the church again. I've already told her I'm Catholic.'

'Just tell her a straight no, dear. They'll trap you the first chance they get. I should think they'll be grateful that you're just attending the fete. I don't know how you can stand it personally, with all those blasted children running around.'

'Oh, I don't mind,' she said pleasantly. Jeffrey snorted.

'That doesn't sound like the woman I married,' he said. Lady Keating remained silent.

The clock continued to tick as the sounds from the cutlery came to an end.

'I'm sure I shall find some excuse,' said Lady Keating, emerging from a deep train of thought. Jeffrey picked up the wine bottle and offered it to her.

'Are you sure I can't tempt you?' he said. Lady Keating covered the top of her glass with the palm of her hand.

'Very well,' he said, refilling his own. He took a large gulp. 'Oh, we won't be having the workmen round tomorrow. I've put them off.'

'I didn't know we were having them anyway. What was being done?'

'Oh…just a few minor renovations,' he said dismissively. 'There was some leakage to be fixed in the women's bathroom, and a few other minor things to be done in there. It would have been out of bounds for a few days, but it wouldn't have affected you. I've put them off anyway, so there's no need to worry.'

From somewhere outside the room came the sound of a thud and a plate smashing.

'They must have dropped something in the kitchen, the bloody fools,' said Jeffrey. 'I'll have words with them again before long.'

Lady Keating sipped her water and looked out across the sunny lawn, having stopped listening to him long ago.

'It's such lovely weather,' she said. 'I'm going to finish reading my book out by the summer house, I think.' Jeffrey looked up at her as she rose to leave.

'Well, don't stay out there too long, will you – you don't want to catch cold. You know how the midges get you,' he said.

'Yes, dear,' she replied.

'I don't know how you stomach all that old Russian nonsense anyway,' he added, as she left the room.

Jeffrey looked at his watch, at first a little concerned, but then seeing how early it was, he sat back in his chair, relaxed a little, lit a cigar and leisurely finished his second glass of Claret.

Stephen was still in his room, knowing now that he could not possibly fall back to sleep. He lay on his bed looking up at the ceiling with Sandra's words still ringing in his head. '*I know what she was…*' Silly little bitch. The words angered him. They seemed to cheapen his memory of Catherine, not least because they had come from the lips of someone like her.

It's time I left here, he thought. He got up and started pacing about the room. In his pocket he still had the tickets that would have taken the two of them off to America. He could still use one of them, at least.

It seemed to him that almost everyone in the house was deceitful. Even Samuel, his new 'friend' as he now saw him, was not immune. Why was there always some kind of pay-off required for any show of kindness or human decency?

As he looked at the plate of cold Yorkshire puddings sitting on the table next to the bed, his anger suddenly overtook him. He lifted the plate up in the palm of his hand and threw it with full force against the adjacent wall. The white ceramic smashed outwards and shot back at him in numerous tiny pieces. The brown morsels of pudding and gravy clung momentarily to the deeper brown of the wall's panelling, before dripping down and landing limply on the thick pile of the rug. He knew he had to leave.

He went to the wardrobe and looked for a suitable jacket, pulling out each set of neatly ironed suits and throwing them down onto the bed. I'll go to the pub and drink myself stupid, he thought, overlooking the obstacle posed by the Sunday licencing laws.

Finally, he found the right jacket and swung it on over his shoulders. He looked down at the mess on the floor and on the wall above it and felt half-tempted by his sense of duty to clean it up. He only just stopped himself from doing so.

I'll be leaving soon, he reasoned, as he headed out of the room instead.

Descending the stairs into the hallway, he passed Lady Keating on her way to get her sun hat from the bedroom. She saw that he was in a rush.

'Stephen, I've spoken with Lord Keating,' she said, stopping him. 'You can take as much time as you need.' As she looked at him, she noticed a deep anger in his expression and it made her want to look away. He looked down at the volume she was carrying.

'Thank you. I'll let you get back to your book,' he said, and continued down the stairs.

Lady Keating watched him as he strode towards the front door and slammed it shut behind him, causing the hallway to rattle. Sandra appeared from the kitchen.

'Did someone break a plate?' said Lady Keating, looking down at her.

'No, M'Lady, though I did hear something,' she replied.

'Go up to Stephen's room and check if everything's in order will you? Tidy it up if you need to – before Jeffrey finds out.'

'Yes, M' Lady,' she replied.

It was not until ten past eight that evening that Stephen reappeared. Sandra and Samuel were busy drying the last of the dishes, polishing the cutlery and putting them away in the drawers. Sandra glanced eagerly at her watch, only half listening to Samuel as he recounted the list of impressive persons he had worked for. Then the door opened, and Stephen walked in.

'Been out then?' she said, looking him up and down. His shirt collar was a little loose.

'Yes, Sandra. I've been out,' he replied slowly. There was a calmness in his manner and he seemed completely sober.

'Out on your own?' she added.

'It's got nothing to do with you. But if you must know, I needed to clear my head.'

'Don't worry about that mess in your room,' she said facetiously, 'I've tidied the whole lot up – all the food, cleaned the walls, swept and scrubbed the rug. I've even put your clothes away for you.'

'Thank you, Sandra. Please accept my apologies,' he said, without looking at her. He crossed the room. 'Is there any food left?' he added. Sandra turned to him.

'Not for you there 'ain't! Have you gone mad?'

'Never mind,' he said, with very little concern in his voice.

Samuel put the last of the plates away and closed the cupboard door then turned to Stephen.

'How are you feeling?' he said. Stephen poured himself a glass of milk.

'Much better, thank you,' he said. 'I'll be back down tomorrow.'

'I don't think you're in a fit state for that,' said Sandra.

'Yes, maybe it would be wise to take a little more time,' added Samuel.

'I'll be back tomorrow,' he repeated insistently.

'Suit yourself,' shrugged Sandra. She looked at her watch again. 'Have we got any candles?'

'Try the cupboard under the stairs. We should have boxes of them,' said Stephen. Sandra picked up a box of matches and walked out of the kitchen. Stephen turned to follow her.

'I'm glad you're feeling better,' said Samuel, as Stephen opened the door. But he did not reply.

Ten

'Good weekend?' said Justin. He took a last puff on his cigarette and stubbed it out in the ashtray.

'He hasn't said a word,' replied DI Lisson, 'not even after a bit of friendly persuasion. He doesn't look like he's about to crack either. You could have a go at him if you like.'

'There aren't any marks on him, I hope.'

'Nothing visible.'

'Well, he can wait till we get back. We've got enough on him to keep him in anyway; he's not getting out, even if he thinks he is.'

The door opened, and DC Cameron came into the office.

'Morning, sir,' he said to Justin and then turned to Lisson.

'Not a peep out of him, son,' said Lisson, before he could ask the question. 'He's all yours.'

'Thank you, sir,' he replied. Lisson turned and left the office.

'I'll be with you in a minute,' said Justin, sorting out some papers and putting them away in his desk drawers. 'We can get ourselves out to Horsham sharpish.'

'Aye, why not,' sighed Cameron.

Chief Inspector Andrews appeared behind the mottled glass of his office door. The door swung open.

'I need to see you for a minute, Lamoureaux,' he said. 'And I'll see you as well, Cam.' They followed him into his office.

'He hasn't broken yet then, sir?' said Justin. Andrews did not answer; his eyes were on the desk in front of him.

'Good weekend?' he said, looking up at Justin. Justin paused before answering.

'Not bad, sir, thank you,' he replied. Andrews picked up a manila envelope from his desk and tossed it across to him.

'Have a good look at those,' said Andrews. It was happening again.

Justin picked up the envelope, looked briefly at Cameron, then slowly pulled out a set of grainy photographs.

'There's nothing according to forensics that points directly to the knife you found being the actual murder weapon,' said Andrews.

Justin's breathing slowed back to its normal pace. Andrews noticed his discomfort.

'Aye, they're not the prettiest of pictures,' he continued, pointing to the autopsy photographs, 'but you should be used to that by now. They reckon the cut doesn't really tell us much. It could have been a shorter knife apparently. And the bruising around the incision could be either the impact of the hand that was holding the knife or from the handle itself. It's anyone's guess. Maybe it was a fist, I don't know. Anyway, the point is that this puts us in a rather difficult position with regards to keeping the suspect in.'

'He'll be a danger if we let him go now, sir,' said Cameron. Justin passed the photos back without comment. Andrews shrugged his shoulders.

'I don't know if we can get a conviction or not, but we're gonna have to play along nicely for now,' said Andrews.

'How do you mean, sir?' said Justin, having regained his composure. Andrews paused before answering.

'Listen, I've got a lot of pressure on me coming from all sides, and as I've said before, we can't be seen stepping on too many toes. Now, if we can get a conviction, that's fine, but we need to be pretty bloody sure of that, and we've got nothing directly linking Vardy to the killing.'

'What about Gormally, sir?' said Cameron.

'Aye, the same applies to him if we're not careful,' said Andrews.

'But we've got the photos of the corpse from the back of Vardy's car, sir,' said Justin.

'True,' said Andrews, 'but there's nothing to say that Mr Vardy was actually involved, the Fingerprint Bureau's come back with nothing…and let's face it, son, that story doesn't even fool me. I can't believe you even tried it on, if I'm quite honest.' Justin looked down at the envelope on the desk. 'Besides,' continued Andrews, 'that car's used by a number of people other than Gormally, so even with him we're on dodgy ground. I think we might be lucky to do either one of them for this, if I'm to be quite frank,' he said, and lit a cigarette.

'I suppose he just happened to be driving it at the time, sir,' said Justin.

'Anyway,' said Andrews, ignoring him, 'that was the bad news. The good news is this: I had a little chat with Mr Vardy on Friday evening and he's offered to say that the photographs came from his offices, so long as they're nothing to do with him and there are no charges coming his way – and also, so long as Gormally doesn't twig.' Justin looked at him in disgust. 'That way we can forget about the complaint that's just come in from the tailors,' he added.

'All right, look, sir,' began Justin, 'we haven't quite played it by the book on this one. Obviously, you've worked out that we didn't find the photographs in the car.'

'Really? What a surprise.'

'Yes, but we had no choice other than to go to the tailors. It was the obvious place to look and that's where we found them.'

'I know all of this – they've said as much already. And it's gonna look just fucking grand when you tell them that in court. What made you think you were going to get away with doing something as stupid as that?'

Neither officer answered, both of them surprised that Andrews had not exploded with rage.

'To protect the girls?' said Andrews, foreseeing their most likely answer.

'Look, sir,' began Cameron, a little reticently.

'Don't you fucking tell me to look, son,' said Andrews.

'Aye, sorry, sir,' he said, sitting up uncomfortably, 'but as it was Vardy's office, and Vardy's car – and it's Vardy who gives the orders. Haven't we just as much chance of doing him as we do Gormally?'

'On inadmissible evidence?' he replied. He turned to Justin. 'You should know better than this,' he said, waving his finger at him.

'We had to try to protect the girls, sir,' replied Justin.

'Forget about the fucking girls,' said Andrews, 'you've lost them, and they were just a couple of whores anyway.' Andrews stubbed his cigarette out as he got up and started pacing around his desk. 'I don't know what's the fucking the matter with you. I admit, I must've bent every rule in the book in my time, but not with the likes of these two bastards.' He sat down on the edge of his desk. 'Do you not understand? There are powerful forces at work here – bigger than anything the likes of you or I should ever have to deal with.' His expression changed from that of frustration to one of defeat. 'You're not going to get Vardy,' he continued. 'One of his men'll get to you before that happens, and that's only if you're lucky. If you're going to convict Gormally, you're going to need Vardy to testify against him, and it'll be on his terms. Other than that, I don't know what else you can do.'

'Why's Vardy suddenly calling the shots?' said Justin. 'I don't understand how Lisson let this happen.' Andrews smiled.

'It was Lisson who suggested it. And he's done all right too – a man like Vardy can't be seen to turn on his own men too often if he wants them to stay loyal. I reckon he's given us this one for free.'

'But if we could get vice squad onto the girls, sir–' began Justin.

'Forget about the girls,' said Andrews, his voice rising with anger. He paced back around the desk. 'There's no guarantee they'll testify anyway. They're fucking gone! And if you're not careful, you'll lose these two fucking rats with them!'

Justin stood up to leave.

'Where do you think you're going?' said Andrews.

'I don't believe we haven't got enough to pin it on Vardy,' he replied. 'It's obvious to anyone that he gives the orders.'

'I'm telling you now that you'd better start believing it!' said Andrews. Justin left the office. Andrews turned to Cameron.

'Don't let him do anything else bloody stupid! Am I understood?'

'Perfectly, sir,' he replied, and went to catch him up.

'So, we'll ask Jeffrey about his "trips downstairs" then, sir?' asked Cameron, as they motored south towards Horsham. Justin turned to face him, having lost himself again in the open fields.

'Absolutely…and anything else that comes to mind. Even if Jeffrey's only played the most meagre of roles in this, I want him! We're not leaving until we've spoken to Stephen as well. One of those two must know something; the only question is which.' He looked out again at the curving pastures. 'He's right you know,' he said, after some time. 'We're going to have to drop Vardy.'

'Madness,' said Cameron, shaking his head.

'Andrews is obviously feeling the pressure from above.'

'He knows they're both guilty as hell,' said Cameron. 'Anyway, he'll be back in Ireland soon enough, sir.'

'Well, if this all goes to shit we'll be lucky to be sent there with him.'

Justin turned back to the window. In the distance he could see a secluded farm house, peaceful looking, surrounded by only a few trees and the open fields.

'If they were to kick us off the force it wouldn't be the end of the world,' he said. 'There are worse fates than losing *this* job, you know.'

'Aye…I think I'll become a milkman,' replied Cameron.

'You'd be better-off financially.'

They crossed a junction and headed along one of the narrow hedge-lined country lanes.

'What's all this chummy "Cam" business anyway?' said Justin. 'None of the rest of us get that.'

'Andrews you mean?' said Cameron, shaking his head. 'I've no idea, sir. A bit of favouritism perhaps – the Celtic connection?' He thought for a moment. 'That reminds me, sir – are you French?'

'French?' Justin looked at him, confused. 'Oh, no, it's a Huguenot name,' he said, 'somewhere back on my father's side. God knows where.'

Cameron nodded, though without quite understanding what Justin meant.

They passed a row of shops with a pub stuck on the end, seemingly as an afterthought. Cameron took a right turn and put the car into low gear as it began to climb the final hilly road leading up towards the house. The oak archway came into view and they could see a couple of journalists hanging around outside the property.

'Pull over by these two, will you?' said Justin.

The car stopped, and the two men came over. Justin opened the passenger door and stood behind it.

'Put that camera down and I'll talk to you,' he said. The young photographer let his brand-new camera drop and dangle on the strap around his neck.

'Are there any comments you wish to make, officer?' said the other, his pencil poised over his notepad.

'Only to say that we've made an arrest and that we suspect there may be links with organised crime.'

Cameron's face dropped as he sat listening.

'Prostitution actually,' continued Justin. The reporter's face lit up as he started to scribble something on the pad. 'That'll be "vice" to your readers.'

'And your name, sir?' he said looking up.

'Goodbye.' Justin pulled down the rim of his hat and got back into the car. 'Let's get moving,' he said to Cameron, and the wheels spun on the gravel drive.

'What did you do that for?' said Cameron.

'I thought it might be of interest to them,' Justin replied. 'I also think it's not going to look very good in the eyes of the Great British public if the police release someone who then goes on to murder another young woman…even if she is a prostitute.'

'That's a bit risky, sir,' he said, through a worried smile. They parked-up at the front of the house.

'That's life, I'm afraid. If the force wants to get rid of me, they'll be doing me a favour. I'm sick of all these games. Pull your hat down when you get out, if you don't want to be on the front page of the bloody Mirror.'

They got out and crunched up the path, careful to keep their faces hidden from the reporter's camera. Justin rang the bell.

'I wonder if your little admirer will answer the door, sir,' whispered Cameron.

'Don't,' he replied. The door opened.

'Oh, good morning,' said Samuel. Cameron smiled and turned his head away then pulled down his hat, only just remembering about the photographer nearby.

'Good morning, Mr Wallace,' said Justin. 'Do you mind if we come in?'

'Certainly, sir.'

Cameron and Justin followed him into the hallway.

'If you'll bear with me for just a moment, I'll inform Lady Keating,' said Samuel.

'Is Lord Keating in?' said Justin.

'No, I'm afraid not, sir. Should I still inform the Lady?'

'Yes, please do.'

Samuel knocked on a door in the hallway and went in, pushing the door shut behind him. Justin turned to Cameron.

'We'll speak to Jeffrey later on, even if we have to wait here all night.'

The door opened, and Lady Keating appeared in the hallway, dressed in a mohair sweater and a blue tweed skirt. She had not been expecting visitors.

'Can I help you, officer?' she asked Justin.

'Yes, we have some questions to ask your staff,' he replied.

'But haven't you interviewed them all already?' she said, looking perplexed.

'Yes, we have, but a number of things have cropped up which we'd like to clarify. I'd like to speak with you also, if you wouldn't mind.'

'Yes, of course. Come into the library,' she said, turning to lead them into the room.

'Actually, we'd like to address everyone together first of all. Is Lord Keating available?'

'No, I'm afraid he's gone to Westminster. I can't say when he'll be back.'

'Never mind. Is it possible to speak to everyone else – in the kitchen perhaps?'

She nodded. 'Please, go on through.'

A few minutes later they were standing in the kitchen. Justin informed Stephen, Samuel, Betty, Lady Keating, and Sandra, that they had made an arrest and that he would like to conduct more interviews. From their expressions he could see that the news was not welcome.

'We would be very grateful for your cooperation,' he continued. 'Mr Hollis…I'm glad to see you've returned. I'd like to speak to you first, if you wouldn't mind?' Stephen nodded.

'You can use the drawing room,' said Lady Keating.

'It's this way,' said Stephen. Cameron and Justin followed him down the hall.

'How are you feeling, Mr Hollis?' said Justin, as he sat down at the table opposite him.

'Much better, thank you,' said Stephen, his manner suggesting that it was the truth.

'Good. We just wanted to ask you a few questions about–'

'May I ask whom you've arrested?' said Stephen, butting in.

'Yes, of course. We wanted to speak to you about that actually. Just before we start, there seems to be some confusion about who arranged for Catherine and Sandra to swap shifts on Wednesday night. Did Catherine say anything to you about this?'

'Just that Lord Keating had asked her, and that she didn't mind since she was feeling a little tired and was happy to get away,' said Stephen.

'And do you know when it was that he asked her?'

'Yes, it was that afternoon – that Wednesday.'

'And you're sure of that?'

'Certain. Up until then she had expected to be working.'

'All right.'

'But listen, Inspector, please…about these arrests…'

Justin shifted uncomfortably in his seat.

'The arrest came after we received some information concerning Catherine's past. I take it you know what I am referring to, Mr Hollis?'

Stephen sat looking up at him, motionless.

'Yes…I know all about that,' he said, finally. 'She told me everything – or so I believe.'

'I see,' said Justin. He wondered if she had really told him all.

'I know what you're thinking: that she wouldn't have told me that she had once been a prostitute. But she did. She told me everything she thought I needed to know.'

Justin nodded, but remained silent for some time.

'And how did you feel about it all?' he said.

'How you might expect,' replied Stephen. 'Deeply shocked at first. Then, of course, I was bloody angry. I felt that she'd deceived me…but then I realised that it wasn't her fault, you see…she was just a child when it all happened.'

'Yes, I agree,' said Justin as he scribbled something down on his notepad.

'So, who is it you've arrested?' said Stephen.

'Someone connected to her past, we believe. A Mr Jack Gormally.' Stephen's eyes darted about the room as he tried to place the name. 'I don't think he's anyone you would know,' Justin said softly. 'Now, Mr Hollis, I must ask…did anyone else in the house know about her past?'

'Yes. Sandra knew. She's the other girl who works here.'

'Yes, we know who she is.'

'And Lord Keating.' Justin looked up from his pad and sat forward in his chair.

'How did Lord Keating find out?' he said.

'I don't know how he knew,' said Stephen. 'Would you mind telling me more about the arrest you've made?'

'We will in time,' he replied. 'How did Sandra find out about Catherine – can you tell us that?'

Stephen shook his head. His eyes had glazed over.

'Again, I don't know,' he said.

'So, when you agreed to marry Catherine, you already knew about her past; is that correct?'

'Yes, of course. Like I say…it wasn't her fault what was done to her. She was a victim of one kind or another almost her entire life. It was forced upon her.'

'I fully understand, Mr Hollis,' replied Justin, 'and I'm not casting aspersions with regards to your own conduct or hers. But, can I just ask, when exactly did she tell you?'

'Oh, I don't know exactly how long ago it was. It'll be over six months ago now. She chose to tell me as soon as things became serious between us. And certainly before I proposed to her.'

'And obviously you still did propose. I mean, this kind of thing would put a lot of other men off – but not you?'

'It did at first,' said Stephen, looking down and rubbing his hands together. 'I did wonder if I must be mad. But like I say, I thought about it and I knew deep down that it wasn't her fault.'

'So, you made the arrangements to get married,' said Justin, 'what happened then?' Stephen took a deep breath.

'I didn't make the arrangements; Lord Keating saw to them.'

'Lord Keating? Why did he do that?'

'He said he would see to it, that was all.'

'And did he ask you for money to secure the church?'

'It was a registry office. He paid for the whole ceremony up-front.'

'He paid for the ceremony?'

'Yes. As a wedding present,' said Stephen.

'That seems very generous.' Justin turned to his colleague. 'We must have got him all wrong.'

'I must say, I am surprised,' said Cameron. 'I'm usually such a good judge of character as well.' Stephen was beginning to look agitated.

'I think there's something you're not telling us, Mr Hollis,' said Justin.

'I've told you exactly what happened,' he insisted.

'That time before, when you left the house – Lord Keating told us about it. He said that you resigned and took your belongings, and moved down to Brighton, but then you changed your mind and came back up to Horsham. Is that what happened?'

Stephen paused for a moment.

'What does this have to do with anything?' he said.

'I would appreciate it if you would just answer the question,' said Justin.

'Well…I left. I'd had enough, but then what with Catherine still being here, I decided that I wanted to be near her.' Cameron spoke next.

'Had the two of you had an argument?' he said.

'Myself and Catherine? No, not at all. We never argued.'

'And yourself and Lord Keating?' he said.

'I don't see how this is relevant.'

'It could be very relevant,' said Justin. 'Lord Keating doesn't seem like the type of fellow to allow his employees to chop and change their minds – and then to go and pay for their wedding. What happened between yourself and Lord Keating, Stephen?'

'Nothing…I just–'

'How about Lord Keating and Catherine?' said Cameron.

Stephen looked angrily at him.

'How dare you suggest that–'

'Oh, come on Stephen,' said Justin, raising his voice now, 'we know what he's like. Sandra told us all about him.'

'If I were in your position,' said Cameron, 'I wouldn't have
wanted to leave my fiancé with someone like him. Do you
see how it might look a bit strange to us that you would even
consider doing that?'

The room was quiet.

'Yes, I can see that,' sighed Stephen eventually. 'And you're
quite right; I didn't leave. Lord Keating told me to go.'

'Why did he do that?' said Justin.

'I never found out the reason exactly. It might have been to
do with Catherine, though I'm certain that nothing ever
happened between them. And, as you say, I was worried
about her being here alone with him.'

'And all of this happened before you found out that
Catherine was pregnant?' said Justin.

'Yes, of course…a long time before.'

'I see…' said Justin. 'We have to ask these things, Mr Hollis
because, you see, we have a pregnant girl whose employer
seems to have a certain fondness for his female staff, and
who, for some unknown reason, is falling over himself to
first arrange, and then pay for, your wedding. Do you see
how it could look?'

'Yes, I see how it looks,' replied Stephen resignedly. 'But
the child was mine.' He shifted in his chair and slid his hand
into his inside pocket. 'Do you mind if I smoke?'

'Not at all.'

He lit a cigarette and pulled the ashtray towards him.

'The actual truth is this,' he began, 'Lord Keating asked me
to leave – and I honestly have no idea why – but that's what
he did. I went back to Brighton with the intention of fixing
positions somewhere for the both of us. But when I got
down there, I realised that I didn't want to leave her here –
not even for that limited period. I had already decided to ask
her to marry me and I knew that I had made a mistake in
leaving her here. But the thing is…I knew some things about
Lord Keating that he would not want Lady Keating to find
out about.'

'I see,' said Justin. 'Like what exactly?'

'Places he goes to in his spare time,' he continued, 'places that…you know…you know the kinds of places. Brothels.'

'Right. So, you wanted to come back here, and he didn't want Lady Keating to find out about his dalliances, and so you–'

'I blackmailed him,' he said.

'Why didn't you just take Catherine away with you to Brighton?' said Cameron.

'I thought I could sort some work out for us quickly and then bring her down, but by the time I got down there, the vacancies had gone, so I came back up.'

'Well, that makes perfect sense,' said Justin. 'There was no suggestion of jealousy on Lord Keating's part when he found out about the two of you, was there?'

'No, there was never any suggestion of that.'

'Right. So, he kept Catherine here, but he told you to leave, and you don't know why. I suppose we'll have to settle for that, for now. How about Lord Keating and Sandra? How long has he been pestering her?'

'I don't know. Since she arrived here, I think. I don't know about "pestering" her exactly though – it would be a bit like pestering a rat to eat cheese. I believe she got into trouble at one point, but I can't say for certain.'

'You mean?' said Cameron, patting his stomach.

'Yes. Lord Keating's, I presumed. Listen, what are all these questions about?' he said, 'I don't see what any of this has to do with what happened to Catherine.'

'We just need to make sure that we know exactly what the situation was in the house, that's all, so that we can be certain of Catherine's movements, and that we're not overlooking anything,' said Justin.

'And so, you think Lord Keating was involved?'

'We're not suggesting anything,' said Justin, shaking his head, 'it's just routine.'

'But you think someone in the house had something to do with it?' said Stephen, starting to look flustered.

'We have to cover all possibilities,' said Justin.

'But you do…I mean, you think he had something to do with it!' said Stephen, rising angrily now from his chair.

'Please calm down, Mr Hollis,' Justin began. He leaned towards him. 'The truth is that we need to conduct some investigations inside this house and in order to do this, we really don't want to be drawing any attention to it or it's just going to create obstacles for us. Our job is to bring those responsible to justice, but we need to get at the truth, and we need all the evidence we can get if we're going to see the right people swing. Do you understand? I'm sure you want to see justice done just as much as we do, if not more.'

Stephen tried to listen, but he was not hearing the words.

'I need to get out of here,' he said, 'I need to get some air.'

'Listen Stephen,' said Justin, 'I know this is difficult for you, but we are going to need your cooperation. We need firm evidence in order to bring him in.'

Stephen looked around the room as he collected himself.

'And we need you to keep quiet about it,' Justin added.

'I will,' said Stephen, as he pushed his chair away and quickly left the room.

Justin got up and closed the door behind him.

'Poor bastard,' sighed Cameron.

'Yep. Hopefully he won't do anything stupid.'

'Who's next, sir? Should I call in Sandra?' Cameron moved to get up.

'No. Call in Lady Keating. I need to have a think about what to say to the girl.'

As Cameron got up, Justin grabbed him by the arm.

'Listen,' he said quietly, 'she may be a sweetheart, but I think a bit of pressure on her wouldn't do us any harm. I doubt she knows much about her husband's philandering and I think it might be useful if we shake things up a little bit. We might be able to raise her suspicions and, if we're careful enough, maybe get her on our side. I don't want her suspecting her husband in Catherine's murder – not yet anyway – just in case she says something to him. We want him with his guard down when we see him.'

'Right, sir. I'll bring her in.'

Cameron led Lady Keating into the room and pulled out a chair for her to sit on. She fumbled with something in her cardigan pocket and then pulled out her cigarettes. Justin leant forward and lit one for her.

'Will Lord Keating be returning to the house at all today?' he said.

'No, not until the evening, at least, I'm afraid. He's at Parliament, but he should be at home all day tomorrow.'

'Is that definite?'

'I heard him say so on the phone. He's usually at home on Tuesdays.'

'All right then, I think we can wait until then.'

'How was Stephen when you spoke to him?' she said, looking at them both earnestly.

'Better,' Justin shrugged. 'He was as helpful as he could be.'

'I know it's none of my business, but…I think we could all help him more if we knew exactly what was going on.'

'You will do in time, Lady Keating. It's our intention to have everything cleared up very soon. Then hopefully you can all start to move on.'

'Do you know when you'll be able to release the body?' said Lady Keating. 'I'd like to make sure she has a decent funeral, at least.'

'No, but I understand,' said Justin. 'There are a few small things to clear up first before we can do that. Anything you say to us is strictly confidential. We were wondering actually if you could give us a bit more background information regarding Catherine's past. Did you know much about it while she was working here, Lady Keating?'

'Oh, call me Joanna. No, nothing. What was it about her past?' she replied.

'So, you still don't know? All right then.' Justin got up to stretch his legs then leaned forward on the back of his chair. 'Catherine Smith was a former prostitute who—'

'A what?' she said.

'A prostitute. She worked – or was forced to work as the case may be – in a brothel when she was very young.'

'My God.' There was a short silence while she took in the news. Justin watched her eyes as they aimlessly scanned the room.

'Yes, it does sound as though she wasn't the type you'd expect it from,' said Justin, 'but there you go. Anyway, that answers the first of my questions.' He returned to the table.

'Did Stephen know about this?' she said, looking up at him.

'Yes, he did.'

'And yet he was still going to marry her?' she said incredulously.

'Yes, he had…forgiven her, I suppose. I think that's the correct term.'

Lady Keating shook her head.

'The poor girl. Knowing all this, I feel even worse for her,' she said, 'for all the girls like that really. I myself didn't exactly come from an affluent background but…a prostitute?'

'I know. It's hard to believe,' he said, hoping that the well-used line of his would move the conversation on. 'Anyhow, could you tell us a bit more about how you and Lord Jeffrey met?'

Lady Keating looked up at him, confused and a little suspicious of what was suggested by the tangent.

'Jeffrey and I? But I've told you about that already.'

'How exactly did the affair begin?' said Justin.

She paused for a moment as though carefully searching for the right words. 'Well…as you know, I was working at a hotel in London in which he used to stay – but I object to you referring to our relationship as an affair.'

'But did Lord Keating approach you, so to speak, while you were working? I mean, he couldn't have just suddenly proposed to you one day, surely?'

'No, of course not. But to be honest I don't quite remember. We just gradually got to know one another; it just happened over time. But what does any of this have to do with…well, anything really?' she replied.

'Oh, nothing much,' he said reassuringly. 'As I said, we just wanted to get a little more background information. Like I say, anything you tell us is in the strictest confidence.'

Cameron, who had stayed out of the conversation thus far, shifted forward in his chair.

'What sort of an employer do you think Lord Keating is?' he said.

'What do you mean?' she said, turning to him.

'Well, how would you have felt about being a member of his staff?'

'Perfectly fine I should imagine,' she said a little offhandedly. 'All of the staff are paid on time, they are all provided with good living spaces. I suppose he does expect high standards from them, but that's to be expected.'

'Of course,' replied Cameron.

'And would you say he expects the same high standards from both his male and female staff members?' said Justin pointedly.

'Yes, of course he does.'

'That's good. So, going back to yourself and Lord Keating, how exactly did you go about starting things off?'

'Well, I don't remember exactly – it just happened gradually over time. I know that we began writing to each other after we had met a couple of times. But I don't really see how this is–'

'So, you were just friends at the time?' he said, eyeing her suspiciously. 'It's just that you were very young at the time and well…he obviously wasn't.'

'We felt a mutual attraction to each other,' she said. 'Why, what are you suggesting?'

'It was purely platonic at that stage?' he said.

'Yes,' she said, with a slight hesitation.

'Anyway, I think we're going a little off the point. How are your relations with Lord Keating now?'

'I don't see how this is any of your business,' she snapped.

'No, you're quite right,' he replied, seemingly taken aback. 'It's just that there's quite a high turnover of young female staff at this house and I was wondering if you had any idea as to why that might be?'

'I don't know,' she said, her feeling of agitation growing. 'They're probably just not good enough. I don't have much to do with the running of the house – you really should talk to Jeffrey about such matters.'

'We intend to,' said Justin, pausing to light a cigarette. 'Stephen left the house before, didn't he?'

'Yes, that's correct.'

'It was a little strange really…he told us that he had had a falling out with your husband, moved back down to Brighton, then came back again and Jeffrey took him back as though nothing had happened. But I suppose you don't know anything about that either?'

'Like I say, you need to speak to my husband,' she replied, under his stern gaze. 'I don't know anything about these things.'

'I think there are people in this house who know a lot more than they are letting on, Joanna, and it would help us very much to know what they know. That way, we can put this to rest as soon as possible – and allow you all to do the same.'

'I wish for nothing more,' she said. 'Now if you don't mind Inspector…' She stalled, having forgotten his name.

'Lamoureaux,' he said.

'Inspector Lamoureaux. I have things I need to attend to.' She got up.

'We'll call you if we need you again,' said Justin.

She nodded grudgingly, ignoring Cameron, then turned and left the room. Justin pushed the door shut behind her.

'You went for her there, sir,' said Cameron, as Justin sat back down.

'Yes. We could be here forever otherwise. I'm sure she can handle it; she obviously saw a bit of money in old Jeffrey and knew that she had it in her to make a bit of an investment. It's the same old story.'

'You can't really blame her for that, sir.'

'No, I suppose not. Anyway, I think we should get that Sandra girl in now. She definitely knows more than she's letting on.'

'I'd put money on it, sir. I think it's her day off today so she should be upstairs.'

'Well, that'll save Jeffrey a trip downstairs then, won't it?'

'Aye,' laughed Cameron, and he left the room.

Cameron found her in the kitchen and brought her back with him to the drawing room.

'Would you like a cigarette?' he said to her as she sat down.

'No thanks, I don't smoke,' she replied.

'That's fair enough,' he said.

Justin came back over to the table and sat down, having been watching the journalists from the window. Looking at Sandra now, it was clear she felt far more comfortable being interviewed this time than on the previous occasion. He wondered why.

'You're not working today, are you?' he said, glancing down at her floral blouse.

'It's my day off.'

'We'll try not to keep you too long then.' Justin put out the cigarette he had been smoking and lit another. 'So, you would have been at the apartment at Green Park today; is that correct?' he said.

'Yes, I would.'

'But obviously you don't want to be there now.'

'No chance. Anyway, it's being sold.'

'Of course it is.'

Thoughts of the antiques dealer popped into his head, along with Jeffrey's assumed name and the photographer in the flat upstairs.

'I know I've asked this already,' he continued, 'but I wanted to make sure: those times that you stayed at the apartment – did you ever notice anything unusual about anyone who stayed over? Have you remembered anything since we last spoke, about anyone either you or anyone else might have brought back there?'

'What do you mean "brought back there?"' she said.

'A male friend perhaps.'

'I didn't bring anyone back.'

'Well, last time we spoke you told us that you sometimes had visitors and that, quite rightly, it was none of our business.'

'Yes, but never anyone dodgy.'

'That's all right then – that's all I was asking.'

Cameron had gotten up out of his chair and was now leaning on the backrest.

'I doubt Lord Keating would have stood for it anyway,' he said. Her eyes darted towards his.

'What do you mean by that?' she said.

'He wouldn't have stood for anyone dodgy staying at the apartment,' replied Cameron.

'No. Well, of course not, it's his flat.'

'That's right. Plus, he wouldn't be too happy about you having a bit on the side, would he?' he added.

'I don't know what you're talking about,' she said, crossing her arms in front of her.

Justin sat forward.

'I think I may have misjudged you the last time we met,' he said, looking her in the eye. 'I passed you a note asking if Lord Keating coerced you into sexual relations with him, but I now think I did you a disservice in painting you as the helpless victim. It's not quite like that, is it Sandra?'

'There's nothing like that going on. That's disgusting.'

'We know all about it already, Miss MacGuire,' he said. 'But it's not something we're particularly interested in.'

'Did he get you into *trouble*, Miss MacGuire?' said Cameron.

'What?' she snapped back at him.

'What about Catherine?' he continued, 'was she involved with Lord Keating?'

'Of course not,' she said, unable to believe what she was being asked.

'You knew all about Catherine's past though, didn't you, even though you told us you didn't know much about her? Did she tell you herself or was it Jeffrey?'

Sandra looked blankly at him, refusing to answer.

'It wouldn't have been Stephen,' he said. 'Was it the cook perhaps?'

A wry smile spread across Sandra's face.

'How did you feel about that – living and working with a former prostitute?' said Justin.

'Pretty disgusted,' she said.

'And did you tell anyone else about her?'

'No-one,' she insisted. 'I wasn't that interested to be honest with you.' She looked at her watch. 'It's my day off. What do you two want?'

'Just one more thing,' said Justin. 'Has Lord Keating ever asked you to pick anything up for him from the tailors shop?'

'What tailors?' she said. The look of confusion on her face seemed genuine.

'The one in central London, not far from Green Park. Berwick Street. Does that ring any bells?' he said, studying her reaction.

'I don't know what you're talking about,' she said. Justin sat back in his chair.

'Thank you very much for your time,' he said. He followed Sandra to the door, making sure that it was closed behind her.

'She doesn't know anything about Berwick Street,' he said to Cameron.

'No, I thought as much.'

'Still, it was worth checking. I don't think any of them are going to drop Jeffrey in it, even if they do know something.'

'Is it worth re-interviewing the others, sir?'

'I don't think so,' he said, looking at his watch. 'Besides, I don't think I can face it, can you?'

They collected their jackets and went out into the hall where Stephen was waiting for them.

'I'll let you out,' he said, leading them towards the front of the house. They stopped at the door to pull their hats down before going outside.

'There's quite a crowd now at the end of the driveway,' Stephen warned them as they stepped outside. 'They seem to have congregated steadily since this morning.'

'They must have got the whiff of a story,' said Justin.

Stephen lowered his voice.

'Are you getting any closer?' he said. He could see a camera being pointed at him as he stood in the doorway, but he no longer cared.

'A little. We'll be back tomorrow morning to interview Lord Keating. We'll let you know exactly what happens then. Just keep quiet and keep your eyes open, and we'll get there. Now get yourself inside. You don't need this kind of attention on top of everything else.' They went off to the car.

Stephen stood alone in the hallway for some time, trying to make sense of what they were asking of him. As he went off along the hall, he looked up to see Lady Keating standing by the door to the library.

'Have the police officers gone?' she asked him.

'Yes, they have, M'Lady,' he said.

'Good. It must be very unpleasant for you to have to keep dragging everything up again. How are you feeling? Are you still fit to work?'

'Yes, I think it's best, M'Lady,' he said, with a flatness of tone that somehow hinted at the turbulence inside.

'Well, it's up to you. They said they'll be back again tomorrow, but hopefully they won't need to bother you again.'

'No. Hopefully not.'

She thanked him and turned back into the library.

Stephen looked at his watch. It was half-past two. He knew that Lord Jeffrey could be expected home sometime after seven. He could already see him coming in through the door with his arrogant, nonchalant greeting, passing his hat to whoever happened to be standing nearby. Stephen knew it could not be him this time.

He walked along the hall wondering if he could trust himself to wait for the police to do their job, while in the meantime, continue to serve their main suspect in the manner he had come to expect.

One of the reporters had jumped into a motorcar and followed them right up to the gates of Scotland Yard. Having shaken him off at the inviolable perimeter of the grounds, Cameron parked up and they made their way up to the office. Detective Chief Inspector Andrews was waiting for them when they got there, having left his office door ajar. They sat down at Justin's desk.

'I admire your guts, I'll say that for you,' they heard him call out. Then he appeared at his office door.

'How do you mean, sir,' said Justin.

'I'm gonna get a lock put on this for however long I'm still here,' he said, wrapping his knuckles against his office door. He had been looking over the complaint from the tailors shop. 'Not that that'll stop you, no doubt. No-body's safe with the likes of you around.' He turned back into his office, kicking the door shut with his heel.

'We had better interview Gormally,' said Justin, turning to Cameron. 'We'll tell him what Jeffrey's just told us.'

'And what's that, sir?' he replied.

'Everything. Weren't you paying attention, Detective Constable?'

'Oh, aye,' he said.

They sent a message to get Gormally brought out of the cells then went down to meet him in the interview room. The light from the bulb cast shadows under the bags that had recently appeared beneath his eyes.

'Your friend Lord Keating has been very vocal about your involvement in all of this,' began Justin. Gormally forced a smile that seemed to use up the last of his energy. His face straightened.

'And what's that, exactly?' he said.

'I think old Jeffrey's seen a way to dig himself out of a hole.'

'Sounds like you think he should be arrested.'

'I think we've already got the man we want. And so does he. Why don't you help yourself out a bit?' Justin slid a packet of cigarettes across the table.

'Do you really think I'm that stupid?' said Gormally. He took the cigarette box and lit one up.

'You've had dealings with the law before, haven't you, son?' said Cameron.

Gormally smiled again.

'How old are you then, "son"?' he said.

'Seems like you feel quite at home in these surroundings,' replied Cameron, ignoring the question. He looked around at the stark brick walls of the interview room. 'It suits you,' he added.

'Are you ready to tell us where the girls are?' said Justin.

'What girls?' he replied, sighing with boredom.

'It's all right if you're not, we've already got enough to hang you. I just thought you might want to give yourself a chance. But never mind, Mr Vardy will be able to tell us.'

'We both know he won't do that. You know as well as I do he'll have me out of here before much longer.'

'I wouldn't be too sure of that,' said Cameron. 'The street outside is swarming with press and photographers. Do you really think Mr Vardy wants that kind of attention?'

'I doubt he's going to pick me up personally,' he replied.

'I think you're missing the point Mr Gormally,' said Justin. 'Firstly, we can't be seen to release someone who poses a danger to anyone, even if they are only prostitutes. And secondly, if Mr Vardy is given the choice of saving himself or saving you, who do you think he's going to choose?'

Gormally leaned forward in his chair.

'What do you mean "choice"?'

'One of you is going to have to take the fall. You should try being up-front with us before he does.'

'It doesn't work like that and you know it,' he said in a low tone.

'Honour amongst thieves, hey?' said Cameron. 'I wouldn't rely on that if I were you.'

Justin got up from his chair.

'Right, well I think we're done here,' he said brightly. 'We'd best get back to Lord Keating; we don't want to keep him waiting.' Cameron nodded his assent as he got up. 'Do let us know if you remember anything in the meantime, Mr Gormally,' said Justin. 'Then we can see whether or not we can help each other out.' Gormally watched them leave.

Back upstairs Justin dialled the workmen's number while Cameron sat at his desk, looking on. It was four o'clock and he guessed that they should have finished work for the day.

'John Peters speaking. How can I help you?' said the voice on the line.

'This is Detective Inspector Lamoureaux from Scotland Yard.'

'Oh yeah?' came the uneasy reply.

'It's nothing for you to worry about. I just wanted a few details concerning some work you're doing at the home of Lord Jeffrey Keating. It's the big manor house out in Horsham.'

There was a pause.

'We're not doing that job anymore,' he replied.

'And why, may I ask, is that?'

'He called and cancelled it yesterday; we were supposed to start it today. He's signed the contract as well. I don't suppose there's anything you can do about it?'

'Contractual agreements aren't really police business, I'm afraid,' said Justin, shaking his head impatiently. 'It sounds like you need a lawyer.'

'Oh.'

'Could you tell me what kind of work he had you doing at the house?'

'Yes, he wanted a mirror fitted.'

'A mirror? That sounds like a pretty small job. Does he really need you just for that?'

There was a cough at the end of the line.

'It was a certain type of mirror…for security, he said. And he wanted the space cleared out behind it, he said, and a way of accessing it without being seen.' The penny dropped.

'Where in the house was this?' said Justin. The workman laughed.

'Can't you guess? Listen, are you sure there's nothing you can do about it? We've put work back to make time for this. That costs money, you know.'

'Yes, thank you for your time, sir,' said Justin. He put down the receiver.

'Let me guess, sir. A special type of glass?' said Cameron. Justin nodded.

'Somewhere where he could spy on his female staff, no doubt.'

'Full of surprises that one.'

Justin walked back over to his desk.

'Where's Andrews?' he said. The silhouette was no longer present behind the mottled glass.

'Gone home, I think,' said Cameron.

'Fancy a drink?' Justin pulled a whisky bottle out from his desk drawer.

'Nah, nah. I'd better not…I've got stuff to do.'

'Suit yourself.' Justin half-filled his coffee cup and swallow-ed the lot in one. 'I'm getting out of here,' he said, putting on his suit jacket and replacing the bottle in the drawer. 'We'll head out to Horsham again tomorrow morning. Hopefully we'll get old Jeffers to incriminate himself and have this case cracked by lunchtime.'

'A nice easy day then, sir,' said Cameron.

'It shouldn't be too difficult.' He went out the door.

Half-way along the street, he was already regretting not having taken another decent slug from the whisky bottle. He hailed a cab which took him up through Trafalgar Square and on to Bloomsbury, then he climbed the steps and knocked at the door.

'Is Lord Henry at home?' Justin said, taken aback as yet another new servant opened the door.

'He's just this minute returned from The House, sir. May I ask who is calling?' the servant replied, somewhat timidly, Justin thought.

Lord Henry appeared at the end of the hallway.

'Oh, it's all right. Let him in!' barked the voice of the ex-soldier, and he disappeared into the drawing-room.

Justin paused in the hallway to prepare himself before going in, having previously witnessed many of Henry's irascible moods. Summoning his courage, he stepped into the room and found Henry sitting on the couch.

'Is this a bad time?' said Justin warily.

'Oh, it's that bastard Salisbury. Bastard! Bastard!' he boomed with a passion that rendered the mid-section of the word little more than a whisper. 'No, it's all right young man. Have a seat.'

Justin sat down. Henry looked at him angrily, his mind still on his rival. Justin felt as though he were looking straight through him. Henry's index finger shot up threateningly.

'If someone gives you their word…' he began, but then his voice tailed off. 'Oh, forget it,' he growled. He sighed and sat back, and his demeanour softened, seemingly as a result of Justin's presence.

'And what can I do for you?' he said, rather more warmly.

'I don't mean to be impertinent Henry, but I could certainly do with a drink.'

'Of course, of course. What a bloody good idea!' He turned in his seat. 'Jenkins!' he boomed once again. The door opened. 'Bring us some single malt, will you?'

The servant nodded and disappeared.

'Another new servant?' said Justin.

'Oh, it's the other one's day off,' said Henry, his voice having fully softened now to its familiar clandestine purr.

The servant returned and placed the decanter on the table then swiftly left the room.

'I made a big mistake with this one,' said Henry, pointing over his shoulder with his thumb. 'He can bugger off back to his little fiancé as soon as the other boy returns.'

Justin smiled.

'You know it always amuses me, Henry; you really are two completely separate people. I can never quite tell which is you and which is the other.'

'Well, you know all about my penchant for *the other*. And I think you'll find that you know the real me only too well.'

He set the two glasses down and poured an inch of whisky into each. They both knocked them straight back. He poured them another.

'Shouldn't you be a little more discreet with all these new faces hanging around?' said Justin.

'Not usually – you see they'd only be incriminating themselves. But yes, this one could be a liability.'

'I shouldn't think he would say anything, Henry. I was thinking more of the guests that were here the other evening. I'm just surprised you manage to keep things so quiet.'

'Oh, I only ever invite my most trusted acquaintances to my dinners. And I certainly vet them thoroughly when it comes to *desert*.' He sipped his whisky. 'But I must say Justin, you did let me down dreadfully the other evening. At least now I have the pleasure of telling you that you missed out on a quite wonderful evening!'

'Never mind,' replied Justin. 'You know full-well that that's not my kind of thing, Henry.'

'Well, more fool you! You look as though you could do with letting your hair down. You are looking tired, my boy. What on earth is the matter?'

'It's this case I've been lumbered with – the one at Green Park. You know the feeling when you put in all the hard work, but you can still feel it slipping through your fingers.'

Henry's left eyebrow arched as he cued up the double entendre, but then seeing the look of suffering on Justin's face, he fought the temptation to elaborate.

'Too much work, that's what it is,' he said, eventually. 'You know how the saying goes: all work and no play makes poor little Iustus a very boring little bitch!'

'I don't think that's quite it, Henry.'

'Not to mention the quite ruthless neglect of your friends. You need time to relax, Justin. I worry sometimes that you are not making the best of your short, and somewhat vulgar, little existence.'

'I'm all right, I'm just busy,' he replied.

Henry leant forward.

'Take some advice from someone much closer to death than you are – though I admit, your drinking habit does throw that assumption into quite some doubt. But nonetheless, the final result is the same for us all. It's how one plays the game that's important – you should remember that! And it is just a game.'

Justin had finished his drink.

'Do you mind?' he said, reaching out for the bottle.

'It's not that I mind so much,' said Henry, 'you can have as much as you like.'

Justin refilled his glass.

'The orgasm,' continued Henry, embarking now on some reverie, 'as the French say, is "*un petite mort*," and how right they are. A little bit of death will teach you all there is to know about life. Alcohol has its charms, Justin, as I myself well know. But as Nietzsche so rightly pointed out, its numbing effect will stunt your development. Hence, it is the recreation of the philistine – and that is not you! When did you last make it to the opera?'

'I don't have time for things like that these days.'

'"*Divertentè*" say the Italians,' continued Henry, appearing to ignore him, 'a "diversion" from life. That's what you need, not wallowing in it. You can waste a whole lifetime like that, and then before you know it, you're dead.'

'I don't fear death anymore. I've seen enough of it.'

'Yes, I dare say you have. And there's another one inevitably coming your way. But natural death is something quite different. If I regret one thing about my life – and I don't regret much, I'm pleased to say – it would be that I didn't give nearly enough thought to the finality of death at a young enough age.'

Justin nodded.

'So, you don't regret much then?' he said.

'Indeed, I don't.'

'I don't mean to offend you, Henry, but isn't it only the obstinate and the stupid who have no regrets?'

'The stupid yes, but also those of us who have lived our lives fully. There are things I would change, of course, looking back, even if only to go back and do things a little better. But that can't be helped now. Regret only leads one down a blind alley. One must free oneself in the present while one still has the time. Do you understand what I'm saying to you or am I wasting time for us both?'

'No. I know exactly what you're saying. It's not as though these things don't cross my own mind sometimes…with alarming regularity in fact,' he admitted.

'Which is why you should have stayed a little later and enjoyed the fruits of my wisdom. That reminds me actually, I did need to speak to you. Our friend out in Berkshire had a man sat outside the post office for a couple of days, but he's got nothing to go on and there's only so much police time he can find excuses for having wasted. He made a few enquiries with the staff as to who might have posted your parcel, but none of the customers seemed to have stood out, and after all, he doesn't even have a description to go on.'

'No, I realise that,' said Justin. 'It was a shot in the dark.'

'He's taken his man off of it, I'm afraid.'

'Of course; I forgot about it, in fact. Tell him thanks.'

'You know, if I were you I would give serious consideration to the idea of employing a private detective. It's what I believe the Americans refer to as a private dick.'

'I'll think about it,' said Justin. 'This whole thing's driving me mad. I went down to the Harrow Road baths the other day.'

'Really?' said Henry, sounding intrigued.

'Oh no, nothing like that,' continued Justin. 'It was a mistake. I just wanted to check the cubicles where the photographs must have been taken, that's all. I don't know what I expected to find. Sometimes I even think I'm trying to get myself caught.'

'I should keep well away from that place, if I were you,' said Henry.

'Yes, I shouldn't have gone there. Anyway, I don't have the time to deal with all that now.' He took a sip of whisky and shook his head. 'Why do I get caught-out when you always manage to keep things a secret with such ease?'

'Because I don't go gallivanting around in Turkish baths,' said Henry.

'But still, you're hardly the most discreet. Look at that man you had me sitting next to at the party the other night – Sir Burfield. Surely if the likes of him found out it would put an end to your beloved freedom.'

'Oh, Justin,' laughed Henry, 'you can be so very naïve at times. I have things on Sir Burfield which would force him to go into hiding within the hour. This, I'm afraid, is how my world works.'

'I see. And how about Lord Keating?'

Jeffrey sat up; the mention of his name seemed to have caught him by surprise.

'Oh, well played. Very professional. Perhaps you're not so naïve after all. I shall not fall into that little trap.' He sat back again. 'There is honour you know, Justin, even amongst scoundrels. Besides, I'd be very much surprised if Jeffrey could afford my company these days anyway.'

'What do you mean?'

'Well, it's common knowledge that he's been feeling the pinch. It's all this Socialist nonsense you see; it's been playing havoc with the finances of many of my caste.'

'He's had money troubles?'

'Yes, of course. Though he does his best to keep it all *hush hush* as you might expect. Still…I should think he has a good excuse to sell his London apartment now.'

Justin put down his glass and reached for his hat.

'Where are you going?'

'If you'll excuse me, Henry, there's somewhere I need to be.'

'But why the rush—'

'My apologies, I'll explain later,' he said, as he shot across the room and out the front door.

Justin got on the tube and headed west across London, waiting impatiently as he stood in the aisle, counting off the stops on the map and swaying with the jolt of the carriages. He alighted at Ealing Broadway and walked the rest of the way into Acton.

All along the way he toyed with the possibilities of what the photographs might show. If Jeffrey needed money, then blackmail might provide him with an easy option. Those images must be of value to someone. Surely, he would have mentioned them by now, he reasoned, and in his heart, he knew that it was beyond absurd. Still, he had to make sure.

He pressed the doorbell on the side door of the antiques shop and waited for the photographer to answer. He pressed again, waited a few moments and then decided to knock on the door of the antiques dealer. Eventually the old gentleman appeared at the door.

'Yes, what is it?' he said rather moodily. Justin held up his ID, at which point the man recognised him.

'Oh, good evening, officer.' The door opened a little wider.

'Good evening. Is Mr Turner in?' said Justin, nodding towards the staircase leading to the upstairs flat.

'I believe he may be. That bell of his is out of order. It's a dreadful pain in the neck – I've had the man come over twice already to fix it.'

'Can you let me up?'

'Yes, of course. Come in.'

Justin followed him up the windowless staircase towards the photographer's flat then stopped him at the first-floor landing.

'If you don't mind,' said Justin, 'I'll go the rest of the way myself.'

The old man turned to face him.

'It's really no trouble,' he said, pleasantly. 'The old knees are a bit–'

'No, really. I'll take it from here. Thank you.' Justin passed him on the staircase then turned and waited for him to leave. The antiques dealer descended the stairs back to his own flat and closed the door.

Justin went up the final few steps and gave the door a loud knock. He could hear the sound of footsteps and some shuffling from somewhere on the other side. The hinges creaked as the door opened.

'Good evening,' said the photographer. The words had the sing-songish intonation of a question rather than a greeting. Justin stepped closer into the light. The lack of recognition in the man's eyes told Justin that Jeffrey's photographs could not be images of himself.

'Mr Turner, I was wondering if I could discuss some business with you – just quickly? I'm in a terrible rush.' Mr Turner looked him up and down.

'Just quickly then,' he said. The door opened a little wider.

'I need to secure a photographer on quite short notice and you've been recommended rather highly. The work doesn't need to be done until August, but I must have someone lined up.' Justin looked past him into the room, half of which was in semi-darkness.

'You can come in if you wait a second,' replied the photographer. 'I must just see to something first.'

He closed the door and Justin could hear the sound of further shuffling. A drawer slid shut, and the door re-opened.

'Come on in,' said Mr Turner, flicking on the main light as Justin entered.

Long, heavy curtains had been pulled shut across the small dormer windows, blocking out the evening light. There were two washing lines stretching across the room, each with a selection of photographic prints pegged onto them.

'You'll have to excuse me; my studio doubles up as a darkroom,' said the photographer. He had a kindly face.

'Oh, that's no bother,' Justin replied.

'Did you say you were in a rush? I was just about to make a pot of tea.'

Justin checked his watch.

'I'm sure I have time to take you up on that offer,' he said.

'I'll just heat the kettle.'

Mr Turner disappeared into the backroom and turned on the light.

'What exactly was it you were after?' came the voice from the kitchen.

Justin moved over to a nearby set of drawers and pulled gently at the top handle.

'Oh, I work for a family out in Datchet,' he said. 'They have a large wedding planned at the start of August and the reception is to be at the manor house.'

One by one Justin slid out the drawers and closed them again gently, failing to find anything of interest. 'I heard that you might be well suited to the work.'

'Wedding photographs, do you mean?'

'Yes. But the guests are of a very exclusive set. Would you be interested in such work?'

Justin pulled out the bottom drawer and began to flick through the folders.

'Yes, that sounds most agreeable,' came the voice from the other room, sounding as though it were moving closer. Justin stood up.

'Do you take sugar?' said Mr Turner, appearing in the doorway.

'Yes, two please.' Mr Turner went back into the kitchen.

'Do you do much work in country houses?' said Justin. He reached into the drawer and felt amongst a set of folders. A bundle of loose photographs had been pushed to the back of the drawer as if they had been dumped there in a rush. There was the sound of tea being stirred.

'Yes,' said Mr Turner, laughing gently to himself. 'I often take up work at country houses.'

The spoon came to rest on the table top and Mr Turner came back into the room carrying the two cups of tea. No longer needing to be quiet – having now found what he was after – Justin kicked the drawer shut.

'What are you doing?' said Mr Turner. Justin held up two images out of a set of black and white prints.

'Pornography,' he said, reaching into his pocket for his ID. He held it up. 'I'm a policeman.'

'You can't just come in here–' Turner began, still holding the two teacups in his hands.

'Calm down and listen to me,' said Justin, 'I'm not interested in you or what kind of work you do. I'm only interested in a certain client of yours. His name is Lord Jeffrey Keating.'

'I've never heard of him,' said Turner.

'I think you have,' he replied, waving the photographs in front of him. 'How about Mr Edward Collins?' Turner's expression dropped. He put the two cups gently down on a table nearby.

'Is that a yes or a no, Mr Turner?'

'I…' The sentence turned into a sigh. The look on his face was now one of such utter defeat that it almost made Justin feel sorry for him.

'Look, Mr Turner, don't mess me around. I'm really not interested in what you do, but I've got more than enough here to send you away for a while…if that's what I choose to make of it.' He looked at the images again and frowned. 'Yes, I've got some colleagues in vice who would be very interested in these. But it's up to you. Just show me the work you've done for Edward Collins and I'll forget that you even exist.'

'All right,' he said. 'Come over here.'

Justin followed him over to a box file on a shelf at the other end of the room. He pulled it down and extracted a file marked F.D.

'What do those initials stand for?' said Justin.

'It's just how I file them. It's the client's initials but moved one letter on. I'm sure you can understand why.' He pushed the file towards him and Justin began flicking through the images.

'Do you still have the negatives for these?'

'Yes, of course. I keep everything.'

'And these are all of the images for this client?'

'That's the lot.'

Justin could see by his shamed expression that he was probably telling the truth.

'Do you normally do stuff like this?' asked Justin.

'Not normally, no. And I didn't take these photographs, I only developed them. I just do what I'm paid for.' He pointed up towards the exposed rafters and around the room. 'You can see I'm not exactly a wealthy man.'

'And what happens to them once they leave your hands?'

'I don't know. I have nothing more to do with them then. I suppose they are sold on.'

Justin stared at him, wondering how far he should push his questioning.

'Are the images always posed for?'

'How do you mean?'

'Do the people in the photographs always know that the images are being taken?' He watched the photographer's reaction closely.

'Well, of course they do – they're in the nude.'

'What I meant is…look, never mind.' He decided that it was just not worth it. 'Where do you keep the negatives for these images?'

'They're all in the back of the file.'

Justin checked that they were there.

'Good. I'm seizing this file,' he said, and moved towards the door.

'But what am I to tell the client?'

'You don't tell him anything! There's a delay, that's all. I might be returning these to you – maybe not. It depends what's on them. You might find yourself working with us for a while. I hope you don't mind.'

'Well, I–'

'Thanks for the tea.' Justin pulled the door shut behind him.

Eleven

'Here, have a look at these.' Justin tossed the folder across his desk. 'I've had a good look through them, though I think they might be more to your taste than mine.'

'Photographs?' said Cameron. 'Where did you get these?' He pulled a handful of them out of the folder.

'I went to see that photographer over in Acton, the one old Jeffrey recommends so highly.'

'Looks like someone's been a naughty boy,' said Cameron, smiling.

'Yes. And look who the naughty girl is.'

'Aye…Christ, you'd think she'd at least try to disguise her identity,' he said with a grimace.

'Not our Sandra.'

'Is that what you think of me, sir?'

'What do you mean?'

'That they're more to my taste than yours.'

'Oh, well…you just seem the type,' said Justin amiably.

'It's all right, sir, I'm not easily offended. Though I'm not sure my predilections stretch as far as her,' he said, as he continued to flick through the images. 'Joking aside, sir, do you think some of these were actually taken downstairs in the house?'

'I should think the summer house is more likely. It would be nice to think the place is being put to good use. And I'm sure I recognise some of the furniture from the Green Park apartment in a couple of them. It would have been a pretty convenient place for it, don't you think?'

'Are they all like this?' said Cameron, still only half-way through the set of prints. The look on his face spoke of fascination as much as disgust. Justin had never seen such concentration.

'Yes, they're all pretty similar, or at least Sandra seems to be the main attraction in every one of them. I came back here last night and checked all the negatives. I don't think there's anything more disquieting in the set than what you're currently staring at.'

'Well, that's something. Do you reckon these are Lady Keating's clothes?' said Cameron, squinting and turning the photographs round as if a change of angle would give him a better view.

'Very possibly. I would have thought the jewellery definitely is. Still, I don't suppose it matters much – it doesn't look like she was wearing any of it for very long.'

'Aye, I can see that. Who do you think the bloke is?'

'God knows. It's definitely not Stephen.'

'And it's probably not your little admirer, sir,' smiled Cameron.

'No, I should think not. And it's not Jeffrey either.'

Cameron reluctantly started to put the prints back in the file.

'Is it worth following up, sir?

'It could be, but I doubt it.'

'I think I've seen enough,' said Cameron, quickly stealing one last glance.

'Good,' said Justin, as he rose from his chair and put his hat on. 'I think we'd better get out there then, don't you?'

Cameron knocked on the door as the two of them waited. The sky overhead was blanketed in thick grey cloud that thinned out into white tufts towards the horizon.

'I've had enough of this place already,' said Justin, looking out towards the adjacent fields. The door opened.

'Good morning, Mr Hollis. Is Lord Keating at home?' said Justin.

Stephen simply nodded in reply; the darkness of his mood clearly evident behind his tired expression.

'We'd very much like to speak to him,' said Justin. 'We're confident that this will be the final time,' he added pointedly.

'I think we would all appreciate that,' replied Stephen.

His mistrust of the two officers had grown overnight, fuelled by the circular reasoning brought on by his extreme lack of sleep.

'Come this way,' he said, letting them into the hall. Stephen led them into the drawing room and made them take a seat.

'Whereabouts is Lord Keating?' said Cameron, eyeing the door, wondering if he might be listening in.

'I don't know,' said Stephen flatly. 'In the summer house perhaps. I shall have to find him.'

'That's all right, we'll wait,' said Justin, putting his hand up to stop Cameron from saying any more. Stephen closed the door behind him.

'We'll stick to what we spoke about, all right?' whispered Justin.

'All right, sir,' Cameron nodded.

They sat down on the couch and waited quietly for some time, listening to the mechanical tick of the grandfather clock. Cameron got up and went over to one of the book shelves at the far end of the room.

'It's an impressive house,' he said, blowing out tobacco smoke as he ran his fingers over the gold and maroon spines of the leather-bound books.

'You get used to them,' said Justin.

'I'm sure you do. I bet you grew up in one just like this, didn't you, sir?'

'Not quite. They can seem imposing to visitors – that's the whole point of them. But after a while, a door just becomes a door and a window is just a window…'

'Relative to what you're used to,' replied Cameron, returning to the couch and making use of the crystal ashtray.

'Precisely. It's all just posturing. That's why it's so easy to lose it all through gambling and drinking it all away. At least I've had the privilege of seeing all that first-hand.'

A baritone voice was beginning to make itself heard along the hallway. The door opened, and with an audible huff, in walked Lord Keating.

'No, you two remain seated – make yourselves at home,' he said, raising his hand to them as he came into the room. He went directly over to the whisky decanter and poured himself a drink then sat down opposite them.

'Should I be ready for another grilling?' he said facetiously, sipping his drink.

'Was there a first one?' said Cameron. Jeffrey's eyelids drooped.

'Yes, well, we've got a few things to get through,' said Justin, lifting a leather satchel up onto his lap.

'Well, we'd best get on with it then,' said Jeffrey. 'I may have other *guests* to entertain.'

'We appreciate your hospitality,' Justin replied. 'I'll get straight to the point then. Last time we were here we had a brief discussion about your personal involvement with various female members of your staff.'

'I seem to remember some implied accusations.'

'I'd like to give you the opportunity once again to tell us if you have any non-professional, shall we say, involvement, with any of them.'

'I am much obliged for the opportunity, but no, of course I bloody well don't. And certainly not with that Catherine girl, if that's what you're leading up to.'

'I think we're jumping the gun a little,' said Justin.

'There's some interesting characters working here, aren't there, sir?' said Cameron, looking up at Lord Keating.

'What do you mean?' he replied.

'Well, I'm not too sure how aware you are of this, sir, but there seems to be some illicit activity taking place within this house.'

Justin unbuckled the satchel he had brought with him. As Jeffrey's eyes moved across to the bag, it seemed as though he had stopped breathing. Justin pulled out the file and revealed the photographs.

'Maybe you could help us identify the locations, and then maybe, together, we can identify the photographer. I'm only guessing that these images were taken at one or more of your properties.' He passed them across the table and Jeffrey peered down at them without attempting to pick them up.

'How disgusting!' he sneered.

'My thoughts exactly,' replied Justin.

'Where did you get this filth?'

'They were seized a few nights ago. They were at a photographer's studio. What was his name again?' said Justin turning to Cameron.

'Mr Edward Collins wasn't it, sir?' Cameron replied.

'No, no it wasn't Edward Collins. Edward Collins was the client. It was…Malcolm Turner, yes that was it. He seemed like a very pleasant fellow, if you don't take these into account, of course,' he said, indicating the photographs. 'Bit of a shame really.'

Jeffrey sat watching him carefully.

'You recognise the girl in the photographs don't you, Lord Keating?' said Cameron.

'Yes…yes,' he replied shortly, 'it looks like that little tart who works for me. I understand what you're getting at.'

'How do you mean, sir?' said Cameron.

'Well, you obviously think I have something to do with it. And I don't! Who's this Edward Collins anyway?'

'Well, Mr Collins also sold some antiques to the gentleman downstairs, and, when I had them traced, it turned out that each of the pieces belonged to you. Are you sure you don't know who he is?'

Jeffrey chose not to reply.

'Anyway,' continued Justin, 'these are the interiors of your house, are they not?'

'So-what if they are?'

'Are you saying that these were taken without your knowledge?' said Justin.

'Aren't they Lady Keating's clothes in the photographs, Lord Keating?' added Cameron.

'I have no idea,' he replied. 'And there's no reason why my wife should know anything about these either.'

'I'm sure she doesn't,' said Justin, 'but someone must have known about it; some of the images look as though they were taken in daylight.'

'Maybe we should just ask Lady Keating, sir,' said Cameron. 'It'll save us all time.'

Jeffrey sat up.

'Look…I don't want this kind of business affecting my wife, all right? She's in a fragile enough state as it is.'

'So whose photographs are they?' said Justin.

Jeffrey let out a deep and prolonged sigh.

'Who's Edward Collins?' said Justin in a flat, impatient tone. He reached into the bag and produced another selection of photographs. 'These ones are even better. Of questionable legality though, I might add, sir. You do realise that, don't you?' Justin held up a photograph of Sandra in front of the lion skin which hung on the wall at the Green Park apartment.

Jeffrey swilled the drink around his glass while the two officers waited for his reply. Cameron could feel himself becoming restless. The quietness seemed to magnify the ticking of the grandfather clock. His patience ran out.

'We'll just ask Lady Keating,' said Cameron, getting up.

'Wait…wait,' said Jeffrey, leaning forward and covering his forehead with the palm of his hand. 'The photographs are obviously mine,' he said, defeated.

'Should the identity of Edward Collins also be obvious to us?' replied Justin.

'You know full-well it's me,' sighed Lord Keating.

'Well, we got there eventually,' said Justin. 'Listen, sir…a piece of advice. If you're going to use a pseudonym in future, please make sure that you cover the invented person's tracks as well, otherwise all of the paths might just lead us back to the same place.'

'I shall keep that in mind,' he replied.

'Still, no harm done,' said Justin. 'So, these were all taken in your properties; is that correct?'

'Yes, it is.'

'And for what or whom were they intended? Like I say, the creation and distribution of pornographic material is illegal in this country, sir. So, what did you intend to do with them?'

'I don't know,' he shrugged. 'This is a private matter between consenting adults.'

'Yes…a number of them it seems,' said Justin, perusing the images. 'Who is the man in some of the images?'

'It's just someone she knows,' he answered. 'I don't even know his name.'

'Is there any chance he could be linked to the death of Miss Smith?' said Justin.

'I doubt it very much – he's just some little rat from Bermondsey.'

'And are these all for your personal use?'

'Of course they are. What are you implying?' Jeffrey got up off of the couch and went over to the window.

'How exactly do you go about using these personally, sir?' added Cameron, unable to resist. Jeffrey ignored him.

'Are those journalists still outside, sir?' said Justin.

'Yes, they are.'

'Would you mind sitting back down? There's plenty of time to devote to the press, and I think we have some other things to discuss. I spoke to a gentleman from Peters and Peters – your builders, I believe.'

'What on earth are you talking about now?' he said, moving over to the decanter and re-filling his glass.

'That work you were having done – a two-way mirror in the ladies' bathroom, wasn't it?' said Justin.

'Don't be ridiculous!'

'Mr Peters says he has the receipt. He didn't sound too happy when I spoke to him. But anyway, this is a digression. Like I say, unlike the press, we're not interested in any of this. That's for the vice squad – if, of course, we should decide to involve them. We're only interested in the murder of young Catherine Smith. Please do come and sit down, sir.'

Jeffrey grudgingly returned to the couch.

'Have you ever been to a brothel, M'Lord?' said Cameron, as soon as his shoulders touched the backrest.

'What!'

'A brothel, sir,' he repeated. 'They're illegal in the UK, but you can still find them if you look hard enough.'

Jeffrey stared down at the whisky in his glass.

'I don't think I've ever been so insulted in all my life,' he said slowly, battling to control his rage.

'See, we have reason to believe that you frequent such a place in Berwick Street, in Soho,' said Justin. 'Does that ring any bells?'

'I'll ring your bloody bell in a minute! How dare you! What in the world would make you suggest such a thing?'

'Well, we've already seen you there for a start,' replied Justin.

'You most certainly have not!' he replied in an authoritative tone. He stood back up. 'I consider that a slanderous accusation and I'm warning you, I will have the both of you thrown out – not just from my property, but from the police force as well.'

'Please sit down, sir,' replied Justin. Jeffrey's eyes were tearing into him.

Justin turned to Cameron, sighing.

'You know what, even I'm starting to get bored with these games,' he said, then turned his attention back to Jeffrey. 'I think it's time we started talking like adults, don't you?' He stood up. 'The truth is this: we had you followed from outside this house directly to the brothel in Soho. You were holding an envelope just like this one. My guess is that it too held photographs. I myself, in fact, waited for you to come out, minus the photographs, and then I went inside. Once inside, I arranged a liaison with one of the girls, during which I got the information out of her that led to us finding photographic evidence of Catherine's corpse, along with the probable murder weapon.'

Jeffrey visibly sank back into the couch.

'We have Jack Gormally in custody,' continued Justin, 'charged with the murder, and I am very close to charging you with being an accessory to the act. Do you understand what I have just said?'

Jeffrey looked at him with an expression of genuine shock. The drink he was holding started to spill onto his lap. He righted the glass.

'Do you understand what I have just said to you?' repeated Justin. Jeffrey shook his head.

'No. Not really,' he said, dumbfounded.

'What were you doing at the brothel?' said Cameron.

'I just...I went to see a girl,' he replied. His eyes had taken on a glazed look, as though he were only semi-conscious. Justin decided to push him.

'Was there any other reason you went there? You're better off telling me now,' he said. Jeffrey looked up at him, his mouth open. He shook his head.

'No...I just went to see the girl,' he said.

'It's somewhat of a coincidence, don't you think, that you led us directly to the place where Catherine had been previously put to work, and that the owners just happen to be implicated in her murder, which just happened to take place in an apartment owned by you?' said Justin.

Jeffrey shook his head.

'I...don't really understand what's going on,' he stammered.

'You know Jack Gormally, don't you?' said Cameron, taking over the questioning.

'I know someone called Gormally from that place, yes,' he replied.

'Do you know a man by the name of George Vardy?'

'Vaguely. He's a jazz club owner.'

'Aye, well he also owns the brothel.'

'I don't know about that,' said Jeffrey, still looking dazed.

'Have a drink.' Cameron pointed to what was left of the whisky in his glass.

'No. I'm all right,' he replied.

'How are your finances, Lord Keating?' said Justin, re-joining the conversation.

'Fine. I…they're fine.'

'I'm not so sure about that. There are rumours concerning your money troubles, and I have good reason to believe them.'

'Well, everyone's been hit by this government. We're selling the Green Park flat – we'll manage.'

'But you can't be seen to sell the property while these vicious rumours about your finances are going around, can you, Lord Keating?'

'I can do what I want with it,' he pleaded, 'it's my flat.'

'Yes, but life isn't that simple, is it? Not if you want the best price, and not when you have your good name to uphold.'

'What do you mean?'

'The murder took place in your apartment. You needed cash, and they wanted revenge on the girl who absconded. Now that this has happened, you can safely sell-up without losing face. Is there any part of that which is not true, Lord Keating?'

'I can't say that there is,' he replied. 'Apart from the cash. Who wants to pay top price for an apartment in which a murder has taken place?'

Justin looked at him but remained silent. He had to admit, Jeffrey did have a point.

'But you're right, I do have financial worries,' continued Lord Keating. 'That's what the photographs were for.'

'So they weren't for personal use after all?' said Justin.

'No. I was selling them on to Mr Gormally. He has access to certain trade routes.'

'Couldn't they make their own images?' said Cameron. 'They're hardly short of models.'

'Not of this kind. This is "high-class stuff" apparently: the clothes, the grounds. There's a certain market for it.'

'I see what you mean,' said Cameron. 'You sound like a bit of an expert. Can I just ask you, sir; do you ever tell the truth about anything?'

Jeffrey no longer seemed to be listening.

'Did you have anything to do with them finding out about Catherine's whereabouts?' asked Justin.

'Of course I didn't,' he replied, 'Stephen and Catherine were due to get married and I had already arranged the ceremony. Why would I do that if I intended for her to die?'

'It provides a good cover,' said Cameron.

'This is all too much. I need some air,' said Jeffrey.

'You stay there,' said Cameron.

'Did the brothel owners pay you for the information?' said Justin.

'I didn't tell them anything,' he insisted.

'But you knew about Catherine's past?' Jeffrey sank further back into the couch.

'Yes, I did,' he said.

'How?'

'A friend of mine came round for dinner and he recognised her. He told me afterwards. I asked her if it was true and she didn't deny it.'

'Name?' Cameron demanded.

'John Aston – Lord Aston.'

'Of course it would be,' said Cameron, noting it down.

'See Jeffrey, none of this is making you look any less guilty,' said Justin. 'Every lead we follow seems to bring us straight back to you.'

'I know that. But I swear to you, I had absolutely nothing to do with that girl's death.'

'Under the law you are accountable under common purpose; meaning that if the court thinks you did have something to do with it, and if the death can be shown to suit your aims as well as those of the murderers – which, let's face it, it quite easily can – then you will receive the death penalty.'

Jeffrey looked bewildered.

'Listen to me,' Justin continued, 'this is important: I can almost guarantee that you'll receive a reduced sentence only if you agree to testify against the actual murderers. That means both Gormally and Vardy.'

'But I had nothing to do with it,' Jeffrey insisted.

'I don't know whether you did, or you didn't – not directly anyway. But the court won't see that. If you don't agree to help us, then I'm afraid there's nothing more I can do for you.'

Justin watched Jeffrey as he considered the offer, and for a moment he would have bet good money that Jeffrey was going to comply.

'It has nothing to do with me,' replied Jeffrey eventually, sitting up. He seemed to draw strength from somewhere. 'And I fail to see how any court could find otherwise.'

'Let's discuss something else,' said Justin, getting up from the couch. Even Jeffrey could see that his patience was now wearing dangerously thin. 'What I believe happened is that you tried to advance your relations with young Catherine in some way, shortly before you decided to get rid of Stephen. Is that correct?'

'Absolutely not!'

'Using my better judgement,' said Justin, 'I'm going to say that it is true. So why didn't Stephen take Catherine with him when you asked him to leave? Why do you think he was so eager to come back?'

'You would have to ask him about that,' said Jeffrey. 'Maybe he's the one you should be questioning anyway.'

'What do you mean by that?'

'None of this has anything to do with me,' he repeated. 'Maybe Stephen had something to do with it.'

'Why would he want his own fiancé dead?' said Justin.

'Well, how would you feel if you found out your future wife used to moonlight in a bordello?' he replied.

Justin had moved round to the back of the couch and was now leaning on the backrest.

'Is this how he felt about it?' he said. He came and sat back down.

'I'm not saying anything. I had, and still have, very little to do with either of them.'

'But you paid for their wedding?'

'I thought that that way it would be easier to get rid of the pair of them at once.'

'I think something happened between yourself and Mr Hollis, which is why he left, and I also think there must be a reason why you accepted him back so easily. I'm guessing that the problem was to do with young Catherine – something happened which Stephen objected to – and so you told him to leave.'

'That's absolute rubbish, just like everything else you talk.'

'See, if she were my fiancé,' said Cameron, 'I don't think I'd be comfortable leaving her here with the likes of you.'

'Is it true that Stephen knew about your trips to the brothel,' said Justin, 'and about you and Sandra, then blackmailed you by threatening to tell Lady Keating about it all, in order to regain his position?'

'If you know all this then don't you think he's the one you should be questioning? I had no concern with that young couple. I should have gotten rid of them both! The same goes for that bloody apartment!'

'But you couldn't, could you? You needed a good excuse to dispose of all three of them. Then, when you found out about Catherine's past; bingo! There's your answer.'

'Look, I'm telling you the truth!' said Jeffrey, his voice rising now in anger. 'I've told you everything I know.' He got to his feet.

'Do you enjoy surrounding yourself with vulnerable people, Jeffrey?' said Justin, his voice also rising as he himself rose from the couch. 'A bit of a coincidence, isn't it? Catherine had her past, your wife lost her parents, even the cook seems to have suffered terribly. God only knows about Sandra–'

'Now, I want the pair of you out of here!' he said, staring angrily at Justin.

'Does it make you feel powerful, Jeffrey? Is that what it is? Easier to control aren't they, when they're in a position of weakness? Don't tell me you do it out of the goodness of your heart.'

'I have given you both more than enough of my time. You disgust me, the pair of you, now get out! Get out of my house right now!' he shouted.

'We still have business here, I'm afraid, sir,' said Justin.

Seeing that they had no intention of leaving, Jeffrey turned and marched towards the door.

'Please don't leave the property for the time being, sir,' said Cameron, as the door slammed shut. Lord Keating's footsteps shrank away along the hall.

'What do we do now, sir?' said Cameron.

'We can take him in on pornography charges if we haven't got enough to charge him as an accessory.' He paused for a moment. 'He does have a point though. If Stephen did blackmail him, he could be capable of doing much more.'

'No, I can't see that, sir. It's different if he was protecting his fiancé.'

'We could eventually take them both in anyway; the lesser charges for Lord Keating, and also Stephen on the grounds of blackmail, if we need to.'

'That's only of any use to us though if Jeffrey wants to aid the prosecution, sir. And Stephen doesn't deserve that if he's not involved in Catherine's murder.'

'It's not about what he deserves. It's about the law. I don't really know what to think of any of them anymore. I want to speak to Samuel again though, just quickly. I don't really believe Stephen had anything to do with Catherine's death; every fibre of my being tells me so. Hopefully we can find out what Samuel really thinks about the idea, and then we can go. Go and find him, will you?'

Cameron left the room, shutting the door behind him and leaving Justin with the ticking clock. Justin sat back and let his eyes drift over the two adjacent walls that were covered floor to ceiling with leather-bound books. A rolling ladder was perched at the far end of the room, looking as though it was rarely used. He got up and went over to it, and confirmed his suspicions by finding a thin layer of dust on the upper treads.

On the opposing wall hung a couple of large gilt-framed portraits; proud stances and noble countenances – ancestors of Lord Keating. Below them, just above the oak panelling, was a small impressionist painting which seemed to stand out from all the others. It was a Menzel piece, or so Justin thought, a duplicate of course, the original of which, if he remembered correctly, was still hanging in a German museum. The young girl looked timidly out from the canvas, lighting her view with the flame of a candle, while behind her there sat a conspicuous shadowy figure, the face hidden in the half-light. He followed her gaze across the room, towards the door, and past it to the whisky decanter. Hearing no footsteps or voices nearby, he went over and poured himself an inch into one of the wide crystal glasses and swallowed it in one. He shook the glass to drain the last drips of it out onto the floor then, hearing a sound from outside, he went back over to the couch and sat down.

There was a knock at the door and it swung gently open.

'It's a bit quiet out there, sir,' said Cameron as he led Samuel over to the couch opposite him.

'Oh?' said Justin.

'Someone must have said something to upset M'Lord,' said Samuel, taking a seat. He did not look happy about it.

'Yes, well I imagine his moods probably cast quite a long shadow in this house,' said Justin. Samuel chose not to reply.

'All right, Samuel. I know you've not been here very long,' Justin began, 'but we need to know exactly what you've heard within the house in the time you've been here.'

'And from your time away with Mr Hollis as well,' added Cameron.

'How do you mean?' he replied.

'Let's start with Stephen, shall we?' said Justin. 'You've worked with him before, haven't you? At another house?'

'Very briefly,' he replied. 'We didn't know each other then.'

'Would you say that you do now?'

'As well as could be expected,' he said to Justin, with a meaningful glance.

'I'll presume that, because it was you who took him away from here straight after the tragic event, if anyone knows what kind of state he was in, it would be you.'

'Yes, I agree with that,' he said.

'So, how was he?'

Samuel grimaced at the ridiculousness of the question.

'How do you think, officer? He was in the kind of state you might expect after such an event; one of the deepest pain and shock.'

'What did he talk about while you were away?' said Cameron.

'He didn't say anything much for the first couple of days, which came as no surprise. Then, once I had managed to coax him into talking, he just kind of broke down.'

'Did he say much to you about Catherine during this time?' said Justin.

'Of course, it was all about Catherine. He was in a total state of shock, totally bewildered. He spoke about their plans for marriage and the move he had planned for them, to go to America…'

'And it all seemed totally genuine?' said Cameron.

'Absolutely,' he replied. 'I can't believe you'd think he had played any part in it.'

'We didn't say that,' said Justin.

'It's what your questions implied.'

'No, not really. We just need to be sure.' There was a short pause then Justin continued. 'Moving back to the house: has there been anything unusual – anything anyone has said or done that has aroused your suspicions in any way? Made you think that there might be something going on behind the scenes that you don't know about?' Samuel smiled.

'Well, I'm sure there are many things that I don't know about, but I think I'm probably better off that way. Don't you?'

'Please think carefully, Samuel; this is important,' said Justin. He turned to Cameron. 'Would you mind leaving us alone for a few minutes? Just go and make sure there's nobody outside listening in. Check along the hallway if you would.'

'Aye,' said Cameron, looking a little surprised. 'I'll wait for a knock on the door when you want me to come back in,' he said.

'Make sure you check all of the rooms along the hall,' said Justin, as Cameron left the room.

Justin listened for his footsteps to fade away before continuing. Then he leant forward, looking Samuel in the eye.

'Listen to me. I'm not sure exactly where your loyalties lie, but it's vitally important that you tell me the truth about this.'

'Of course,' he replied. 'And my loyalties, for that matter, are with precisely the people I need them to be,' he added, hoping to make his point clear.

'Good. Now, is there any possibility in your mind that Stephen might have had anything to do with Catherine's murder?' Samuel shook his head.

'Absolutely, definitely not,' he said. 'When I managed to get the words out of him he was inconsolable. I didn't know what to do with him at first; he wasn't making any sense. I thought I might need to call for a doctor…I thought he might need some kind of psychiatric assistance.'

'And he definitely didn't say anything to raise your suspicions?'

'Nothing at all. I've seen him at his lowest ebb – it's absolutely inconceivable to me that his intentions towards her were anything other than one hundred percent genuine.'

'All right. Thank you, Samuel. I appreciate your help. What about your feelings regarding Lord Jeffrey?'

'Well, he's no Lord Henry, I can tell you that. He wants the doors left ajar at all times – I think it's his paranoia.'

'Is that what it is? I thought there was something a bit odd going on.'

'Yes, well…he's quite the opposite in fact to Lord Henry.' Justin smiled.

'Yes, I'm aware of that, but can you think of anything at all that might suggest a link between him and the murder?'

'I have to admit, the thought had crossed my mind,' said Samuel, after a short pause. 'I don't know why. It may just be the fact that I don't think he's at all fond of me. And I suppose the feeling is mutual.'

'I can't say I blame you,' replied Justin. He stood up. 'That'll be all, I think. Thank you, Samuel. Please can you send Detective Cameron back in on your way out.'

'Hopefully we shall meet again,' said Samuel, offering his hand. Justin shook it.

'Under better circumstances, I'm sure we will,' said Justin. Samuel turned and left the room.

Cameron came back in with a look of amusement on his face.

'Did you work your magic, sir?' he said. Justin shot him an aggrieved look.

'He's certain of Stephen's innocence.'

'And he's definitely telling the truth?' said Cameron.

'I think so. I'm pretty good when it comes to reading people.'

'Aye. Well, I wouldn't want to read too much into that filthy sod,' said Cameron.

'Yes. Quite,' he replied.

'He's probably right though,' said Cameron. 'Mr Hollis doesn't seem the type to be involved in something like this. So, what do we do now then, sir?'

'I don't know. All we can prove against Jeffrey is the pornography charge. That'll have to do if there's nothing else. But it's far from ideal. We'd need very strong evidence against someone in his position, especially if we're to make him stick his neck out and testify against Vardy, knowing full-well that in doing so he'll be setting himself up for a long stretch as well. If we can't do that then we may as well leave it. We might just have to pin it all on Gormally and let this one go.'

'Aye, it's not easy though.'

'No, it isn't. Anyway, let's get out of here; I've had enough.'

Samuel left the dining room and headed straight back up to his room, ignoring the footsteps coming along the hall behind him. He was in no mood to speak to Sandra, nor anyone else for that matter. He went in and closed the door, turning the key in the lock to keep it shut.

There was a knock at the door. Ignoring the disturbance, he opened his wardrobe to see if there was any clean linen up on the shelf, but there was none.

Another knock came.

'Oh, for God's sake,' he said to himself in a whisper, as he remained dead still. Surely whoever it was would get the message, he hoped. He would tell them later that he had been asleep, even if it was an obvious lie.

A third knock came, even louder this time. He crossed the room and sat down on the bed, but in doing so, made one of the floorboards squeak loudly. Cursing it, he got up and went to the door.

'Can I come in?' said Stephen quietly, the moment it opened a touch.

'It's not really a good time at present, Stephen. Can we just talk later?' he replied.

Stephen pushed the door fully open and strode in.

'I need to talk now,' he said, ordering Samuel to close the door. He did so. 'I need to know what you told them.'

'I didn't tell them anything,' said Samuel, sounding very irritated and surprised at Stephen's audacity. 'What's got into you? I told you I wouldn't, so there was nothing to tell,' he added.

'You know what I'm talking about. I've got enough problems without those two getting their wires crossed and hounding me!'

'I told them nothing you wouldn't have wished me to. I told them that you are completely innocent,' said Samuel, in the kind of light-hearted tone that somehow made the words sound disingenuous.

'I hope you did!' said Stephen, fixing him with an intimidating stare.

'Of course I did,' replied Samuel calmly, refusing to back away and relinquish territory. 'What's the matter with you?'

A tense moment seemed to stretch itself out interminably, as Stephen refused to answer. Finally, he left the room.

Very little was said in the car on the way back to London, though neither of them noticed. The change of scenery, as the open fields gave way to an increasing trickle of suburbia, brought them both out of their private thoughts.

A pub caught Justin's eye; a light from within making it look like it might be open. He checked his watch – it was already past afternoon closing. They drove on.

Cameron turned the car into the traffic at Parliament Square and they continued on towards The Yard.

'How long do you think we can keep Gormally in?' said Cameron, as Justin's attention drifted back into the car.

'It depends on Vardy. If he testifies like he says he will, then it's no bother. We haven't got enough on him though, so why would he keep his word? Otherwise, we can hit Gormally with the pornography charges as soon as there's any talk of us having to release him. But we'll need to bring Keating in on the same then play him off against Gormally, and I don't really want to do that just yet.'

'You don't think Jeffrey might abscond?'

'No, he's too high profile. He won't go anywhere. I think we should have a drink when we get back to the office and have another think about it.'

'Sounds good to me, sir.'

Back at The Yard they sat waiting for Andrews to pack up and leave for the day. Justin looked up, hearing the door go.

Andrews looked across at him with a half-smile then nodded and left without a word.

Justin opened his bottom drawer and pulled out the whisky bottle. It was a new one, almost full. Cameron appeared at his desk, fully prepared, holding out his coffee cup. Justin poured him a decent slug.

'Cheers.' He raised his cup and they both downed their measures. With a nod towards the bottle, he permitted Cameron to refill them, then sat back and lit a cigarette.

'There must be something we're overlooking,' he said, as he took a deep drag and slowly let out the grey smoke.

'Aye,' nodded Cameron. He looked tired.

Justin turned over the sheet of paper he had been writing on and started to scribble something.

'Now, I've narrowed it down to four possibilities – if it wasn't Jeffrey of course. One, is that Sandra has told someone else – which could be anyone, possibly the man in the photographs – and they tipped off the brothel.

Two, is that Jeffrey's friend John Aston has tipped them off, which is quite possible if he still frequents the place. He could even have done so without realising the ramifications of what he was saying. These explanations, of course, don't tell us how they knew that Catherine would be alone at the flat.

Three, is that she was seeing someone else outside without our knowledge. I'm not too sure about that, but then I don't really know what to think anymore,' he said, and downed some more whisky. He reached for the bottle. Cameron's eyes widened.

'It's been a long day,' was the excuse Justin offered, adding, 'Help yourself.' He continued, 'Four,' Justin felt himself hesitate to say the words, 'is that Stephen was in on it.'

'Nah, it wasn't him, sir,' said Cameron.

'You're sure of that?'

'Sure as I can be. There's nothing in my mind that would point to his involvement in it, not from what he said or from the way he was acting. Even what Samuel said suggests to me it wasn't him. Which makes me think, sir – what about Samuel?'

Justin shook his head.

'No, it definitely wasn't him,' he said.

'What makes you so sure, sir?'

'He'd only just met her – all of them in fact. I'd be very surprised, and probably quite worried, if it turned out to be him.'

'Didn't he know Stephen from before though, sir?'

'Yes, that's true. But unless he's had some long-kept secret designs on Stephen, I think we can rule him out.' Having said it, he now wondered if it could be possible.

'So anyway,' said Cameron, interrupting his train of thought. 'What do we reckon about Stephen?'

'I honestly don't think he was involved. The wedding was arranged, he'd left the house and then came back, seemingly just to be with her. He had bought tickets to America… There's nothing I can see that would point directly to him.'

'That sounds about right to me, sir,' he said with a sigh.

'Oh well, sod it,' said Justin. He looked at his watch. Cameron reached for the bottle and poured himself another measure, just in case Inspector Lamoureaux was thinking of going home.

'You can certainly put them away, sir – if you don't mind me saying.'

'Do you blame me?' replied Justin. 'Besides, I'll make sure I work it off at the gym.' He got up to stretch his legs.

'Where did you learn to box?' asked Cameron.

'School. Then the army. It's the best thing I ever did.'

The door opened and in came a uniformed constable.

'Sorry to bother you, sir, but there's someone here to see you,' he said, addressing Justin.

'Fine. Bring him in.'

'It's a young lady, sir, I'll bring *her* in.' He left the office, closing the door behind him.

'Who the hell is that?' said Justin.

'Better not be my fucking wife,' said Cameron. Justin picked up the coffee cups and put them away in a drawer, along with the whisky bottle.

The door opened, and Lady Keating came into the room. Both Cameron and Justin stood up. She walked up to the desk, greeted them both and then sat down. Cameron pushed her chair in behind her.

'I shan't keep you long,' she said.

'What can we do for you, Lady Keating?' said Justin. She looked at him for a moment, as though wondering if she was about to make a huge mistake, then turned her eyes to her lap.

'I think I can help you with your enquiries after all,' she said, 'but I don't want to be involved in a court case, in naming names and having to give evidence.' Justin subtly drew a pad and pen towards him. 'It would bring all sorts of unwanted attention to the house,' she continued.

Justin looked up at her, a little confused.

'Well, I'm afraid that's going to happen anyway, given the circumstances.'

'Is there no way of keeping things quiet?' she said.

'The press is already involved, unfortunately,' said Justin, receiving a knowing glance from his colleague. 'What's done is done, I'm afraid.'

'Can I get you anything?' said Cameron. Justin gave him a look which told him to keep quiet.

'I know who was involved in organising Catherine's murder,' she said quietly. 'I think I have done all along. But if you try to draw me into all this then I shall deny that I ever told you anything,' she insisted.

'Take your time, Joanna,' said Justin, trying to contain his excitement. The pen twitched between his fingers. 'Get the Lady some water,' he said to Cameron.

There was silence while Cameron was away. He returned, placing a glass on the desk in front of her.

'There are some things I think you should know,' she began, 'things that have been going on at the house.'

248

'It would be good to hear your side of things,' replied Justin. 'Your husband has not exactly been forthcoming, though the conversation we had with Mr Hollis was very enlightening.'

'I see,' she replied.

'Is there anything concerning your husband that you think we ought to know about?'

'Well…where would I begin?' she said.

'Jeffrey and Stephen,' he said. 'I understand there's been some tension between them. Can you tell us why that is?'

She looked at Justin in a way that suggested she might be having second thoughts.

'I don't know about that,' she replied. 'But I know it was something to do with Catherine. I'm not sure of the details. Anyway, I'm not here to tell tales on people.'

'Then, if you don't mind me asking, what are you here for?' said Justin.

'To do the right thing.' She looked down at her lap again. 'Maybe I shouldn't have come…'

'It's all right,' he said, 'everything you say will remain off the record. We just need to know if we are on the right track.' He decided to change tack. 'Let's start outside of the house, shall we? Jeffrey's away a lot, isn't he? Can you tell us what you know about that?'

'Not much, I'm afraid. Although perhaps I should be grateful for that. Things are easier when he's away, as you can imagine. To be honest, as I'm sure you've already been told, the relationship between us has been over for a while. But still, things are easier when Jeffrey's not there. It's been very strained in the house, but obviously we've done all we can to keep our business our own.'

'Yes, I understand,' Justin replied.

'Was it his involvement with other women that put an end to your relationship?' he ventured. She looked back at him a little startled, as though she were not willing to let the extent of her naivety be known.

'I didn't know he had been involved with anyone else until recently,' she replied, 'and I'm not sure I know that much about it now.'

'Well, he's a free man, evidently, when he's away from the house. Prostitutes, trips to brothels, trips downstairs…' Justin was willing to throw everything he could at her now if it meant he could win her over. She looked back at him as though she could not take it all in.

'I suppose I should have expected that,' she replied after some time.

'In any relationship, Joanna, it's fair to expect some loyalty,' he said gently.

'Who knows?' she replied. 'What did you mean when you mentioned "trips downstairs"?'

Justin coughed uncomfortably, suddenly aware of his impropriety. It had been the whisky talking.

'I'm sorry to bring this up, but did you know anything about his involvement with your other maid, Sandra?'

She paused before answering.

'*Trips downstairs*,' she said, looking past him over his shoulder. 'Oh, I see what you mean. How quaint, after what I've just told you,' she said bitterly. Justin wished he could take the words back. She sighed and sat back. 'Given what you've told me, I shouldn't be surprised. I suppose I didn't want to know about it.'

'But you did know?' he said, pushing on.

'I must have suspected something was up. Somewhere in the back of my mind I must have known of his "trips downstairs," as you so eloquently put it. I suppose I was happy just to ignore things so long as they remained reasonably comfortable – so long as there was a chance of getting things back to how they had been before.'

'So, you think he had something to do with Catherine's murder?'

'That's what I'm telling you,' she said. Then she thought for a moment. 'I shouldn't be saying this. I don't know what's possible and what isn't any more. I shouldn't even have come here,' she said anxiously. 'I suppose it's all very amusing to you with his *trips downstairs.*'

'I'm very sorry,' said Justin. 'It's just a phrase I use out of habit. Nobody's thinking anything bad of you.'

'Well, I just wish he would've gone – and taken her with him if he had to. I wish he'd never come back up. I'm leaving now.'

'You're holding something back, Lady Keating,' said Justin sternly. 'If there's anything you know, then you need to tell us it now!'

'I've already said enough. I don't want to be dragged into all of this, and I'm certainly not here for your entertainment!' She rose from her chair. Justin grabbed hold of her arm.

'You're already in all of this,' he said. 'Listen to me, Joanna. We can offer you full protection if you help us get the information we need. You need not testify against your husband.'

'Testify against Jeffrey?' she said. Saying the words out loud seemed to have startled her, as though it all suddenly seemed too real. She looked bewildered. Slowly, she sat back down. Justin could see the thoughts tumbling through her mind. 'No, I must go now,' she said, getting up.

'Please, Lady Keating,' said Justin, 'let's just discuss this a little while longer…' But she had already turned and was gone, slamming the door shut behind her.

Justin poured them both one more measure.

'This'll have to be last,' said Cameron. The door opened, and DI Lisson appeared.

'I want a word with you, Lamoureaux,' he said. 'What's this I hear about some fine-looking woman at this manor house? No wonder you wanted to keep me away from the place.'

'I think I've just scared her off,' Justin admitted. Lisson looked down at the whisky bottle sitting on his desk.

'Well, I wouldn't say no,' said Lisson. Justin looked up to see that he had already found a coffee cup and was aiming it at the rim of the bottle. Justin poured him a measure.

'Cheers,' he said, and they both drank.

'Here, what did you say to her to make her run off like that? Then I'll know not to try it,' said Lisson.

'Oh, nothing much,' he replied. 'She's just a girl really, who got caught up in things. She didn't want to give evidence anyway. She even asked if it would be possible for us to keep things quiet! With the press outside her house and with Jeffrey's public profile! How ridiculous can you get?'

'Aye, she did say that,' Cameron confirmed with a smile. 'That's some naivety.'

'Or wishful thinking,' added Justin. He poured himself another drink. 'I suppose if she's been in denial this long—'

'So what are you going to do now?' said Lisson.

'Keep pushing Lord Keating till he cracks, I suppose,' said Justin. 'To be honest, I'm starting to enjoy it.'

'Well, I'll be with you from now on,' said Lisson. 'I'm not getting anything out of that scumbag downstairs…and if the lady of the house lives up to her reputation—'

'If you insist,' replied Justin. 'But I think you'll find that the maid would be a better match for you. I suppose it didn't help much, you letting Vardy off the hook the way you did.'

'It's better one of them than none of them,' he replied. 'We've all been waiting around for you to work your magic at your end, but it looks like you've fouled it up.'

Justin shifted himself uncomfortably in his chair.

'You know what I think, anyway,' Lisson continued, 'and I'll say it again. It's odds-on the girl's fiancé was involved all along. It's always the same, especially when you take her past into consideration. We want to get hold of him before he pisses off back down to – where was it again?'

'Brighton,' said Cameron.

'Brighton. You're gonna regret it if we don't.'

'I think there's more chance of him pissing off over to America, if anywhere,' replied Justin. 'But anyway, he's not going to. We know for a fact it was Lord Keating; his wife just pretty much told us so.'

'She said that, did she?' said Lisson, his voice taking a less aggressive tone.

'Pretty much,' replied Justin, 'but she refused to help us any further.'

Cameron sat sipping his whisky and staring off into the distance.

'She said that she wishes he had never come back up,' he said.

'That's right,' replied Justin. His face froze as he thought about it for a moment. 'You mean she wishes he would never come back up – from his trips downstairs.'

'Nah, the way she said it, I'm pretty sure she meant it in the past tense,' replied Cameron.

'Well, so what? When he'd taken his trips downstairs, she wishes he'd never come back up.'

'But taken the girl with him?'

'What the fuck are you two talking about?' said Lisson. They both ignored him.

'Downstairs?' said Justin, looking confused.

'No, it wasn't that, sir,' said Cameron. 'She wished he'd taken the girl with him if he had to.'

'Meaning Sandra,' said Justin.

'She wouldn't have been referring to Catherine by any chance, would she?' he replied.

'Stephen,' said Justin, looking straight ahead at Lady Keating's vacated chair. 'Get the car round,' he said to Cameron, as he rose from his desk.

The wine had been set to chill, and the places laid for dinner, out at the house in Horsham.

'Will we be on time?' asked Stephen, standing just inside the kitchen door.

'Of course we will,' replied the cook, her annoyance evident in her tone. 'You can start serving in fifteen minutes.'

Stephen let the door swing shut as he left the kitchen and went off along the hallway.

'Good,' he whispered to himself. He had been finding it hard to keep his thoughts on anything for very long lately, but now his focus was back. 'I'll get ready to serve the wine,' he added, leaving the empty hallway and entering the dining room.

Stephen had been early in setting out the two places for supper; one for Lady Keating at one end of the table, the other for her husband several yards away from her, down at the other end. When they ate together – which seemed to be an increasingly rare occurrence – the long, polished mahogany rectangle separated them like two rival lovers preparing for a duel.

Sandra came in through the side-door, pushing a trolley on which sat a bottle of cognac and the bottle of chilled wine.

'Is M'Lord on his way in?' Stephen asked her. He picked up a serving napkin from the trolley and reached out towards the uncorked bottle that was laying on ice.

'Probably in a minute or two. He's on the vodka though, so I wouldn't pour the wine just yet,' she replied.

'Very well,' he said, withdrawing his hand and carefully replacing the napkin.

Stephen had paid special attention this evening to the exact positioning of each napkin and each piece of cutlery on the pristine white table cloth. He wanted everything to be perfect. He moved Lord Jeffrey's chair out just a little further – just a mere fraction of an inch – and squared it with the table, in preparation for his arrival. He checked the position of the bread plate and its diagonal dimensions from the exact centre of the placing then smoothed the napkin which was already perfectly folded and positioned directly below it. Sandra leant on the trolley, watching him.

'What are you doing?' she said, breaking his deep concentration and startling him a little. He felt his heart skip out of its natural rhythm.

'Setting the places, of course. What are *you* doing?'

'Watching you acting all weird,' she said, then turned her head away and glanced at the grandfather clock. It was seven minutes to seven.

'Why don't you go and wait outside?' he said offhandedly. 'Or go and see if he wants anything. He doesn't usually turn you down.'

'That's true enough,' she said, and stuck out her tongue at him. 'I'll be in the drawing room, if you want me,' she said over her shoulder as she left the room.

The clock behind him was ticking. He knew it was madness, but he simply could not stop himself from checking again and again that the bread knife was on the exact angle that was expected. Its rounded tip glistened benignly, having been perfectly polished, reflecting the light that shone down onto it from the chandelier. He looked across at the wine bottle again and then at the clock, and his pulse quickened even further. The empty room with the table perfectly set, the cutlery glistening and the polished rays of the oak wall panels spreading and weaving out opulently; it was a fitting scene for a just revenge.

The door opened and in walked Lord Keating. Sandra had been right; he was on the vodka. He looked a little tipsy. Something about him brought life into the room as he entered, breaking the stillness in a way that was quite intimidating. Sandra followed him in.

Jeffrey looked at the place that had been set out for Lady Keating and waved his free hand towards it.

'You can get rid of that one – my wife will eat later,' he said. 'God only knows where she's got to this evening.'

Sandra began loading the plates back onto the trolley while Stephen neatly pulled back the chair for Jeffrey to sit down.

'It looks smarter than usual,' said Jeffrey, laying his glass down clumsily so that some of the liquid spilt out onto the table cloth. 'What's the occasion – have we slaughtered the prize pig?'

'I believe it's venison, M'Lord,' replied Stephen.

'Oh good. Make sure mine's rare – the bloodier the better.'

'I'm sure you won't be disappointed, M'Lord. Should I serve the wine?'

'Yes, do so.'

Stephen picked up the napkin and bottle then moved slowly back to where Jeffrey was sitting and poured him a glass.

'Why are your hands shaking, Stephen? Have you been at the whisky again?' he said.

'No, M'Lord,' he replied, steadying his pouring hand with the other. 'I might have gotten a bit of a chill when I went outside earlier.'

'In mid-summer? It's as warm as anything. In fact, open a window, would you?' said Jeffrey, despite the fact that he was feeling not in the least bit hot. He pulled his red silk cravat away from the skin of his neck and poked in the end of his napkin. Stephen opened a window.

From outside, he could hear the sound of a car racing up the gravel drive and crunching to a halt.

'I should think that's her,' said Jeffrey. 'You can leave that place setting where it is,' he said to Sandra, who had just finished putting it all back on the trolley. 'Go and see if she's ready for supper, will you?' he added. Sandra turned, leaving the trolley where it was, and left the room.

Good, thought Stephen as he watched the door swing shut behind her. That'll spare her the scene.

Jeffrey reached out for the wine glass.

If I do it now, I'll also spare Lady Keating the sight of the killing, thought Stephen. He could hold the door closed if he had to and keep everyone out until the struggle was over. He reached down and felt the blade of the knife in his pocket, running his fingers along the serrated edge and then back up onto the polished handle. His fingers shook as they tightened their grip.

Jeffrey tilted his head back as he brought the glass to his lips, exposing his neck for a second at the perfect angle. It was just as Stephen had pictured it. Suddenly, Lord Keating turned around.

'What are you doing, standing there behind me?' said Jeffrey. He must have heard his breathing. 'I might expect it from that other little pervert,' he added.

Stephen took a step backwards.

'Where is he today, anyway?' continued Jeffrey, turning back around to face the table.

Stephen's hand and the knife began to emerge again from his pocket just as the door opened.

'Stephen!'

It was Inspector Lamoureaux. The knife shot back into his pocket. DC Cameron appeared in the doorway next to Justin.

'Where's Lady Keating?' said Justin.

'Do you mind!' said Lord Keating. Justin turned to him.

'Quickly! Where's your wife?'

'She's not here!' he said belligerently. 'What the bloody hell do you think you're doing?! I–'

'I said, where is she?' Justin shouted.

'She drove into London earlier today. I thought that was her now but–'

'I know that,' replied Justin, 'but why's her car now sitting at the end of the driveway?'

Jeffrey got up from his chair, went over to the window and looked out towards the archway. Sure enough, her black Citroen was perched on the grass verge underneath the cover of the nearby trees.

'It can't be,' said Jeffrey, 'she's…'

Sandra came back into the room.

'Lady Keating's upstairs,' she said. 'She's not been back long – she came in through the kitchen.'

Justin turned to Stephen.

'Come with me!' he said. Stephen followed without a word.

'Now, just wait a minute!' came Jeffrey's voice from the dining room doorway, as Justin ran up the stairs with Cameron and Stephen following close behind. But they had already reached the landing.

They turned and shot down the hallway, past each of the half-open doors that led only onto darkness. Behind only one of them – the only one that was closed – there was a light visible through the gap at the door's edge.

Joanna Keating was the picture of calm as her mind raced through all she would need for the inevitable travails ahead. Her small brown leather suitcase was lying open on the bed, and into it she flung two diamond rings and a tangled coil of glistening bluish pearls, which landed softly on top of the crumpled shades of black satin and oriental silk.

She looked up at herself in the mirror, her creaseless dress and her evening bag; its black beads glistening modestly in the room's half-light. She was glad to see that she was successfully maintaining the appearance of self-possession. She had made a respectable go of things. Now, at last, it was time to leave.

The sound of raised voices came up from downstairs. Her eyes shot to the door as she listened carefully to the male tones; sharp and guttural, and increasing in volume, along with the rumble of footsteps that seemed to be getting closer to the door. She latched one of the buckles on the front of the suitcase and slid it down onto the rug next to the bed. The door swung open.

'Lady Keating,' said Justin breathlessly. Pausing at the door, he looked up and saw her standing peacefully at the foot of the bed, her hands folded neatly in front of her waist. 'May I ask what you are doing?' he said.

'I'm standing in my bedroom, Detective,' she stated calmly, as another suit appeared behind him in the doorway. 'And may I ask what the hell it is you think you're doing?'

The gentle goodness that had struck him the moment he first looked at her now seemed to have vanished. In its place was a threatening tranquillity and a lack of hesitation in her reply.

'I'm afraid you'll have to come with us,' he said, taking a step towards her, a little reticently.

'I'm sorting out a few belongings,' she replied, as if she had not heard him. 'I need to get away from here – for a while at least. It's been a tremendous strain, all that has happened.'

'I don't think you're going on any trips for the time being, Lady Keating,' he replied, 'and I think you know why.'

Stephen appeared in the doorway behind Justin. Joanna's eyes met his.

'Look, I can explain…' she began, looking again at Justin. She reached into her evening bag, her face retaining its look of calm as Justin stepped closer. She turned to him again.

'Stay where you are,' she said, her tone remaining gentle. Just visible in the half-light was the dark barrel of the pistol she was now pointing at Justin's chest. Justin froze.

'Don't come any closer,' she warned him. She turned to Stephen. 'I never wanted any of this to happen,' she said, still aiming the gun at Justin.

Jeffrey now appeared in the room, his napkin still fluttering from his collar. She cocked the gun.

'Joanna!' said Jeffrey, 'whatever are you doing?'

'Shut up!' she said flatly.

'Is that one of my pistols?' he replied, dumbfounded, his mouth hanging open. She altered the angle of her hand and aimed it at him.

'Shut – up!' she said again.

'Put the gun down, Lady Keating,' Justin said firmly. She pointed it at him again, then looked at each of the men in front of her.

'There are six bullets in this,' she said. 'Now, I'm taking my case from the floor and then I'm going out of this room through that doorway behind you.'

'Joanna!' said Jeffrey. She ignored him and looked at Justin again, and for the first time he got a hint of the maelstrom of suffering behind her eyes.

'All right,' said Justin, putting his hands up and stepping away from her towards the door. 'Everyone out of the room!'

Joanna knelt down and shifted the suitcase in front of her feet, taking neither her eyes, nor the gun, off of Justin. Slowly they moved out along the hall and onto the landing.

Stephen and Jeffrey sloped down the staircase side-by-side, both utterly bewildered. Justin followed. Cameron was the last one left on the landing. Joanna waved the gun at him.

'You too,' she said. He turned his back to her and descended the staircase. She kept the gun pointed at the two officers all the way.

'Keep your hands up where I can see them,' she said. Justin smiled acidly.

'I led men into gunfire for three straight years, Lady Keating,' he said, 'but now I surrender.'

They made their way down the stairs and towards the front door where the whole group of them then gathered. Again, Joanna waved the gun at them.

'All of you, outside,' she said, then turned. 'Where's Sandra?' she said, looking at Stephen.

'I don't know,' he replied quietly.

'*You* should know,' she said turning to Jeffrey, 'you spend enough time with her.'

Jeffrey looked back at her, his expression blank. He looked like he was about to faint.

'Go on, get out!' she said. The group stepped out under the portico, and then further out onto the gravel. She looked down the driveway and knew that she had left her black Citroen too far away to be of any use to her now. The blue Bugatti was parked nearby. She turned to Jeffrey.

'Give me your keys.'

Without even answering, and with a look of the deepest resignation, Lord Keating complied.

Stephen turned to her.

'I had no idea it was you,' he said. 'I had no idea that you knew anything about Catherine's past.'

'I hear everything in this house,' she replied, 'what with the bloody doors hanging open all the time. It's been the only benefit of Jeffrey's ridiculous paranoia.'

Her expression changed. It became sensitive once again; expressive of deep and genuine sympathy.

'I never meant for this to happen, Stephen,' she said, 'and I swear to you – I swear to God, I never knew she was pregnant.'

'What *did* you expect to happen?' Stephen replied.

'I just wanted her away from you…away from the both of us…so that we could get things back to how they were. That was all I cared about.'

'I told you long ago that it was finished,' he replied. 'Even on Sunday…'

Justin smiled to himself as all of the pieces fell into place.

'I know that,' she replied. 'And it was killing me; returning to formal tones and pretending that nothing had happened. But I hoped it wouldn't always be like that, not while you had something over Jeffrey. I heard you blackmailing him and his threats in return; what he knew about Catherine. I thought that if I could get her away from us, it would be all right. There was a parting letter for you.'

'A parting letter! One penned by you, I suppose,' replied Stephen. She lowered her gaze.

'I swear to God, I had no idea they intended to kill her! They had a bag with them – I didn't even know they had a camera,' she said.

'You mean to say you were there!' he said, aghast. He saw that tears had now formed in her eyes. She wiped them away.

Joanna stepped backwards and moved around the car to the passenger's side, then dropped her suitcase onto the seat. 'I would never have done it if I had known they intended to harm her in any way,' she insisted. Justin stepped a little closer.

'How did you know where to find the brothel?' said Justin.

'I didn't. But I know Mr Vardy's jazz club. Jeffrey's taken me there a couple of times. We're treated as special guests, and it didn't take too much snooping around to find out why. They asked me about a girl named Emma at first. Someone had mentioned to them that she worked at the

house. I thought at first they must mean Sandra, but then
when I mentioned her name, they just laughed. Catherine
was the only other girl here.'

'And I suppose you knew all along about Jeffrey and
Sandra?' said Justin.

'Of course I did. And all the other harlots. So long as he
left me alone, I was happy enough with the situation. It
wasn't him that I cared about anyway. It was only today that
I found out about Stephen and Sandra.'

'What?' said Stephen.

'I think you may have your wires crossed, Joanna,' replied
Justin.

'Where is that little slut anyway?' she said, ignoring them
both and turning to Jeffrey. He remained silent.

Police sirens could be heard in the distance. Lady Keating
opened the car door and got in.

'This is all a bit pointless now, isn't it, Joanna?' said Justin.
'How far do you expect to get?'

'It really doesn't matter anymore,' she replied.

'Of course it matters. There are other ways out of this.'

'We both know that's not true,' she replied.

'Of course it is! We need your evidence. And besides,
you're not going to get far. A woman travelling alone at
night–' he began, but she had already switched the gun over
to point it at Stephen.

'Get in!' she said to him.

'It'll be my pleasure, M'Lady,' came his withering reply. He
got into the car and took the keys from her, and the motor
roared into life.

Stephen reversed the car slowly, moving it around in a wide
crescent, as Lady Keating leant on her suitcase to steady her
hand, keeping the gun trained on Justin. There was a click of
the gears and a burst of revolutions. Then, throwing gravel
up into the air, the wheels span round and the car moved
off, carrying the two of them away.

The police sirens were getting closer. Sandra appeared
under the portico and watched as the car sped smoothly and

aggressively along the driveway towards the main entrance. Justin lowered his hands and looked across at Cameron. They would wait until the car was safely out on the road before running hopelessly to the Crossley and attempting to give chase.

Suddenly, from the end of the driveway came a scrape and screech from the Bugatti as it skidded violently and swerved across the gravel. Lady Keating screamed momentarily as the engine continued to power up with a deep, rising rumble.

It soon reached the oak archway, and with a smash of glass, and a thud and crumple of metal, the vehicle hit one of the trees, and shot up into the air, lifting like a piece of tin swept up on a strong breeze. The branches above them shuddered and swayed in recoil from the impact as, with a loud and permanent thud, the front of the chassis crumpled in on itself and the car overturned, coming back down to rest on the grass next to the undisturbed Citroen.

Justin and Cameron ran over to the wreckage where Stephen's body lay limp, crushed and sprawled under the remains of the car's bonnet. Joanna had been thrown clear. Justin knelt down and pulled her head up from the hideous angle to which it had slumped. There was no pulse left to be felt; just the handle of a steak knife sticking out from the side of her neck. A police car turned the corner and skidded as it stopped.

Twelve

They both looked tired.

'Do you mind?' Justin reached across his desk for Cameron's packet of cigarettes as he sat down.

'No. Take the packet if you're all out, I've got more,' replied Cameron, sitting at the far side of the desk in his shirt-sleeves. He looked down again at his notes. 'Bloody hell!' he sighed.

'Yep.' Justin pulled the whisky bottle out of his desk drawer and unscrewed the cap.

The office door opened, and Detective Chief Inspector Andrews appeared with a heavy bag hanging from one shoulder and a selection of files under his other arm. He tottered over to Justin's desk.

'I thought you'd already gone, sir,' said Justin.

'I did, son, I just came back up for my keys,' he replied, putting the bag down and placing the files on Justin's desk. He looked at the whisky bottle that was standing half-empty in front of him. 'You two been having a wee celebration by the looks of it.'

'I'm not sure celebration is the right word for it, sir,' he replied. He offered Andrews the bottle.

'No, I don't drink. And I hope you've not been making a habit of drinking that in here!'

'Wouldn't dream of it, sir.'

'Cheeky sod!' he said with a smile. 'You're lucky I've got a ferry to catch.' He looked down at the notes that Cameron was studying. 'So, it was young Lady Chatterley then, was it?'

'Aye, you could say that, sir,' replied Cameron.

'Except he'd long ended the arrangement,' added Justin.

'And she tried to take revenge?' asked Andrews.

'On the girl, possibly; though I don't think that was her motive. On Stephen, definitely. Apparently, they ended up meeting in the summer house last Sunday afternoon, and whatever happened there, he ended up reiterating the fact that it was all over. That's what angered her enough to come and talk to us.'

'Why didn't the servant tell you about his relationship with her earlier?' said Andrews.

'I think he thought it was unrelated. For all he knew, it couldn't have had anything to do with Lady Keating, so why bother telling us? To be fair to the bloke, based on the information he had, it was probably a wise decision. I would have suspected his involvement right from the start had we have known anything about an affair between the two of them.'

'But you might have also suspected her,' Andrews pointed out.

'I like to think we would have made that connection,' Justin replied.

'Well, he's paid for it now, sir,' said Cameron.

'He certainly has,' said Andrews. 'But what about this Keating character? Didn't he change the shifts around the night the girl was murdered?'

'Yes, he did. But other than that, he had nothing to do with it, sir,' said Justin. 'He only changed the girl's shifts so that he could have Sandra on show to one of his dinner guests – one of the recipients of her exotic images, I believe. When Lady Keating found out about the shift swap she saw her chance to get rid of Catherine and so she put a call through to her friendly host Mr Vardy, to arrange what she thought would be Catherine's abduction. Then, later on, when everyone in the house at Horsham was fast asleep, she must have crept out, driven into London and let them into the flat. No, as far as the murder goes, old Jeffrey Keating is an all-round honourable fellow.'

'Sounds like it,' replied Andrews. 'Bring him in on the porno charge.'

'I charged him twenty minutes ago, sir. He's just left.'

'And you don't think he'll abscond?'

'I doubt it, sir. He's too high profile. Anyway, if he runs, he runs. We don't need him for anything else now that we have witnesses to Lady Keating's confession.'

'No, I suppose not. So…the poor, delightful Joanna. Was she present at the crime scene?'

'Joanna Zdanowska her name was, sir. And yes, she was, I'm afraid – along with both Gormally and most probably Vardy.'

'What the fuck was she doing running around with them two? Christ, you just can't tell nowadays can you!' said Andrews.

'They were only vague acquaintances of hers – made through Jeffrey, of course. She said she didn't know that they had intended to kill Catherine, and to be fair, I believe her. She'd written a letter from Catherine to Stephen, and she arrived and left separately from the other two, so it would suggest to me that she wasn't expecting the girl to be murdered. At least not there and then. She wasn't entirely without conscience, sir; that's why she didn't raise our suspicions. She seemed perfectly respectable to everyone who knew her. She'd once been a chambermaid at The Ritz.'

'Ah, well she didn't have to go far then.'

'No, just across the park. She'd been an orphan. Then she'd managed to catch Jeffrey's eye and he became her kind of benefactor.'

'I bet he did.'

'If she hadn't have come into the office and tried to pin it all on Mr Hollis, I would probably never have suspected her. But we were certain by that point that it wasn't Stephen – that's when I realised it must have been her.'

Cameron coughed loudly.

'DC Cameron played an important part in it as well,' added Justin.

'Thank you, sir,' said Cameron flatly.

'So, if she'd kept her mouth shut then she would have gotten away with it?' said Andrews. 'I'll remind my wife of that,' he added. Then he thought about it. 'No, actually maybe I won't.' He swung his bag up over his shoulder. 'Anyway, I'd better be off. You've done a good job.'

'We did our best, given what we had to go on,' said Justin. 'It was all quite simple in hindsight. If we'd just been a bit cleverer about it, we could have saved a couple of lives and been certain of getting Vardy as well. She never actually said he was involved. I just hope he's not going to end up walking.'

'You still might get him if you're lucky; you've got witnesses to the Lady's confession, at least. Anyway, there are better men than you who've made bigger mistakes than that, I can tell you. Not that I'll admit to it – and I suggest you don't either.' Andrews picked up the files and one dropped out; it was a manila envelope. 'It's all over now. You can let it go,' he said.

'Yes, sir,' Justin replied, picking up the envelope and passing it to him.

The door opened and in walked Inspector Lisson.

'Ah, glad I caught you before you left, sir. I wanted to say goodbye,' he said, extending his hand. Andrews shook it.

'I should think you're happy with the new appointment,' said Andrews. 'Have you heard?' he said turning to Justin, 'Chief Inspector Bradley's moving across to take my place. Lisson here knows him well.'

'We grew up on the same street,' said Lisson. 'He used to play football with my brother.'

'Excellent,' said Justin. He turned to face the window.

'Right, I'm off,' said Andrews. They had said their goodbyes.

'Enjoy Ireland, sir,' Lisson called out after him.

'Aye, what's bloody left of it,' he replied, as the door swung shut behind him.

'Right, I'm out of here too,' said Lisson.

'Me too, sir – if that's all right?' said Cameron.

'Of course. I'll stay here for a bit,' said Justin, still staring out onto the street.

'I'll see you in the morning, sir,' said Cameron.

'Yes, I'm afraid so. Shut the door behind you, will you?' said Justin.

The office was empty.

Justin reached down to his desk drawer, unlocked it and pulled out the incriminating photographs. Why did I bring them back here? he thought, as he sat, perching on the edge of his desk. Perhaps it was the gamble.

He lit a cigarette and slid the images out of the envelope for one last look at them then introduced them to the cigarette lighter.

'Everywhere cunning,' he thought, 'everywhere small feuds and hatreds…feebleness of purpose.'

He watched them eagerly as they began to melt, knowing that he should never have even considered keeping them. The flames consumed his profile, and he shuffled over to the open window to let the grey smoke escape up into the evening sky.

It was rush hour below. There was movement in the street running alongside the Thames. Someone was looking up. He moved away from the window and dropped the last of the remnants into a wastepaper bin then reached for his jacket and hat.

James S. Holmes lives in Wellington, New Zealand.
This is his first novel.

www.ingramcontent.com/pod-product-compliance
Lightning Source LLC
Chambersburg PA
CBHW031956050726
47590CB00006B/1932